St. Patrick's Cross

A Larry Macklin Mystery-Book 18

A. E. Howe

Books in the
Larry Macklin Mystery Series
(in order):

November's Past	September's Fury
December's Secrets	October's Fear
January's Betrayal	Spring's Promises
February's Regrets	Summer's Rage
March's Luck	Autumn's Ghost
April's Desires	Winter's Chill
May's Danger	Valentine's Warning
June's Troubles	St. Patrick's Cross
July's Trials	Memorial Day's Escape
August's Heat	Independence Day's Search

Copyright © 2022 A. E Howe

All rights reserved.

ISBN-13: 978-1-7346541-8-9

This book is a work of fiction. Names, characters, places and incidents are the product of the author's imagination or are used fictitiously. Any resemblance to actual events, locales, business establishments, persons or animals, living or dead, is entirely coincidental.

Except as permitted under the U.S. Copyright Act of 1976, no part of this publication may be reproduced, stored in a retrieval system or transmitted in any form or by any means, electronic or mechanical, including photocopying, recording or otherwise, without written permission from the author. Thank you for respecting the hard work of this author.

CHAPTER ONE

I could feel spring in the air as I walked across the sheriff's office parking lot on a Wednesday morning in early March. On a day like this, the last thing in the world I wanted to do was give a talk on crime-scene preservation techniques to a bunch of deputies with better things to do, but there I was.

The hour-long presentation was part of my punishment for disobeying orders. Had I deserved it? Yes, but… The "but" didn't get me anywhere with my father, who was also the sheriff. Did it help that my future lieutenant, Phil Eccles, was sharing my pain, having also broken the rules? Misery does love company.

We were slowly getting better at making presentations together. The first—entitled "Sheriff's Office Rules of Conduct"—had been rocky. The second—"What is the Chain of Command and How Does It Apply to the Adams County Sheriff's Office?"—had gone a little easier. My father had picked out the topics, which were clearly aimed at reminding Phil and me of all the rules we had broken. Dad had specifically required that we discuss our failure to follow proper procedure in detail.

That morning, I was hoping that the third time would be the charm for a perfect presentation. I thought the odds rose when Phil joined me in the training room bearing a box that smelled like sugar.

"Alpha shift is a rough one," he said. "I brought donuts to bribe them."

"They're better than Charlie," I said, thinking of the first group we'd addressed.

The department ran on four shifts. On any given day, three of them would be on duty for eight hours each, while the fourth would have the day off. Some civilian employees, such as dispatch, were assigned to the four different shifts, while others worked a standard eight-to-five schedule, five days a week. Investigators like me were also on the eight-to-five schedule, but often our days and weeks were much longer, especially if we were on call.

"Has your dad said how many of these dog-and-pony shows we're gonna have to do?" Phil asked, placing the handouts I'd prepared on a table by the door so the deputies could pick one up as they entered.

I shrugged. "The only time he talks to me is when he's telling me it's time to babysit his pet moose." Dad's favorite son was his one-hundred-and-ninety-pound, four-year-old Great Dane, Mauser. "Just thank your lucky stars that he isn't making you participate in that part of the punishment."

"My wife would never put up with all that drool in her house."

"Dad doesn't drool that much… Oh! You meant Mauser," I joked.

"Keep making comments like that and we'll never get out of purgatory. The walls have ears." Phil pointed to the security camera mounted in the corner of the room.

The door opened and Sergeant Jack Hannah came through with his usual swagger. Phil pointed to the handouts and Jack took one.

"I've been working the road for fifteen years; I think I know how to secure a crime scene," he grumbled.

"Gee, I think I remember an eight-year-old picking up a twenty-dollar bill from an armed robbery scene you had secured," Phil said, making air quotes around the word "secured."

"The damn kid was short. I didn't see him go under the crime-scene tape."

"Don't kibitz our presentation," Phil warned him.

"Whatever," Jack muttered as other deputies started to file in.

"You two still here. I thought you were fired?" The next smart-aleck comment came from Randy Spears.

"You'd miss us if we were gone," Phil told him.

"You hear anything about those promotions?" asked Susan White, a twenty-three-year veteran of the department.

"You hoping they'll reopen the positions?" I responded. I was sure that everyone in the room knew that the promotion committee was going to meet next week to decide whether Phil and I would be allowed to keep our promotions to sergeant and lieutenant. The department had the most extensive and efficient grapevine in the world.

"No, no. Just wondered if we had to respect you two or not," came a comment from another member of the peanut gallery.

"I don't mind the teaching; it's the heckling I can't stand," I muttered to Phil, who chuckled.

"It's a locker-room mentality," he said loud enough for all of them to hear, which just got us more abuse.

An hour later, we'd finished the presentation and I was headed back to my desk when I got a text from Pete Henley that read: *Come to my crime scene ASAP.* Two things were odd about that. First, Pete would normally just call me and, second, I wasn't currently his partner. Dad had me working alone as more of my punishment. If I needed assistance on a case, I had to ask Major Sam Parks first.

Another thing that triggered my mental alarm was that Pete didn't use "ASAP" lightly.

I didn't bother stopping at my desk. I texted Pete that I was on the way and radioed dispatch for the location of the crime scene. Marti gave me the information and told me it was a suspected homicide.

I drove to a construction site south of town where several warehouses were going up. I'd noticed bulldozers clearing the land a month ago. When I arrived, there were two patrol cars, an ambulance and Pete's unmarked car parked outside the chain-link fence surrounding the site. As I got out of my car, Shantel Williams and Marcus Brown from our crime-scene department pulled up in their van.

Pete stood by the ambulance's open back door. When I walked over to him, I could see two EMTs who I recognized but didn't know well sitting on the bench seats inside, talking to a figure lying on the stretcher. Pete turned to me.

"He's been asking for you. Come over here." Pete took my arm and started to lead me away before I had a chance to see who was in the back of the ambulance. "I need your help to get him to the hospital where he can be evaluated."

"Who is it?"

"Robin Hennessy. He's either drunk or high or both," Pete said.

I groaned. "Is he hurt? Dispatch told me there was a homicide."

"*He's* not hurt. At least not that I can tell from the state he's in. But Drew King is dead," Pete said through clenched teeth.

"Oh, Pete…" Drew King had retired from the department almost nine years ago, not long after I'd joined. He'd been Pete's field training officer, mentor and good friend.

"We got a call from one of the construction workers when he got to the site and found the body inside the office." Pete pointed to an old trailer that served as Blue Land Development's onsite office. King had started the company after he retired.

"Is Robin a witness?"

"Suspect. *Chief* suspect," Pete said darkly. "He was passed out inside the trailer when I got here."

"Robin is a lot of things, but he's not a killer," I

protested, thinking of my old school friend and receiving a skeptical look from Pete.

"He still had the baseball bat in his hand. Or at least near his hand."

"I…" I wanted to argue that Robin didn't have a mean bone in his body, but I knew better. Under the influence of drugs, good people can do horrible things that would be completely out of character under any other circumstances. I also knew that Pete was an excellent investigator and not one to jump to conclusions without good evidence. "What do you want me to do?"

"Escort him to the hospital where he can be evaluated. The EMTs have already drawn blood for testing. See that his blood is put into capable hands and, of course, collect all his clothes. I wish I could have stripped him here. I've searched his pockets as best I could. Do it again."

"And after they've evaluated him?"

"I'll write up the paperwork to have him charged with breaking and entering. Which will give us some time to see what we're looking at."

Pete didn't say anything else, so I started to turn back toward the ambulance. But then he added, "I have a picture of him passed out with the damn bat four inches from his open hand."

"I'll keep a good eye on him," I promised.

Both of the EMTs had climbed out of the back of the ambulance. I finally remembered that one of them was named Jayden, but I still couldn't come up with the driver's name.

"We're ready to transport him," the driver said.

"Thanks, Vince," Pete said, unknowingly coming to my aid. "Larry's going to ride along. Your patient is unofficially a prisoner. If he's pronounced fit to be released, he'll be charged with B-and-E."

"Off the record, there's nothing wrong with him that a detox won't fix. That's assuming his liver hasn't decided to surrender to the inevitable," Vince said.

"Any idea what he's on?" I asked.

"We've dealt with Robin several times in the past six months. A better question is: What *isn't* he on?" Vince turned and headed for the wheel while I climbed in back.

"If you're riding back here, then I'll be up front," Jayden told me. "I need the fresh air." He closed the doors behind me, leaving me alone with Robin.

I looked down at the man and tried to remember the last time I'd seen him. He was a common presence in Calhoun's more seedy neighborhoods, but it had been years since we'd talked. We'd been best friends all through elementary and middle school, but that had ended long ago, and we'd stopped acknowledging our acquaintance.

Robin lay on the stretcher with his eyes shut. His clothes were a bloody mess and judging by the smell emanating from them, he'd been wearing them for at least a week. He looked ten years older than me, though I knew he was exactly one month younger. His hair was poorly cut, greasy and already showing a few strands of grey.

Growing up, teachers and our families had joked that if they saw one of us then the other wasn't far behind. Mom had even kidded about how much we looked alike. Now I looked down at him and saw what could have happened if I'd made other choices in my life.

As the ambulance pulled out onto the main road, Robin opened one of his eyes and looked around. When he saw me, he closed the eye again, then opened it and squinted as if to clear his vision. He tried to reach up and wipe his eyes.

"Hey." He strained against the straps holding his arms down. "Hey!"

"Your arms are strapped down for your own protection," I told him. A part of me didn't want to get into a conversation with him.

Robin opened both eyes, which were milky and bloodshot. He looked toward me and, with a great effort, focused on my face. "I know you. Yeah, sure, it's Larry!" He was still trying to pull his arms up. "What's the game, Larry?"

The words were thick and he seemed to be fighting to make the sounds necessary for speech.

"Robin, you're in a bunch of trouble."

"You're not shitting me. My arms are tied down!" He strained some more, then yelled again at an ear-piercing volume, "Hey! Let me out! Help!" His eyes were panicked.

"Robin, calm down. I'm Larry, remember? You asked for me." I was trying to get him to focus again. "You're okay. We're taking you to the hospital."

The word "hospital" only ramped him up more. He began to thrash wildly on the stretcher.

"I don't wanna go to no damn hospital. No! Help! I don't want to dry out! Help!"

"Robin, you were found with a dead man," I said when he paused to take a breath. I wanted him to understand that this wasn't some kind of intervention.

"You're a cop," he said and eyed me nervously. "Why do you wanna do this to me, Larry? I never done nothin' to you." Like a rollercoaster, he was rolling down from a panicked high into a trough of self-pity.

"We'll get this all cleared up," I said calmly. "Can you remember what happened last night?"

"Not a thing. I never remember what happens. That's the point."

"I know."

"So what you askin' for?" he asked sullenly.

"I'm trying to help you."

"You wanna help me, you'll let me out of here. Help!"

"Robin, I know you aren't crazy. Stop yelling."

"You're right. I'm not crazy and I'm *not* going to the hospital." He yanked hard at his restraints.

"You can't break them. All you're going to do is hurt your arms."

"You'd like that," he said nonsensically before dropping back onto the stretcher.

"Did you know Drew King?"

"Never heard of him," he answered, so quickly that I

knew he hadn't listened to the name.

"Drew King. He used to be a deputy."

A spark of recognition appeared in his eyes. "King Tut. That's what I called him. 'Cause he was always tut-tutting me when I did something he didn't like."

"When was the last time you saw him?"

"I don't know," Robin lied.

"When?"

"I told you. I don't know."

"Okay." I didn't want to push him. He hadn't been read his Miranda rights and, honestly, I didn't see the point in asking him questions when his mind was still half clouded by whatever cocktail of drugs he currently had circulating through his veins.

"Yeah, that's right, okay," he muttered.

We rode in silence for a while. Slowly, Robin seemed to become fully aware of his situation.

"I fucked up this time," he said as we stopped at the first red light on the outskirts of Tallahassee.

"I hope not," I said and meant it. As I sat with him, I had an irrational desire to save this sad, alternative version of myself. I knew the impulse was stupid. Every good cop, social worker and teacher learns early on that you can't save people who don't want to be saved. If you try, then they will come to hate you and you'll learn to hate them.

"Hey, Larry, stay with me, man," Robin pleaded as Jayden and Vince started wheeling him into the hospital.

"I'll be here the whole time," I promised, walking beside the stretcher.

"That's good. Yep, that's good. We had some great times as kids. Didn't we?" He smiled for the first time.

"We sure did." It felt like someone had turned on a projector in my brain. I saw images of us sliding down a giant sand pile in front of my house, playing paper football at a picnic table outside our school and pedaling bikes so fast that we thought we could fly.

Robin was wheeled into a small cubicle in the emergency

room and, despite some arguments, a nurse managed to take his blood pressure, pulse and temperature.

I recognized the expression on the doctor's face when he finally saw Robin. It was a mix of pity, anger and disgust, but mostly resignation. Here was another lost soul who wasn't going to do anything to help himself. Still, the doctor had a job to do, even if the job entailed nothing more than spinning his wheels.

Doctor Metcalfe, a tall black man in his early thirties, looked at the paperwork that the EMTs had filled out.

"Robin, can you hear me?" he asked his patient.

"Hell, yeah, I can hear you!" Robin snarled. "Now you hear me. Untie my arms!"

The doctor looked at me. I shook my head.

"We need to do a thorough evaluation first," Metcalfe said, flashing his penlight in Robin's eyes.

"I'm fine," Robin grumbled, trying to avoid the light.

The doctor continued his examination and made copious notes.

"How long have you been drinking?"

"Don't remember when I wasn't," Robin said with a crooked smile.

"Can you tell me what drugs you've taken in the last forty-eight hours?"

"I thought that's what you were goin' to tell me?"

"You need to answer the doctor's questions as best you can," I said sternly.

"I don't even know what day it is. I guess yesterday I was hanging at the Fast Mart down by the tracks. Think Scratch got me some… tranks and maybe… I always want some demmies, must have got some 'cause I ain't hurtin'." He laughed.

"No wonder you were passed out." The doctor shook his head. "Alcohol and downers, along with some pain pills. You're lucky to be alive."

"I don't want any treatment," Robin stated firmly.

"I recommend a three-day detox to start with," Metcalfe

said in an equally firm voice.

"I can't do three days."

As I watched this exchange, I tried to imagine Robin beating someone to death. I had personal experience with people out of their minds on drugs and knew the damage they could cause. But if Robin was right about the drugs he'd taken, then he was more likely to slip into a coma than go on a rampage. Take a mild-mannered guy and cram him full of downers, you don't expect him to go berserk.

"He's as healthy as you would expect a thirty-something drug addict living on the streets to be," Metcalfe told me when I followed him down the hall out of Robin's earshot. "I'll be back when I can to finish the examination. He'll need to be stripped."

"Right," I said, gritting my teeth and cussing Pete for leaving me with the chore of supervising the stripping and searching of Robin's filthy body.

"You know, there's no medical reason for the restraints." The doctor gave me a look that made it clear he didn't approve.

"He was found at the scene of a homicide."

Metcalfe cleared his throat. "Well, do what you have to."

I went back into the cubicle and, with some trepidation, helped the male nurse unstrap Robin. I was more worried he'd do a runner than attack someone.

"Don't make me put handcuffs on you," I told him.

"What'd I do?" he asked.

"We're going to try and figure that out."

"Nothin', that's what I did." Robin looked at the nurse, who matched my six feet in height but outweighed me by at least a hundred pounds. The man looked like he could pick Robin up and toss him across the room without breaking a sweat. I appreciated that the doctor had sent backup.

"Get undressed," the nurse ordered after we had helped Robin up from the stretcher.

"Here?"

"You can step behind that curtain," the nurse said,

holding out a hospital gown.

Reluctantly, Robin took the gown and sullenly walked behind the curtain. When he stepped back out, even the flimsy hospital gown was a huge improvement over the bloody and filthy clothes he'd been wearing.

When the doctor came back to examine Robin, he found the scratches and abrasions you'd expect to see on someone living rough. What he didn't find were any wounds from a struggle. Not that that proved anything. If you hit someone in the head with a bat hard enough, they wouldn't have much of a chance to defend themselves.

I explained that I would be taking Robin back to Calhoun and booking him into the county jail.

"He'll go through withdrawal," Metcalfe warned.

"He won't be the first." The deputies that worked at the jail were very familiar with withdrawal symptoms. The nurse on staff would see Robin through the worst of it.

Deputy Matti Sanderson picked us up in her patrol car and drove us to the jail. She'd brought an orange prison jumpsuit for Robin to wear since his clothes had been bagged as evidence and I figured he should get used to the color. I didn't think anyone would be rushing to put up his bail.

"I didn't do anything." Robin was sounding more coherent now, sitting up with his face close to the plexiglass barrier that divided the front of the patrol car from the back. I was crammed into the passenger seat with Sanderson's laptop and other equipment.

"You need to think hard about what you did yesterday and last night," I said.

"I didn't do—"

"No. Think, don't talk. You're going to have plenty of opportunities to explain everything to Deputy Henley, but you better have good answers to have any chance of release."

"I don't know why y'all are doin' this to me."

"What part of 'found in a trailer with a murdered man'

don't you understand?"

"I didn't do anything," Robin whined.

I thought it was entirely possible that he had just been wandering around last night, stumbled upon the trailer at the construction site and crawled inside to sleep. I made a note to ask Pete if the light had been on in the trailer. Was it possible that Robin had wandered in without turning on the light and, strung out as he was, never even noticed that he was in the middle of a crime scene? I couldn't rule out the possibility. I hoped for his sake that the coroner could pin down a time of death that would give Robin an alibi. But that would also depend on him coming up with witnesses who could say what he'd done before he got to the trailer.

We rode the last ten miles in silence. I thanked Sandy for the lift as she dropped us off at the jail, which was located just across the street from the sheriff's office.

Inside the jail, the desk sergeant told me Pete had sent over the paperwork for Robin's arrest. As he talked, the sergeant gave Robin a long look. The man behind the desk had been working at the department long enough to have known Drew King when he was a deputy. Finally, the sergeant released the magnetic lock so I could take Robin into the booking room.

"No! Come on. You can't really do this." Robin was pulling at the handcuffs.

I ignored him and stopped near the fingerprint station, which had come a long way in recent years from the ink-and-roll method I'd learned in the academy. A few quick presses on the digital scanner and we were done—no muss or fuss, except from Robin.

I took him by the shoulders. "Look, Robin, you need to take this seriously. Try to find some inner strength and dignity that hasn't been eaten away by all the crap you've drank, smoked, huffed or injected over the years."

"I never injected nothin'," he said indignantly.

"Fine. My point still stands. Dig deep and find some strength, or you're going to be in jail for a long, long time."

"But I didn't do nothin'."

"Pete Henley is a great investigator, but like the rest of us, he has to work with what he has. If he doesn't come up with any other viable suspects, and you can't give him a good reason to think you didn't kill that man, then you're going down for murder. Right now, there's enough evidence for a jury to convict you."

Robin looked confused. I knew he was muddle-headed from all the abuse he had heaped on his body, but the clock was ticking for him to get out in front of this. If Pete couldn't eliminate Robin as a suspect, he'd spend a lot of time focusing on Robin instead of searching for other possibilities. Of course, I had to remind myself that Robin could very well *be* the killer.

"I'll try." His voice was weak and unconvincing. "Will you help me?"

I cursed under my breath. That was the one request I hadn't wanted him to make.

"Robin, this isn't my investigation. Even if it was, that's not how investigators work. I would have to look at all the facts and, if an overwhelming number of them pointed to you, I'd have to charge you and let a jury decide your fate."

"I remember us playing cops-and-robbers as kids. You were always the cop, just like your old man," Robin said angrily

Against my wishes, my brain showed me an image of him running around with a cap gun as I chased him through my backyard until Mom let Spike, our Great Dane, out of the house. The dog playfully charged and barked at us until we were laughing so hard we couldn't breathe.

I shook off the memory and said, "I'll talk to Pete and make sure he does everything he can to find the person who killed Drew King."

"Thanks, man."

We finished the intake process, then I watched as a deputy took Robin back to a cell.

I still had the eerie feeling that I was watching a darker

version of myself.

CHAPTER TWO

I walked across the street carrying the evidence bag with Robin's individually tagged clothes inside. I hadn't let it out of my sight since they'd been bagged at the hospital, and I was glad to finally check them into the evidence room. With that chore done, I swung by my desk to check my emails, conscious of the solemn mood in the office around me. Many of the deputies and civilian personnel had been friends with Drew King.

An hour later, I caught a ride back out to the crime scene to pick up my car. Shantel and Marcus were picking up and tagging the last of the evidence. I found Pete leaning against his car with his head in his hands, looking exhausted. He wiped at his eyes and gave me a grim look.

"This one's hitting me hard." Unlike me, Pete was normally able to separate his emotions from his job. I knew it made him a better investigator. Letting my emotions get ahead of my brain was why I was on double-secret probation.

"Drew was your FTO," I said with understanding.

"Drew could be such a hard-ass if he thought you were slacking off. At the same time, if he knew you were giving it your all but were still falling short, he'd be the first one to lift you up. It was tough on me when he left the department. As much as I trusted all the other deputies, I still felt like I'd lost my backup."

"We'll find the person responsible for this," I said, looking over at the trailer.

"Justice would be good. But it won't change the fact that I've lost someone I depended on to be there if I needed them. Until today I didn't know what it meant to me, knowing I could call him anytime I needed to." Pete choked back a sob.

"Do you know of any enemies he might have? Ex-cons who might hold a grudge?" I asked a little while later.

"Don't you think I've been racking my brain trying to come up with someone? I don't want it to be your friend Robin. You know why?" There was an edge to Pete's voice that caused me to keep my mouth shut and just shake my head. "Because if it's that little weasel, then this was senseless. I want there to be a reason for a man like Drew to die, and I want to find a very bad person that I can make pay for what they did." He was almost nose to nose with me.

"You know I'm here for you."

"First thing you can do is make Robin Hennessy remember some details from last night. If he didn't do it, then he might have seen something that can give us some leads."

Pete was right, but after the hours I'd spent with Robin that afternoon, my confidence wasn't high that he was going to be any help.

"Drew had, what, three… or was it four ex-wives?"

"Five if you count the last one," Pete admitted. "He separated from her not long ago. He told me he was done after this one. I guess that's kind of ironic."

Marcus and Shantel came over to us.

"We're finished. Unless you have something else you want us to do." Shantel looked almost as tired as Pete. "I hate working on the ones where you know the victim. Drew and I butted heads a lot. Sometimes just for the fun of it." She cleared her throat and looked off into the distance, fighting back tears.

"I checked Hennessy's clothes in," I told her.

"Did I miss anything in his pockets?" Pete asked.

"Some change. A plastic jewelry bag that probably held drugs. Nothing else."

"The sheriff has already given us the go-ahead to work overtime on this one," Shantel said.

Dad didn't like to play favorites. Normally, budget would take priority. He'd given me the lecture more than once about what would happen if we ran out of money before the end of the budget year. But in this instance, while money was important, so was morale. Drew had a lot of friends. Besides, Dad knew that if he didn't give his employees permission to work overtime on this case, then they'd just find a way to work on it at the expense of other cases.

"I'd like to see the crime scene," I told Pete, who nodded and headed toward the trailer.

"This is going to be hard on everyone." Shantel shook her head as we walked away.

The trailer was well used, with all the dents, dings and scratches that you would expect from being set up at a dozen construction sites. Even so, all the windows were intact and the door was secure on its hinges. The trailer was the width of a standard singlewide and roughly thirty feet long. At some point, an extra heavy-duty deadbolt had been added to the door. I made a note to check the back door to see if it was equally well secured.

"There wasn't much of a struggle," Pete said as he held the door open for me.

The inside of the trailer was furnished with standard metal office furniture, including a desk, a supply cabinet and a filing cabinet. Against one wall was an old sofa, a lamp and another chair. Across from that was a small refrigerator and a sink.

"There's a bathroom down the hallway and a bedroom

that's full of equipment, mostly OSHA safety stuff."

The computer and other items from the desk had already been bagged and tagged, but there were still a few things scattered around the bloodied office, including half a dozen beer cans. Everything was covered with fingerprint powder.

"There were twice as many beer cans, most of them empty," Pete told me. "Your buddy was flopped out on that couch when the employee showed up this morning."

By the blood evidence, I could tell where King's body had been lying on the floor, partly behind the desk.

"What are your thoughts on how the attack happened?" I asked.

"My best guess is the assailant got in a blow that staggered but didn't kill Drew, who then flailed around, trying to defend himself before the killer hit him again."

While I wasn't an expert on blood evidence, one look at the wall and furniture made it clear that the blood spatter had come from several different directions. The carpet on the floor, already old and worn, was now smeared and clotted with blood.

"Drew was still in pretty good physical condition." I remembered seeing him a few months earlier at the office Christmas dinner.

"Yeah, he kept in shape." Pete paused and nodded. "I know where you're going with that. How could a man who hasn't been sober in twenty years overpower a man like Drew King? My guess is Robin got in the first blow, leaving Drew dazed. Robin took advantage of Drew being stunned to finish the job."

"If Drew was unprepared, then that would mean the attack was unprovoked and by someone he trusted." I was looking around the room, trying to get a feel for what had happened.

I thought about Robin. Was he capable of this type of brutal attack?

"There is another possibility," Pete admitted. "Drew could put back a few beers at the end of the day."

"The autopsy will be interesting. If he was intoxicated, that would explain him being unable to protect himself."

"And could explain how Robin and Drew got into an altercation that ended in murder," Pete said.

"When did the employee find the body?"

"He arrived at the site around six o'clock this morning. He's the foreman and said it's his routine to get here an hour before everyone else to check all the machines to see if they need any maintenance. He would also meet with Drew most mornings to go over the schedule for the day."

"Were the lights on in the trailer?"

Pete nodded. "He noticed that when he first arrived. He saw Drew's truck and figured Drew had gotten here early, so he went over to the office first thing to find out what was up."

"Did he knock on the door or just open it?"

"He just walked in. When he saw his boss dead on the floor and what he thought was another dead man on the couch, he hightailed it back to his truck where he called 911."

"And Robin was still unconscious when you arrived?"

"Buzzed out of his brain would be more accurate. The first deputies on the scene beat me by about fifteen minutes. I ordered them to secure the area until I arrived. We were acting on the information that Dan, that's the foreman, provided."

"That both men inside the trailer were dead?"

"Exactly. When I got here, I suited up and entered to find that one of the dead bodies was snoring. I took photos before I tried to wake him. The beer cans and the odor told me he was drunk; that and the fact that I recognized him. Once I finished taking pictures, I roused him enough so that I could half drag him out of here."

"What did Robin say?"

"Not much. You know the kind of thing. 'Put me down. What are you doing? Leave me alone.' He never acknowledged the body or all the blood."

Pete pulled out his phone and showed me a picture of Robin lying sprawled on the couch, one hand open and hanging off the side. Under his hand was the bat that had presumably been used to kill Drew King. It didn't take much imagination to picture the hand opening up and the bat falling into the position it had been found.

"Looks bad for Robin," I admitted.

"The only cases I've ever worked that were more open-and-shut than this were ones where the killer was still holding the weapon."

"Which he is not," I pointed out. "It's possible that someone could have placed the bat on the floor under his open hand."

"It's also possible I could win the lottery this week. But not probable." Pete shook his head, then took a deep breath and let it out. "Look, you know I'm not going to railroad anyone, but I'm also not going to swim upstream against the evidence. Right now, the needle is pointing straight at Robin. I know he's an unlikely killer. Still, you have to admit that years of drugs and alcohol can rot a man's soul as well as his brain and body."

"I just want to look at all the possibilities."

"Do you think Major Parks will let you work the case with me?"

Knowing I was still on thin ice with the powers that be, I just shrugged. "Your guess is as good as mine."

"I'm fine with it. There's going to be plenty of work to do, especially if Robin isn't our killer."

"I'll talk to Parks and see what he has to say."

"Not your dad?"

"He's still got me on Mauser duty every weekend. I'm lucky he's letting me come into the office at all."

"I can't say I mind the fact that Phil Eccles hasn't gotten his promotion yet. He's still not talking to me."

Pete, acting as the SWAT team's sniper, had taken a shot at a bad guy holding Phil's wife hostage. Things had worked out fine, but in Phil's opinion, Pete had recklessly endangered his wife. Now, whenever both of them were in the same room, the temperature dropped to subzero.

"You two are going to have to find a way to mend fences," I said as I walked past Pete toward the trailer's bathroom.

"Assuming I reach my fitness goals and get my promotion to sergeant, I'll be moving out of CID and won't have to deal with him." Pete followed me to the bathroom.

"Are you going to tear up the plumbing?" I asked, inspecting the sink.

"Marcus said he would come out tomorrow and take out the traps in the sink and bathtub," Pete said. "He's also going to spray the sink and tub down with luminol. I did check them when I arrived, and both were dry."

"If there's any trace of blood, then you might have a third person."

As I looked through the rest of the trailer, I felt the road to Robin's salvation getting narrower and narrower.

"Have you seen *anything* that would point to another person's involvement?" I asked Pete hopefully.

He shook his head.

"Did you find any drugs?" I asked.

"Drew had a couple of bottles of prescription meds in his desk. I'm no expert, but they all looked legit. Shantel said she'd have an expert make sure the pills in the bottle are the same as what was prescribed."

Exiting the trailer, I walked around the outside of it looking for any signs that someone else had been involved in the murder. I checked the windows and the back door, looking for a drop of blood or any sign of a break-in. Shantel, Marcus and Pete had already covered the same ground, but different eyes see different things. This time, though, my eyes didn't see anything that could be called a clue.

"I'll talk to Major Parks," I told Pete as we walked back to the cars.

"I'll talk to him too. I want to make sure we do this one

right."

Pete and I had worked on dozens of cases together. I felt confident that we would solve this one, but I didn't know if we could do it without sending Robin to prison for the rest of his life. A part of my mind refused to believe he was capable of this murder. Was it possible that he could get into a drunken brawl that ended with someone being killed? Absolutely. But, alcohol or no alcohol, he wasn't a psychopath who could just club a man to death. At least, that's what I thought.

I checked the time and figured I could get back to the office and catch Major Parks between meetings. In addition to managing CID, following Lieutenant Johnson's resignation, he handled the department's budget. This meant he spent half his time meeting with county, state or federal officials, depending on the funding source. He had the least appealing job at the sheriff's office as far as I was concerned. I'd have rather had hot needles shoved in my eyeballs than spend all day crunching numbers.

Having luck on my side for once, I saw Parks in the hallway as soon as I got to the office.

"Hey, Larry. I've got about fifteen minutes before I have to head over to the courthouse," Parks said when I caught up with him.

"I'd like to be assigned to help Pete with the King case." I didn't see any reason to beat around the bush.

Parks didn't say anything. Instead, he ushered me into his office, glancing at his watch. Once inside, he sat down behind his desk and grumbled, "If you and Eccles hadn't gone off half-cocked, I wouldn't still be supervising CID."

"*Mea culpa.*"

"Drew King was a great deputy. I can't believe someone killed him. What I've heard is that Pete has a prime suspect already in custody."

"There was a man found in the trailer where King was killed," I allowed.

"With blood on his clothes and the murder weapon in his

hand." Parks looked at me as though I was a particularly slow student.

"Near his hand, not in it," I explained.

"Why do you think Pete needs your help?"

"He's going to talk to you too. There's more to this than meets the eye." It sounded lame even to me.

"Don't tell me about a hunch. Most of the time when an investigator says he has a hunch, what he means is, he doesn't have any evidence. Are you saying that the man found in the trailer didn't kill King? Is there any evidence to support that belief?"

"Not yet." I frowned. "Full disclosure. The man found in the trailer was a friend of mine growing up. We've since gone our separate ways and I'm not saying he isn't the murderer. What I *am* saying is I think there needs to be someone coming at the case from the angle that he isn't the killer. Just so we don't rush to judgment."

"You think that's a risk with Pete heading up the investigation?" Parks asked, the corners of his mouth turned up in a slight smile. He was a notoriously good debater.

"Pete is a great at what he does. I know that. I just want to be sure we have the right man."

I thought Parks was going to make it harder for me. Instead, he looked at his watch again and stood up.

"Everyone who knew Drew King is going to want to be sure we get this right. Having you come at the investigation from a different perspective won't hurt and could help guarantee that we get it right. Okay. Tell Pete to save his breath." He was already heading for the door.

"I appreciate this," I said, following him out.

CHAPTER THREE

I texted Pete and told him we were good to go, then headed straight for the evidence room. Thanks to Shantel's hard work, and a little federal grant money, it was now more than just a room, with lots of space for examining items, an impressive computer setup and several offices, including Lionel West's IT lair.

"Does this mean you're back in your father's good graces?" Shantel asked when I told her that Parks had assigned me to work with Pete.

"No. I think it just shows that the powers that be are going to do everything they can to solve King's murder."

"As they should." Shantel shook her head. "I will say, your man looks pretty guilty." She pulled up the crime-scene photos on her desktop monitor.

"He's not my man. We were friends as kids, that's all." I was beginning to feel defensive and more than a bit irritated that I was being put in the position of defending Robin. If he was guilty, then I wanted to see him locked up as much as anyone.

"Here, you can click through them yourself," Shantel said, standing up and letting me take her seat.

The first photos were of the yard outside the trailer,

mostly showing dozens of footprints in the sand. The majority were partials and all of them were probably meaningless considering the amount of foot traffic at the construction site. It hadn't rained for a couple of days, so anyone who had been there in the past seventy-two hours would have left imprints of their shoes. There were a couple of clear ones close to the door, but odds were they had been left there by the man who found the body or the first deputies on the scene.

Inside the trailer was where the pictures began to get interesting.

"He was tore up bad," Marcus said.

He'd come up behind me and was looking over my shoulder, but I didn't mind. He could answer any questions I had. Marcus and Shantel were a well-oiled machine when it came to evidence collection, analysis and preservation. Both had worked more crime scenes and had more training than most law enforcement officers.

"Could you tell if Drew was sitting or standing when he was attacked?" I asked.

"Standing and facing his attacker," Marcus said without hesitation.

"Why?"

He took the mouse out of my hand and clicked through until he found the photos of King's body.

"See how the forehead is caved in? There was also at least one blow to the back of his head, probably after he fell."

"Was all the damage confined to his head?"

"Mostly." Marcus clicked the mouse a few times until he came to a clear shot of King's hands. "Though those fingers look broken to me."

I scrolled through more photos that showed King's laptop and phone on the floor, along with a lot of other clutter that had been swept from the desk during his weak attempts to defend himself after the first blow.

"Was Drew carrying?" I asked.

"He had a Sig 320 in a holster on the inside of his

waistband and a Glock 43 in an ankle holster. It didn't look like he'd tried to get to either one," Marcus answered.

"Wow. That first blow must have been quick and unexpected." I tried to see how this might have played out for Robin. "Robin is five-foot-ten and thin as a rail. Maybe a hundred-and-thirty-five."

"Yeah, I getcha. Drew would have had to have his guard down to be taken by surprise."

"Especially by someone who was drunk."

"Maybe he wasn't drunk when he got there," Marcus said, then immediately shot down his own supposition. "No. From what I hear, that man hasn't been sober in years."

"Decades," I agreed.

"And if he *was* sober, why would he get drunk and hang out in the trailer till morning?"

"Something is wrong here."

I flipped through more of the photos, stopping on a clear shot of the murder weapon. The bat was covered in blood, with bits of hair and scalp stuck to the wood.

"What kind of fingerprints did you get off of the bat?"

"Smeared mostly. There were a couple of clear ones near the grip."

I clicked some more, and a close-up of the grip came up on the screen. The bloody fingerprints stood out clearly in the photos.

"That's convenient," I said, frowning.

Most people think that you leave clear fingerprints anytime you touch a surface. The reality is that it's rare to leave clear prints. Usually they're smeared or smudged or not there at all. I was willing to bet that these prints would belong to Robin, but I still doubted his guilt.

I flipped through more of the pictures, looking closely at shots of the couch where Robin had been passed out.

"Not much cast-off blood on the couch." I pointed at the dirty brown corduroy fabric in the picture.

"There are a couple of smears." Marcus leaned in and pointed to some dark spots that were hard to distinguish from the dirt stains.

"Pete said you're going to take the drain traps out tomorrow. Let me know if you smell anything."

"What are you thinking?"

"It's crazy, but I wonder if someone poured any of that beer down the drain." I looked over my shoulder at Marcus, who gave me a puzzled look.

"You think the scene was staged?"

"I don't know what I think. I'm just flailing around."

Marcus took the mouse and clicked around the pictures again. He stopped at a couple that showed the dozen beer cans spread throughout the front room of the trailer.

"You would have thought that someone, even a drunk, would have put a few of the cans into the trash." He shrugged and let me take control of the mouse again.

"Who can predict what a drunk will do?" I said, arguing against myself. I continued clicking back and forth through the pictures without seeing anything else unexpected. "Was there just the one camera on the front of the trailer?"

"Yep, and Lionel has all of King's electronics."

That made me wonder about the business. Had Drew King owned Blue Land Development outright? Did he have partners? How successful was the company? There were plenty of questions that needed answers.

I gave up on the pictures and was on my way to my desk when I saw Pete coming down the hall.

"Want to go talk to Drew's son?"

"Where does he live?"

"Over in Quincy, but he's in the lobby now. I talked to him a couple of hours ago. He wanted to see me in person."

Art King was an eerie reflection of his father. He had the same height and strong build, blond hair, blue eyes and broad forehead. He seemed underdressed for the cool weather, wearing just a polo shirt and slacks. He shifted his weight from leg to leg nervously as we introduced ourselves and Pete invited him back to our small conference room.

"I can't believe this has happened," Art muttered as we took seats around the table.

"We need as much information as you can give us about your father, his business and any friends or enemies he might have had," Pete told him.

"I don't know where to start. Or what I can tell you that would help." His large hands twisted and squeezed each other on the table as he talked.

"Start with the business. Does he have any partners?" Pete asked, mirroring my earlier thoughts.

"No. He started the company seven years ago, about a year after he retired from the sheriff's office. He had planned on just renovating or building a couple of houses he could rent out, but he decided he liked the work, so he got his general contractor license and started Blue Land Development. It's funny because his dad, my grandfather, was a builder. Dad spent a lot of time helping him when he was growing up and always said he went into law enforcement because he didn't want to work construction." Art gave us a sad smile. "He didn't have any partners. The closest thing to that was his foreman. I know he'd thought about making him a partner, but Dad didn't think the company was ready to expand."

"Did he have any customers who were unhappy?" Pete asked.

"I guess there were a few that had complaints, but Dad was good about fixing any problems that came up." He stopped and Pete started to ask another question, but then Art continued, "There was one guy down at the coast, he'd wanted a house built. Problem was, the designs he had didn't meet the current code for maximum wind speed and all that stuff. The guy argued for six months or more with Dad before he admitted that Dad was right and had new plans drawn up that would pass all the zoning requirements. Even after that, the guy wouldn't let up with the bullshit. He paid for all his time, but Dad didn't think it was worth the aggravation."

"What's this guy's name?"

"I'd have to look through Dad's records. It was maybe three years ago. I remember Dad stuck with it 'cause he was still kinda new in the business and didn't think he could walk away from the work."

"What about his ex-wives?" Pete asked, changing direction.

Art shook his head. "Naw, they were all pretty lightweight divorces. Even Mom. Not that there weren't some fireworks, sure, but nothing like real fights. I think he still kept in touch with most of them. I know him and Mom would get together a few times a year. When I was still a kid, I'd get all excited thinking they were going to get back together. Stupid. But I'm glad they weren't mortal enemies like some of my friends' parents. Chris's parents used to try and kill each other if they made eye contact."

"Where's your mom living now?"

"You aren't serious?" Then he sighed. "I get it. You've got to cover all the bases. She lives over in Lake City." Art pulled out his phone and scrolled for her number before sliding the phone over to Pete. "I talked to her when I found out. She's upset. If I didn't feel like I had to take care of Dad and… you know… talk to you all and everything, I would have driven over and told her in person."

"Can you give us a list of his wives?" Pete asked.

"You got a piece of paper and a pen?"

Pete pulled a sheet of paper out of his notebook and handed it and a pen over to Art.

"The more details, the better," I said.

"Two of them were short and sweet. The first one, I never even met." Art was already writing names and dates down on the piece of paper.

Five minutes later, and after consulting his phone a few times, he slid the paper over to us. The list read:

Helen Barrett, 1980-81? Maybe lives in Atlanta?

Madeline Everett (Mom) 1985-1998

Betty, 2000, lasted only a few months.
Katelin Howard, 2005-2010, remarried, lives in Mobile, Alabama.
Shelby Thomas, got married last year, but separated a couple of months ago. Works as a waitress at a local restaurant. I think it's the Palmetto or something.

He had also included phone numbers for his mother, Katelin and Shelby.

"Did your father ever talk about a man named Robin Hennessy?" Pete asked.

"I don't think so."

"Did he ever mention any problems with a homeless guy or a drunk?"

"Is that who killed him?"

"We're just starting our investigation," Pete told him. "I promise you that we'll keep your family as informed as we can."

"Was there anyone that your father complained about?" I asked.

"Not really. Like everyone else, he complained about banks and people stealing off his construction sites."

"Anything recently?" Pete asked, and I made a mental note to check calls for service to see if King had made any reports.

"He'd just started this new project. The last site was down by the coast, and he did have a bunch of lumber stolen from there. I remember him being pretty pissed about that."

"Had he fired any employees recently?"

"I don't know. Dan would know more than I would. Dan Gunter, that's Dad's foreman."

I hoped King and Gunter had kept good records. A lot of construction crews used day labor for menial tasks and were fast and loose with their employee recordkeeping.

We talked with Art for another half hour without getting any more useful information.

"Any thoughts?" I asked Pete after Art had left.

Pete sighed. "There's going to be a lot of ground to cover

with ex-wives, his past as a deputy and a business that attracts a mix of the good, the bad and the ugly."

"The murder of a shut-in would be easier," I joked.

"And whether Robin did it or not, you know I have to do my due diligence. Want to go over to the Palmetto?"

"You want to talk to Shelby?"

"Yep. I think I know her. Not that I've been spending a lot of time at restaurants lately." There was a little sadness in his voice as Pete patted his shrinking stomach.

"You're looking good."

"Thirty more pounds. I did a mile yesterday in twelve minutes."

The conference room was about fifty feet from Dad's office, and when we stepped out of the room, I heard him yell my name.

"Macklin! In my office."

I cringed. I'd gotten pretty good at sneaking around the building. Avoiding Dad had become one of my top priorities since I'd landed in the doghouse.

I turned to Pete. "I'll catch up with you."

"I'll be at my desk," Pete said, giving me a sympathetic pat on the shoulder.

Dad was holding the door of his office open for me, but I knew it wasn't out of respect. He just wanted to make sure I didn't change course and try to escape.

"You'll be on dog duty this weekend," he said when the door was shut behind me.

Mauser was flopped over on his mattress in a corner of the office. Normally he would have jumped up and given me one of his oversize greetings, but this time he just looked at me and yawned. He was as bored with me being his babysitter as I was.

"Dad, don't you think this has gone on long enough?" I asked. When his face turned an ugly color of scarlet, I realized I'd made a mistake.

"Don't." He held up his hand. "Doing a few minor chores isn't going to kill you, and it might make you stop and think the next time you're considering doing something stupid."

"That's not fair. We've gone over this. You know why I did what I did."

"I know you could have gotten people killed. Rules are in place for a reason."

"Fine! Just tell me what I have to do to end this," I said in my most petulant twelve-year-old tone. I was tired of being the whipping boy over a mistake that I wasn't even sure was a mistake.

"No," he said through gritted teeth.

"What?"

"No. *I'm* the one who's tired of being an angry father," he said, giving me the distinct impression that he'd read my mind.

"Good. Then can we just get past this?"

"No," he said again, and for a minute I didn't think he was going to say anything else. Then he stepped forward, putting his nose five inches from mine and focusing on me with those intense green eyes. "I want you to tell me that you aren't going to do something stupid and throw your life away."

His anger was gone, replaced by something even more frightening. Fear. The only other time I'd ever seen fear in my dad's eyes had been the day my mother went to the hospital and never came home.

"I'm not going to get myself killed. You've come closer to dying on this job than me," I reminded him, thinking of that horrible day only a few months ago.

"Damn it, Larry! You take too many chances. If—and it's a big 'if' at this point—*if* you get that promotion, your decisions will impact other people's lives."

The vulnerability in his voice unnerved me.

"I'm not a fool." I should have told him that I would be more careful and that I didn't really want to cut my own life short by doing something idiotic. But to say those things would have been to recognize my own vulnerability.

"That's what frustrates the hell out of me."

After a moment of uncomfortable silence, I finally said, "When do you want me to pick up your moose?" resigning myself to another weekend babysitting Mauser.

"The usual, Friday afternoon. Genie and I are going down to the coast for the weekend."

"Must be nice," I said with enough snark to keep our relationship in balance.

"Someday maybe you'll get to take grown-up vacations. Of course, you'll have to grow up first." He followed that with a short, harsh laugh to let me know he was still the same old man I loved.

Mauser gave a grumbly whine from his corner. He hated any kind of conflict. I opened the treat jar Dad kept on his desk, causing a Pavlovian response that sent Mauser galloping over to throw himself against my legs.

"Stupid mutt." I smiled and let him devour the dog treat.

I wiped the slobber on my pants as I went to find Pete, who was gossiping with some of the deputies from our tactical response team. I had a funny feeling watching him joke and laugh with them. It made his departure from CID seem more real. With him moving out, and assuming I got the promotion to sergeant, I was looking at a whole new work environment. It wasn't a comforting thought.

CHAPTER FOUR

I pulled Pete away from the others and we headed out to the car. The restaurant was only a mile away, so I let Pete drive. When I got in the car, I looked at my watch and saw that it was already after five, so I texted my wife, Cara, that I would be getting home late.

At the Palmetto, the hostess recognized us and called for Mary, the owner, when Pete asked for her. Though Mary's father had been convicted of several murders, she didn't hold any grudges against us for putting her father on death row, knowing that we were some of her best customers and biggest supporters. After a brief greeting, we explained that we needed to talk to Shelby.

"Do you want to use my office?" Mary offered. "I'll send her back there."

Shelby was hugging several menus against her chest as she came to the office door. Her blonde hair fell off her shoulders in a natural way that made her look younger than the furrows on her brow and wrinkles around her eyes told us she was.

"I… Are you… I know you're deputies…"

"You might want to sit down." Pete waved her to one of the chairs in the office.

Still clutching the menus, she lowered herself down into the chair while she looked back and forth between Pete and me.

"I got a call from a friend before I came into work. He said there was… trouble out at the worksite," she said nervously.

"We're sorry, but Drew was found dead in the office trailer this morning," Pete said, delivering the news as gently as he could.

"I don't understand. He was… healthy. I mean, I know he wasn't young, but…" Shelby was searching our eyes for answers. We let her have some time to flounder around with her thoughts. It might seem cruel, but in these moments, people will often fill the gaps with information that they might not ordinarily give an investigator. Instead, Shelby finally reached a point where she just stared at us.

"He was killed," Pete said.

Her mouth dropped open. "Why? How?"

"Those are questions we haven't answered yet," I said.

Pete and I had decided to do a dual interrogation. Sometimes one of us would take the lead and the other would sit back and observe, while at other times we'd both ask questions. This was most effective when we wanted a witness or suspect to be kept off guard. It didn't allow them to focus on just one investigator. Neither of us thought that Shelby was a likely suspect, but from what we knew at the moment, she would probably inherit King's estate, which gave her a classic motive.

"Do you know of anyone who might have wanted to harm Drew?" Pete asked.

Shelby opened and closed her mouth several times, trying to come to terms with what was happening.

"I… Maybe… He could be kind of in your face if he got upset. Like his neighbor, Crenshaw, they got in fights a couple of times when I lived there."

"Fights about what?" I asked.

"Fights might be too strong of a word," she backpedaled.

"They were more like arguments. Mostly they were about Drew's dog. He's a hound dog and barks when he sees things, you know, like raccoons and stuff. Crenshaw would get mad and complain. Drew would tell him to go pound sand. That is… was Drew's favorite phrase. Go pound sand."

"Were you and Drew getting along?" Art had told us that they were separated. I just wanted to give her a chance to lie to us.

"No…" She let it drag out into a pregnant pause. "We didn't do so well living together."

"Did you argue a lot?" Pete asked.

"No. It wasn't like that. I think it was a freedom thing for Drew. For me, I guess it was a security thing."

"Can you explain that?"

"Like he wanted to go out whenever the mood hit him. There were times when he wouldn't come home or call or anything. I mean, geez, it's not like he didn't have a phone with him. I'd text and call and nothing. When I'd ask him why he didn't answer my calls or texts, he just said it made him feel like someone had a leash on him. Drove me up a wall. I never knew whether he was coming home or not. You know?"

I could see the problem. Sometimes my own phone felt like an anchor on my hip, but keeping in touch with Cara and her keeping in touch with me was part of our love. It signaled our connectedness and mutual respect.

"Did you think Drew was seeing other women?" Pete had been walking around the small office, but as he asked the question he stopped and looked Shelby in the eyes. She didn't flinch.

"No. He liked to drink and hang out with the guys or go fishing. He fished a lot."

"But you didn't know what he was doing?"

Shelby seemed confused by the question. For a few moments she looked down, as though thinking hard about her answer.

"I get it. When you lay it out like that, it sounds like he could be sleeping around. Thing is, it never felt like that. This isn't my first rodeo. I've been married before and been in a few long-term relationships. A woman gets a feeling when a guy's stepping out on her. She might not want to admit it, but she knows. Drew didn't even eyeball other women when we were together. He loved being in love, but he didn't like being in a relationship that forced him to answer to someone else."

Assuming we didn't find out that he had a little black book with a hundred names in it, Shelby had probably hit the nail on the head. I knew guys like that. They just felt trapped as soon as they had the relationship they'd been chasing. Cops were the worst. The job demanded so much of an officer that it was hard to answer to anyone else while off-duty.

"Did you all have any public arguments?" Pete knew the value of getting a suspect to make a statement which could be proven true or false.

"No." Her voice was firm.

"How much do you think Drew's estate is worth?" I decided to toss her a question she wouldn't be expecting, and I got a reaction. Her mouth moved like a fish gulping for air for at least ten seconds.

"I never thought about it," she finally managed.

"Technically, you two are still married," I pointed out, letting the weight of the words sink in.

"I never thought... Yes, we are. I... We hadn't really figured out what we were going to do."

"So you'll inherit his estate," Pete told her.

"You can't think... Oh no." She was shaking her head vigorously. "I liked Drew... I maybe even still loved him."

"We have to consider all the possibilities," Pete said. "I'm just looking at the facts."

"I guess I understand." She didn't sound sure at all.

"Can you tell us where you were last night?" I asked, not wanting to give her too much time to think.

"I was with my friend, Nell. I've been staying with her since I moved out of Drew's house."

"What were you doing?"

"Drinking wine and binging on *Yellowstone*."

"Can you give us more details?"

"Sure. I got home from work around ten. I brought food from the restaurant and we ate that while we watched TV. Nell had gotten a couple of bottles of wine for her birthday last week, so we opened one and… I fell asleep about midnight. I'm not much of a drinker. I guess she turned off the TV at some point 'cause when I woke up around two, I was on the sofa and the lights were all out. I got up, got a glass of water and some aspirin before going to bed."

"Nell didn't see you when you got up?" I asked.

"She'd gone to bed. I haven't seen her since we were watching TV. She left for work before I got up." She looked at her watch. "Nell gets home about six."

She gave us Nell's phone number and address.

"Can I look at your phone?" I asked, holding out my hand.

She'd taken the phone out to read off her friend's number. After a brief hesitation, she handed it to me. She didn't have to show it to me, but everyone knows that the quickest way to raise an investigator's suspicions is to act like you don't want them to snoop through your private affairs.

I checked her messages and saw that she'd last texted Drew two days earlier. She had asked about some clothes she'd left at his house, then he had suggested that they get together for dinner to discuss how to move forward. She had answered in the affirmative without setting any specific time or place. I flipped to her recent calls and saw that she hadn't talked to Drew for over a week. Other texts and calls looked innocuous. I handed the phone back.

"You mentioned the neighbor, Crenshaw. Can you think of anyone else who might want to hurt Drew?" I asked.

"A few. I mean, I don't really know them. I just know he talked about people he had arguments with. He talked about how tough the construction business could be. Guys get mad when you fire them. I remember him talking about some of his… What do you call them? Subcontractors that he'd refuse to pay until they fixed problems with their work. That kind of thing." She paused and looked at us. "Then I guess you guys know about his work as a cop. There were a couple of times that he pointed out people he said had threatened him when he was a deputy."

"Do you remember who they were?" Pete asked.

"Not really. We'd be in a bar or restaurant and he'd say, 'See that woman? She scratched the hell out me. She told me she'd rip my…' you know… testicles off if she ever got the chance. There was a guy at the docks once. A big nasty-looking guy. Drew said he threatened to have him killed 'cause Drew arrested his brother."

Shelby didn't remember the man's name but told us he'd been working on a fishing charter boat out of Panama City around August of last year.

We finished with her and assured her that we would let both her and Drew's son know when the morgue would release his body.

"I don't think I should have much say in his funeral. Drew had family and friends that were closer to him than I was."

"The fact is, you're his wife and the law doesn't make a distinction between wives who were close to their husbands and ones who weren't. It's an on-or-off type of deal," Pete informed her.

"Do you want to have dinner?" I asked Pete as we walked with Shelby back to the main dining room.

"I've already had a thousand calories today. I think I'll just head on home." Pete looked mournfully at the plates of food in front of the diners we passed.

"I should get home anyway." I gave him a supportive pat on the back.

Cara was on her phone when I got home. After greeting the menagerie of our Pug Alvin, our very clingy tabby cat, Ivy, and our nine-month-old crazy white kitten, Ghost, I eavesdropped on Cara's call enough to know that she was talking to her father.

"I need to go down to Gainesville this weekend," she told me after ending the call. "Mom's got something going on health-wise. Dad says she's been trying to treat it with her remedies…" Cara put air quotes around the last word. Her parents were professional hippies and her mother in particular had been known to put too much faith in the healing powers of the universe. "Dad thinks she needs to see a real doctor and wants me to try and convince her."

"Why does he think you'll have any more luck than he has?"

"Because it has to do with female—"

I didn't hear the rest because I put my fingers in my ears and started shaking my head. "Sorry, I don't need the images in my brain."

"And I do?" she quipped.

"When are you going?"

"Friday afternoon. With luck I'll be back Sunday."

"That's fine. My only plans for the weekend are babysitting the beast and working on paperwork, including preparing the next talk on proper police methods."

"Your dad's still sore?" she asked sympathetically.

"I think he's angry, and… I don't know… worried." I wasn't sure how much I wanted to share about Dad's recent revelation of his insecurities.

"I can understand that. You scare the hell out of me sometimes." Cara came over and put her hands on my waist and kissed me.

"I get it. It just bothers me that he's questioning my judgment."

"I'm not doing that. Maybe he's not either. You might be doing the son thing and projecting your own insecurities onto him."

"That's Doctor Phil stuff," I said with a small smile. "You might not be wrong. I just want to move on from this."

"He'll ease up soon enough. Any word when the promotion committee is going to make a decision?"

"Maybe next week. I've tried to ignore it. They're going to do what they're going to do. I think Phil will get his promotion. I'm not so sure about mine."

"Would they do that?"

"They can promote him and not me, but not the other way around. 'Cause if they promoted me and not Phil, everyone would see that as nepotism."

"Sorry I won't be here to help you with Mauser," she said to change the subject.

"We'll get along okay. He's been here enough recently that he's bored with it and less inclined to break too much of the furniture. As long as that raccoon doesn't come around."

The branches of an ancient live oak tree curved over our doublewide, and a mother raccoon and her kits had taken to dropping down onto our roof at night and running around. Which was usually okay as they didn't make that much noise. However, it was enough to wake Mauser, causing him to bounce around barking at the ceiling in the middle of the night.

"I'll make him up some special meals before I go," Cara said. There was a soft bark at her feet. "And some for you too. You're still my bestie." She reached down and scratched Alvin's back, making him grunt in pleasure.

"He loves the big idiot more than anyone." I looked around to see Ivy glaring at me from the back of the couch. "I know you're tired of him now, missy." She stretched and scratched her claws on the upholstery until Ghost jumped up and batted at her. She swatted back at him with a corrective hiss that sent him running across the room.

Dinner consisted of salads for both of us. While I didn't *need* to lose weight, I'd reached a point where if I didn't pay attention to what I was eating, my clothes would shrink.

"I heard there was a murder at a construction site," Cara said, trying not to sound too interested.

I wasn't surprised that she'd heard about it. She worked at the only veterinary clinic in town. Everyone in the county that owned a small animal knew Dr. Barnhill and his staff. The clinic grapevine was only slightly slower than the one in the first-responder community.

I thought about how much I wanted to tell her. After more than two years together, I'd learned to walk the fine line between satisfying her curiosity without divulging important evidence. My guide stone was our public information officer. Anything that they were willing to release to the papers, I could tell Cara.

"There was. The victim is Drew King. He retired from the sheriff's office about nine years ago."

"There must be a lot of anger and grief in the department, losing a friend like that."

"Drew was Pete's FTO and they had a close bond. But, yeah, just about everyone at the office knew and liked Drew."

"Are there any suspects?"

I sighed. "That's the kicker. An old friend of mine was found at the scene."

"Did he do it?"

I shrugged as I swallowed a mouthful of rabbit food. "I don't know. He was passed out at the scene and denies that he was involved in the murder. But any way you slice it, it's hard to figure how he can be innocent."

"You said he was a friend of yours?"

"We were best friends back in elementary school. Spent the night at each other's houses and went everywhere together. The kind of friend you can only have before the hormones kick in."

"What's his name?"

"Robin Hennessy."

"I don't think I've ever heard you talk about him."

"We grew apart in middle school. His parents split up,

which caused him to start hanging out with the wrong crowd. By the time we were in high school, he was drunk most of the time."

"Middle school is a tough time for most kids."

"He never recovered and has been drunk ever since."

"Why would he kill a retired deputy? Was he violent?"

"That's what's bugging me. He's never been violent, or even malicious. When I was on patrol, I dealt with him a few times. A pain in the ass, yes, but never violent. Just an addict. My grandfather would have called him a bum."

"Is it your case?"

"Pete's, but Parks is letting me assist."

Cara smiled. "That sounds like you aren't on the naughty list anymore."

"I was a little surprised. But then Major Parks isn't Dad."

"I hope you can help your friend."

"Me too. I just don't think he did it. And that's a bias I'll have to watch out for."

We spent the rest of the evening geeking out by playing a board game based on the movie *Alien*. We wound up dead the first time and only just managed to save ourselves and the ship the second time. It was nice to be engaged in a crisis that we could pack up in a box when we were done.

CHAPTER FIVE

I came into the office on Thursday determined to spend the first hour putting together the next presentation that Phil and I were scheduled to make on Monday. I wanted it done so I wouldn't have to think about it while working on the Drew King case or have to deal with it over the weekend. So much for best laid plans; the phone rang before I was even in my seat. I frowned at it, wondering why we even still had desk phones. Hoping the call would be short and unimportant, I answered it.

"Larry?" a woman asked. She had an accent I couldn't place, yet her voice was oddly familiar.

"Yes, this is Deputy Larry Macklin with the Adam's County Sheriff's Office. What can I do for you?" Not recognizing the voice, I wasn't going to assume that it was someone who should be on a first-name basis with me.

"You don't remember me. I'm Robin's mother."

A host of memories flooded into my mind. "Mrs. Hennessy. Of course I remember you."

"Robin called me last night. He said you arrested him for breaking and entering. And… and… there was something about a murder." Her voice was strained.

"I'd rather talk to you in person. Are you still in the

area?"

"Yes. I live on Lake Loka."

Depending on where on the lake she lived, I could be there in forty or fifty minutes. Seeing my plans for the day go out the window, I asked, "Are you going to be around this morning?"

"Yes."

"Can you text me your address?"

"I don't do much with my phone. Can I just tell you?"

Shaking my head a little, I grabbed a pen and a pad of paper. "Sure."

An hour later, I pulled up to her small cabin near the water. The lake, a major bass fishing destination, had been formed by a damn across the Loka River. I'd spent quite a bit of time on the lake as a kid, and still remembered the historical marker near the boat ramp that explained the origin of the river's name from the Muscogee Creek word *lucv*, meaning turtle. The Muscogee had camped along the shores long before the white settlers arrived.

Mrs. Hennessy opened the door before I could knock. She looked younger than I would have imagined and was wearing slacks and a colorful blouse.

"Larry, look at you!" she exclaimed. "What an impressive young man you've turned out to be." Her words seemed laced with a deep melancholy. "If only Robin could have stayed friends with the likes of you."

I walked through the door that she held open for me.

"It's a little chilly in here. The electric heat doesn't work very well," she said apologetically. "When Roger's here, he makes a fire in the woodstove that heats the whole place, but I'm not comfortable doing that."

"Roger?" I asked.

"My husband. I'm sorry I didn't correct you on the phone. My name is Rose Walsh now. I remarried… Gosh, I guess ten years ago."

"Your husband is away?"

"He's an engineer. Retired, but he still does some

consulting work. He's in Texas right now."

She waved me into the living room. A couch and two overstuffed chairs barely fit in the small space, which would have felt cramped if it wasn't for the huge window that overlooked the lake. Built up on a tree-lined bluff above the water, the cabin was sandwiched between larger homes that each had a boat dock.

"You said that Robin called you last night?" I prompted her once we were seated.

"I didn't understand what he was talking about. How could he be involved in a murder?"

I decided not to mince words. "He was found at a construction site with the body of a dead man."

"That's crazy. I know Robin has his problems, but he's a good soul."

"I want to help Robin as much as I can," I said. "In order to do that, I need as much information as you can give me."

"I'll tell you anything I can."

"Let's go way back. I met Robin in second grade. Y'all had just moved here, right?"

"That's right. We came down from Canada. At least his father and I did. We moved to Tampa right before Robin was born. We came up here when Luke got a job as a forester, managing one of the tracts of land owned by the St. Joe Paper Company."

"I remember spending the night at your house a couple of times."

"I hope the fights didn't keep you up at night," she said ruefully.

I shrugged. "There *was* a bit of tension."

"I apologize retroactively."

"Robin took your divorce hard."

Rose sighed. "It was the classic dilemma: Do you stay together for the child or split up so they have a peaceful homelife? I still don't know if we made the right choice 'cause you're right, Robin was never the same afterward. I blame myself... Oh, not for the separation... That needed to happen. My husband was a difficult man to get along with." She paused, as if struggling to explain herself. "Both of us were from Irish Catholic families—my mother came over from County Clare with her family when she was just a child. And Luke was a cliché of the hard-drinking, hard-fighting Irishman. It was romantic at first, but it's hard to live with."

"That couldn't have helped when you decided to get a divorce," I sympathized.

"My mother didn't speak to me for three years," she admitted, fiddling with a Celtic cross that hung from her neck. "Still, I couldn't live with the man any longer, and he'd started to turn his drunken rants against Robin and me. Sadly, Robin has never accepted the decision. It didn't help when Luke died only a few years later. Even today, if we talk, Robin will blame me for his father's death and the fact that he didn't have a closer relationship with him."

"That seems unfair."

"I don't know. Luke's heart attack was partially a result of his drinking, which became much worse after the divorce. The worst thing I did, and I *do* blame myself for this, was to keep Robin away from his father as much as I could. I'll always regret that. I thought I was protecting him. Instead, I created a hole in his soul that he's spent all these years trying to fill up with alcohol and drugs."

Rose's eyes were growing moist as she searched my face for hope. I decided it was time to address Robin's most recent crisis.

"Robin was found in the office trailer of a construction site near Calhoun. Unfortunately, he wasn't alone. Drew King, the owner of the construction company, was also there and Drew had been murdered."

"I can't make sense of that." Rose wiped at her eyes. "Robin couldn't hurt anyone."

"I hope that's true. Our best investigator, Pete Henley, is heading up the case, and I've been given permission to assist him. Right now, all Robin is being charged with is breaking and entering. He won't be charged with anything else unless the evidence is there." I paused and let this sink in. When I thought she'd had a chance to understand the situation, I let the other shoe drop as gently as I could. "As a seasoned investigator, I should tell you that the situation doesn't look good for Robin."

"Please believe me when I tell you he didn't do this," she begged.

"All I can tell you is that we'll examine all of the evidence very closely before we come to any conclusions."

"What can I do to help him?"

"I don't know if they'll set bail on the B-and-E charge. If so, he'll need someone to post his bond. Beyond that, the judge is going to want to know where he's going to stay. If you could let him stay here, the judge would look more favorably on releasing him."

Rose started to cry. "My husband won't allow him to stay here. He calls him a drunk and… I know it's true. I don't blame Roger. The last time Robin stayed with us, this was years ago, he stole almost five hundred dollars. Since then…" Her voice trailed off into tortured sobs.

"It's okay. If Robin gets out on bail, we'll find a place for him to stay. There are several halfway houses in the county that might let him in."

Rose reached out and touched my arm. "Thank you. Your family was always so good to Robin. He loved staying with you."

I couldn't stop myself from thinking: *He's not staying with me when he's out of jail.*

"Before he called you from jail, when was the last time you talked to Robin?" I asked.

"He only calls me about once a month." She sighed and wiped the last of her tears away. "It's usually close to the first of the month when he knows I get my Social Security check. Sometimes I meet him. Other times, I'll just send him money. A week or so ago, just after the first of March, he called. I met him at the taco truck in Calhoun. We didn't talk long. It was too cold and windy."

"I want you to think hard about this next question. Did he ever mention Drew King?"

Rose furrowed her brow and considered her answer before admitting that she didn't remember ever hearing Drew's name.

"What about Blue Land Development? Did he ever mention anything about the company?"

She shook her head. "No. We seldom talked about… anything really. The days when I would try and encourage him to look for a job or go to AA meetings are long gone. I've learned to accept the fact that, unless he decides to change his life, there's nothing I can do to help him."

"Did he ever do construction work?"

"Robin gets day jobs occasionally, especially if the weather has been bad. Panhandling is not so good when it's cold or raining," she said bitterly.

"Can you tell me the names of any of his friends?"

"Why are you asking me these questions? He's not dead."

"I'm not going to lie to you. Right now, we have to treat Robin like a suspect, and that means getting all the information we can about him. I'll ask *him* about his friends, but now I'm asking you."

"I'm sorry, but I doubt he has any friends, not in the true sense of the word. I guess he hangs around other drunks and drug addicts. Are those friends?"

I felt a little embarrassed. "You're right. I should have asked you who he hangs out with."

"And the answer is that I still don't know." Rose looked thoughtful for a moment, then said, "There *was* a girl. Well, a woman. Robin met her a few years ago. She was… awful. I know how that sounds, but you'd have to meet her. The three times I saw her, she was high. Thin as a rail. Honestly, I was worried she had HIV or some other issues going on. Robin called her his girlfriend." The disapproval was evident in her expression.

"What was her name?" I asked, wondering if it was someone I might have encountered working on another case.

"I think it was Nat. Roger thought it was funny she was named after a bug. I don't know if it was a nickname or short for Natalie or something."

I ran the name through my mental rolodex of the street people I knew. Nat didn't ring any bells. "What did she look like?" I asked.

"Maybe five-foot-four? Very skinny. I don't think she weighed more than a hundred pounds. Black hair that would have been long and straight, but I think she pulled it out because it was thin in places. I wasn't sure that wasn't a symptom of some disease. She just looked… unhealthy."

"Color of her eyes?"

"I wouldn't know. I didn't notice them. She had all these things in her face… piercings."

"Can you be specific about the piercings?"

"There was a large one through her left nostril. Some on her cheeks and lips."

"Anything else?"

Rose hesitated. "I haven't mentioned the worst of it. Her tongue was split. It was very distracting to see someone with a forked tongue."

I stifled a groan. "I know her," I said noncommittally. Her street name was Snake Tongue and she was notorious for spitting at people, especially cops. I didn't look forward to digging her out of whatever hole she'd crawled into.

There were plenty of people living on the streets who were easy to get along with. If there was a problem, it was possible to talk to them and work it out. Others like Snake Tongue were just plain nasty when confronted. Most of the time, she wouldn't even wait to find out what you wanted to talk to her about. As soon as she saw you pull up, she'd either start spitting or screaming or both. Whatever her childhood had been like, it had created one angry person who was almost impossible to work with.

"Curious that Robin would hook up with someone like… Nat," I said.

"She was manipulative. And I'm sad to say that Robin was an easy target."

"Did they break up?" I asked.

Rose shrugged. "He knew I didn't approve of her, so he just quit bringing her around or talking about her. I don't know if he's still seeing her or not."

I couldn't help but think how sad this family was. "Can you think of anything else that might shed light on Robin's more recent activities?"

"Nothing. You must think I'm a horrible mother. I've tried to help him. I've tried being supportive, I've tried tough love… now I just do what I can."

"None of us can see into the future. We just make the best decisions we can," I said, trying to comfort her. I'd seen so many parents that had lost children who were still alive, but would never truly be their children again. It was heartbreaking. The other side of the coin were children who had horrible parents and had never known the support of someone who truly cared. I wished it was possible to make a cosmic trade where children who didn't appreciate their parents could go with the parents who wouldn't love their children, and all the loving parents would get loving children.

"I'll do whatever I can for him," Rose told me.

"The arraignment will most likely take place at the courthouse tomorrow morning. That's when a judge will decide whether to post bail. I don't know what your circumstances are. If you can't afford a lawyer for him, one will be appointed to represent him. In fact, he's probably already been notified of who will represent him tomorrow."

"Should I hire a lawyer?"

I was brutally honest. "We have some good public defenders in our county. If Robin was just facing the breaking and entering charge, then I'd say he'd be fine. But with a possible murder charge, I'd recommend that you hire the best lawyer you can afford."

"Is there anyone you'd suggest?"

"I'll give you the name of a friend of mine who can help

you sort through the options and find the best lawyer you can." I almost left it at that, but then I thought of her losing her house, and maybe even her husband, over this. "Don't ruin your own life in an attempt to save Robin."

"I'm his mother," she said fiercely. "If I have to sacrifice myself for my son, I will."

I thought of a parent plunging into the water to save a drowning child, only to fail and leave the family with two funerals instead of one. Choices aren't always fair.

"Call me if you need anything," I told Rose, leaving her standing at the door looking more lost and scared than when I'd arrived.

CHAPTER SIX

I headed back to Calhoun. As I passed the city limits sign, I saw a police car parked on the side of the road, half hidden behind a wax myrtle bush. I was planning to give a classic country wave to the officer when I noticed that it was my old partner, Darlene Marks, standing near the car with a radar gun.

I turned around and pulled off the road next to her.

"Is this chief-of-police work?" I asked with a big smile as I got out of my car.

"It is when I'm tired of dealing with the crap back at the station." Darlene grinned. "I wish I had the nerve to turn off my phone." She hit an approaching car with the radar gun. "Sixty-one. Six over the limit. By the way, you were seven over."

"Nine, you're fine," I tossed back.

Her face turned serious. "Heard about Drew King. That's a pity. I didn't know him that well, and he wasn't my kind of guy, but all the cops had great respect for him."

"He was definitely a man's man," I agreed. "I remember going to his house with Dad for a family cookout for the department. He and a dozen other deputies dug a mud pit and bet on wrestling matches the rest of the afternoon. But he always managed to stay just below the point of getting loud and obnoxious."

"His ability to know where the edge was, and staying just on the right side of it, was what a lot of the officers liked about him," Darlene agreed. "What's the story with the murder?"

"Robin Hennessy was found in the office trailer with Drew's body."

"Rollin' Robin?"

"Rollin'?"

Darlene nodded. "When I first started with the police department, my FTO and I pulled up on him at the Fast Mart. The clerk had called it in when Robin refused to leave. A customer had complained about the odor and his begging. I get out of the car and Robin is lying on the sidewalk in front of the store. I ask him the usual questions and ascertain that he's just blottoed out of his mind on Mad Dog or some other rotgut. I tell him he has to leave the premises or be charged with trespassing. He tries to get up and can't. I warn him that he'll go to jail if he can't move off the property, but he still can't get his legs to work. Jefferson, my FTO, tells me to load him in the back. I wave him over and, when he gets a whiff of Robin, he tells me to belay that order. That's when Jefferson asks Robin if he can roll. Robin tries it and manages to roll a ways down the sidewalk. Long story short, we managed to get him to roll to a safe enough place under a tree and tucked him in for the night."

"He's not a bad guy."

"Never thought he was. He always tried to comply with my orders and only bothered people when he was really over the moon. Did he kill Drew?"

I shook my head. "I don't know. My gut says no way, but the evidence says he has to be at the top of the suspect list."

"He sleeps like a rock," Darlene said. "Twice we've had calls from people who thought he was dead."

"Really?" I said, raising my eyebrows. "Then it's possible that he *was* passed out in there while the killing took place.

But then why would the killer leave Robin alive? If you were the murderer, would you assume the guy sprawled out on the couch was passed out? I wouldn't."

"Maybe the killer set Robin up. Could have even drugged him, which wouldn't be that difficult. They could have used a substance like GHB, which suppresses memories."

I thought this over. "So the perp buddies up to Robin, slips him a date-rape drug and then takes him to the construction site before killing Drew. After the murder, he stages Robin on the couch and leaves. I like it. We drew blood from him, so we can test for drugs. Honestly, that's the best-case scenario for him."

Darlene gave me a mock salute. "Always glad to be of service. You still in the doghouse?"

"Oh yeah. Literally. I've got moose-sitting duties again this weekend."

"I like your dad."

"Talk to him. He might adopt you."

"Get out of here before I give you a ticket." Darlene looked at her watch. "Hell's bells, I better get back on the merry-go-round. See you around the playground."

Back at the office, I ran into Pete sitting at his desk. He was picking at a salad and drinking iced tea. When he saw me, he raised the glass of tea.

"Unsweetened. I might as well be on a desert island eating berries and drinking rainwater."

"I feel for you," I told him.

He leaned back in his chair as I told him about my meeting with Robin's mother.

"Well, you can let her know that we're going to turn him loose," Pete said, surprising me and looking very unhappy about it. "The State Attorney doesn't want us to keep him locked up without more evidence to hold him on the murder charge. When Major Parks and I met with him, he explained that if we keep Robin locked up, it'll look like our investigation is focused on him. If Robin is charged and the case gets in front of a jury, they don't want it to appear that we didn't do a thorough investigation."

"I guess that makes sense."

"It does, but I think it's short-sighted. I know the B-and-E charge is thin, maybe even bogus, but it keeps Robin out of trouble and covers our butts if he's guilty."

"You have a point about keeping him out of trouble," I grumbled. "I was hoping that he'd be arraigned and the judge would let him out on bail, preferably with some stipulations, like he has to be under supervision."

"I argued that exact point," Pete agreed. "But the State Attorney still thinks that breaking and entering is too thin not to look like an excuse if the case goes to trial."

"In this case, he's the boss."

"We need to find Robin a place to stay where someone can keep an eye on him and keep him sober."

There weren't many options. "We can try the two halfway houses in town."

"Called both of them and they're full through the weekend."

"Great. What about out of town?"

Pete thought about it. "That might be better, because it would keep him away from his old drinking buddies. Trouble is, where? And who's going to take him?"

"Somewhere in Tallahassee? His mother made it clear that he can't stay with her."

"Didn't you say her husband is out of town?"

"Yeah."

"Then maybe he could stay there just for the weekend. The halfway house on Martin Street will have a room on Monday."

"I'll call her."

I called Rose Walsh and explained that the situation had changed.

"You mean he's not under arrest?" She sounded confused.

"That's right. But he's still a person of interest in the

murder, so we want him to stay off the streets."

"I can't keep him sober. Never have been able to."

"We aren't expecting miracles," I assured her. "Do what you can. If there's trouble…" I hesitated for a second, then said what I knew I needed to. "…you'll have my number and can call me. Anytime."

"When will he get out of jail?"

"I'll drop the charges right before he would have been arraigned. That way he's locked up for one more night," said Pete, who'd been listening in on my conversation.

I passed the information on to Robin's mother. "I'll bring him to your house tomorrow as soon as he's released."

"I smell trainwreck all over this one," Pete said, shaking his head as I hung up the phone.

"What are you complaining about? I'm the one she's going to call when he gets drunk at three in the morning."

"And he *is* going to get drunk. I'll do as much investigating as I can between now and tomorrow morning. Maybe we'll get lucky and find some clues that are inculpatory or exculpatory. I'd like to know if we're letting a killer loose… or just an alcoholic."

"One of the people Robin hung around with was Nat," I revealed.

"Who?"

"You know, Snake Tongue."

"Oh God, not her. She gives me the heebie jeebies. You know, I've seen a lot of tattoos and whatnot, but she's… different."

"Yeah, it's people like her that give body modification a bad name."

"Since I'm the lead investigator on this case, I assign *you* to go interview her."

"Thanks, boss," I said, flipping him a casual bird. "When are you going to move out to the range?"

"You're going to miss me when I'm gone."

"Maybe." I smiled. "Guess I'll go see if I can find the snake woman."

I checked recent calls for service and she popped up on a report dated only a week earlier. The report detailed a complaint that a "strange woman" was squatting in a duplex down in the Ditch, one of Calhoun's least savory neighborhoods. The address of the duplex was one that every deputy and cop in the city knew, sort of like how all the teachers learn the names of the troublemakers on the first day of school.

The gist of the report was that the deputy had made contact with Natalie Owens, the current occupant of the duplex, who informed him that she was renting it from the person who had leased it from the landlord. After talking with the landlord, and establishing that the name which Natalie had given to the deputy was not the current signed tenant, the deputy had asked Natalie to step out of the apartment and walk with him to his car. She tried to spit at him, but he'd had dealings with her in the past and was prepared for that trick. The deputy informed her that spitting was a form of assault and that she would be arrested if she did it again. Finally, she had called someone to come pick her up. End of story. Except, luckily for me, the deputy had had the foresight to include both Natalie's phone number and the name and number of the man who had picked her up.

I knew better, but I still tried her phone number first. I wasn't surprised when it went straight to voicemail. *Probably a burner phone*, I thought. Next, I tried the number of Roderick Messer, the man who had picked her up. I was a little shocked when he answered.

"Who this?"

"I'm Deputy Larry Macklin with the sheriff's office. I'd like to talk to you about an incident that took place a week ago. You picked up a young woman who was having trouble with her living arrangements?"

"What?"

"I want to talk to you about Nat," I said, cutting to the chase.

"I don't narc on no one. 'Specially her."

"Mr. Messer, I'd like this call to be all friendly-like. Don't make me do a records check on you."

"I get it," he said without indicating if he was willing to cooperate.

"We'll do it this way. I'll ask some questions and you answer the ones you want. If, by the time we're done, I'm not satisfied with your level of cooperation… Well… we'll deal with that then. First, do you know where she is?"

"That's an easy one. No."

"Have you seen or talked to her within the last week?"

"Yeah."

"Which?"

"Both."

"Where and when did you see her?"

"At a party. Sunday night."

"Where was the party."

"Nah. Not answering that one," he said emphatically, all but telling me that it had been more of a drug den than a party.

"What part of town was it in?"

There was a drawn-out silence. I didn't know if he was trying to decide whether to answer the question or if he honestly didn't know how to describe it. Finally, he said, "Guess you'd say the middle of town."

I thought about the location of the duplex from the report. You could call that the middle of town. "The Ditch?" I asked.

"Yeah, okay."

"Near where you picked her up?"

After more silence, he allowed, "Maybe." Which was a definite "yes."

"Have you seen Robin Hennessy in the past week?" I asked, changing tack.

"Oh, hell, is that what this is about? I heard he killed a dude. Not my business, man!" His voice was becoming hysterical. "I'm not getting involved in a killing."

"I'm just looking for Nat. Right now, all I want to do is talk to her."

He cursed loudly, then said, "You hang around the Ditch between the time it gets dark and… I guess about midnight, you'll see her walking around."

"You didn't answer my question about Hennessy," I reminded him.

"He was at the same party Sunday night."

"Were they together?"

"What the hell do you think it was, the prom or something? I don't know if they were together. They were in the same house. I know that."

He had a point.

"Was Hennessy taking drugs?"

"I don't know. He's always high, but mostly sticks to drinking. But he'll do ecstasy, party drugs, stuff like that."

I asked a few more questions without getting any more useable information.

"I'm going to talk to Robin," I said to Pete after finishing with Messer.

"You didn't find out where Snake Tongue is hiding?"

"I was told that if I hang out for hours at night in the Ditch, that sooner or later she'll wander by."

"That sounds like fun."

"If you want, I'll talk to Robin about being released."

"That'd be great," he said and turned his attention back to his computer monitor.

It was well past noon when I walked out to my car. The jail was literally just across the street from the office, but I thought I might drive around and look for Natalie Owens when I finished with Robin.

At the jail, I put my gun in a locker and signed the guest book to indicate which prisoner I was there to see. Marge Jones, who reveled in her nickname of Large Marge, showed me to an interview room.

"I'll be back in a jiffy," she told me with her friendliest smile as she left to fetch Robin. I was glad to receive the smile. I'd seen her war face once when a prisoner had challenged her, and it could have made me wet my shorts.

Most people look the worse for wear after a day in prison. Robin, on the other hand, looked much better—clean and clear-eyed.

"I feel awful," he moaned after dropping down into the metal chair across from me.

"You don't look awful."

"Sober isn't good for me." He laid his head down on the table.

"You're going to be released."

He looked up at me. "You kidding?"

"No. I'm going to pick you up in the morning and take you to your mom's place."

"What?" He sat bolt upright and stared at me. Those clear eyes looked terrified. "Do I *have* to go to her place?"

"Would you rather stay here?"

"Yes!"

"Well, you can't." I felt he wasn't being very grateful.

"Her husband hates me."

"Roger won't be there."

This news caused him to relax a bit. "Why are you letting me loose?"

"The truth is, the State Attorney wants to find more evidence against you so they can charge you with Drew's murder." I didn't think I was giving away any secrets. If he had a lawyer, they would have told him the same thing.

"I didn't kill him." Robin didn't sound sure.

"If you blacked out..."

"No. No, I couldn't do that," Robin said, obviously trying to convince himself. If he wasn't sure himself, then I thought his chances would be slim to none of escaping a very long prison sentence.

"Where's Nat?" I asked.

Robin's eyes got big. "How would I know? I'm in prison."

"Where do you think I could find her?"

"Why?"

"I want to ask her some questions."

"She won't like that."

"I'm sure she won't."

"Have you ever met her?" He looked nervous, as if he thought she could be listening in on our conversation.

"Yes. I know she's… strong-willed."

"Don't make her mad."

"What's your relationship with her?"

"What?" It was as if the question had never occurred to him. Maybe it hadn't.

"Are y'all having sex?" I said bluntly. "Do you consider her your girlfriend?"

"I don't know."

"You don't know if you're having sex with her?" I frowned.

"No, yeah. I… yeah. We're kinda girlfriend and boyfriend, but she's… different."

"Obviously," I said, knowing that a relationship with her was likely to be difficult. "But what do you think she'll say if I ask her about your relationship?"

"Don't. Please." He was clearly worried.

"What are you scared of?" I asked, knowing that the answer was her.

"You have to ask?"

"Okay, that was a stupid question," I half apologized. "What I want to know is: Why are you hanging out with her?"

"'Cause she wants me to." Robin looked confused.

"Do you want to hang out with *her*?"

"Sometimes."

"When?"

"When she's nice and we're partying."

"What happens when she's not nice?"

"Ha!" he snorted. I let the silence drag out and become uncomfortable until he went on, "She gets real mean. Not just to me. That's part of it. I don't like to see her hurt other people."

"Who does she hurt?"

Robin seemed to take notice of where he was and who he was talking to.

"I'm not going to get her in trouble." He clamped his mouth shut.

"This isn't about her. I'm trying to pull your neck out of the noose."

"I couldn't ever… like… testify against her."

"Is it that bad?"

"She's hurt people real bad."

"Could *she* have killed Drew?"

From the look on Robin's face, this was the first time that he'd considered this possibility.

"That's crazy."

"You don't look like you think it's crazy."

"She's got a temper. I just… Why would she do it?"

"Let me give you a little lesson in solving murders. The murderer has to have means, motive and opportunity. Would you agree that Nat has the means?"

"What's that?"

"Is she mentally, emotionally and physically capable of killing Drew King?" I explained.

"I guess so," he admitted.

"That's one. Now we don't know what her motive is, but my question to you is: Have you ever seen her get mad enough over some petty disagreement that she's hurt someone?"

He didn't answer, but his silence spoke volumes.

"Pure anger could be a motive, so that's two," I pointed out. "Which leaves opportunity. When I talk to her, I'll try to find out where she was on Tuesday night and Wednesday morning."

"I don't think she did this."

"Why?"

Robin shrugged.

"If you didn't do it, then someone else did. Someone

who left you alive. Assuming, of course, that you were there when the killing took place and didn't just stumble onto the scene when it was over."

"I like that one. The one where I come in afterward," Robin said eagerly.

I sighed. "Unfortunately, there are some problems with that explanation. For one thing, the murder weapon was found underneath your hand, as if you'd dropped it. Or someone placed it there to *look* like you dropped it. Also, there was some blood near the door of the trailer that didn't have your footprints in it. It's possible you could have stepped over it, but not without being aware it was there. I doubt you could have done that as drunk as you were."

"Oh."

"That's right. Oh."

Robin rubbed his eyes. "This feels like I woke up after twenty years to find myself accused of murder."

"It's a tough way to get sober," I said with a notable lack of sympathy.

"I've tried to do it a few times before. Mostly pushed into it by Mom. Didn't go very well. Her husband still pisses in my ear about all the money thrown away on rehabs and doctors."

"I'm going to look for Natalie. I'll see you in the morning," I said, standing up.

Robin glanced at the clock on the wall that showed it was almost two. "She should be getting up about now."

"Does she have a car?"

"She doesn't even have a driver's license."

"I knew that." I'd noticed on her record that her driving privileges had been suspended four years earlier after multiple DUIs. She'd never bothered to get them restored. "Still, we aren't talking about the most law-abiding individual," I said and walked out of the room.

I spent the next three hours trying to track Natalie down. She wasn't anyone's favorite topic of conversation. The few people who would talk to me spent half the time looking over their shoulders as if they expected her to leap on their backs in a sneak attack.

Back at the office, Pete told me that King's autopsy had been scheduled for Friday.

"I won't be able to make it," I told him. "I'm delivering Robin to his mom in the morning."

"You on dog duty again this weekend?"

"Don't even start," I grumbled. I wasn't looking forward to being alone with Mauser. He was always more cooperative when Cara was around.

Phil Eccles texted to ask when I wanted to meet with him to go over our lesson plans. Major Parks had informed us that we would be released from this particular punishment after just two more sessions.

From the amount of shit I've been getting from the patrol officers, it will be good to get this behind us, Phil texted. I knew how he felt. The joking from the rank and file was starting to have a sharper edge to it.

Another text said: *The promotions committee is supposed to meet Wednesday.* I replied with a thumbs-up. At this point, I didn't care what they decided. I just wanted it over with so I could move on.

Cara and I intended to make the evening all about us since she was heading down to Gainesville the next day, but we weren't surprised when her mother called right after dinner and spent the next hour trying to convince Cara to stay home. Eventually we were able to enjoy a movie, then a mutual back rub that started on the couch and ended in the bedroom. I would have slept well if my dreams hadn't featured a forked-tongue woman and a giant black moose.

CHAPTER SEVEN

In the morning, I lingered awhile to hug Cara tightly and remind her to be careful on the road, then headed into work. Fridays at the sheriff's office tended to be either sleepy or chaotic. Luckily, this morning appeared to be one of the former. It had been cool enough the night before to keep a hefty portion of the illegal activity in the county indoors and out of public view, so the reports from patrol were light.

I'd been at my desk for an hour, working on my other cases, when Pete walked in.

"I've just been to the jail and signed the paperwork to let Robin go. You can pick him up whenever you want."

"Great. I just hope his mother can keep an eye on him."

"You met her. What are the odds?" Pete asked.

"Not good. She's nice, smart, a little judgmental, but also naïve. What happens is going to depend on what Robin *wants* to happen."

"And?"

"He hasn't been sober in twenty years. The DTs are going to be rough for him."

"Wonderful."

"And from talking to him, I'd say he's not committed to sobriety. In the plus column, his mother's house is down on

Lake Loka, so he'll be isolated… a little."

"At least he doesn't have his phone. It's down in evidence with Lionel."

"That's something. I'll try to reason with him on the drive to his mom's." I thought about what Pete had said and asked, "You mind if I take a look at the phone? I'm still trying to track down Natalie."

"Have at it," he told me. "If you find anything interesting, let me know so I have something to give the senior staff when I brief them. You can help with the briefing if you want."

"Nope," I said. "You're the lead on this one."

I got up and headed down to Lionel's office.

"I've copied all the data from it," Lionel said, handing me an evidence bag containing the phone. "And Marcus already checked it for blood and fingerprints."

I put on gloves before opening the bag. Robin didn't have the phone locked with a password, so it was easy to scroll through all of his contacts and texts.

"Ha!" I said when I found a contact labeled "Nat."

I read the texts between them, which mostly consisted of Natalie telling Robin what to do. *Pick me up here. Bring me food. Bring me cigarettes. Bring me an array of alcohol and drugs.* I wondered where she expected Robin to get the money to meet all of her demands, as his answers back were usually along the lines of: *I'm busted. They won't give me credit. I'll have to beg some.* Her responses were always petulant and demanding.

There were half a dozen locations mentioned in the texts she'd sent over the course of the last month. I made notes on my phone. Most of them seemed to be in some sort of code that I'd have to ask Robin to translate. I re-bagged the phone and handed it back to Lionel, then headed for the jail.

The deputies at the jail were always happy to see someone leave.

"Good weather will have the riffraff partying this weekend. I predict we'll be hanging out the 'no vacancy' sign by Sunday night," Marge said while I waited for Robin to change clothes.

He came out wearing a pair of county overalls since the clothes he'd been wearing had been tagged into evidence.

"They're big on me," he complained.

"We can go pick up your stuff if you want."

"Yeah, that would be good."

Robin had been staying at an informal hostel run by a character named Trojan who was always two inches on the right side of the law. He took in the homeless and the recently paroled, providing an important community service, and if law enforcement wanted to come in and look around, he never objected. But there was always a feeling that he turned a blind eye to any illegal activities that went on there. Some even speculated that he profited from deals that went down under his roof.

Trojan met us at the door of the house.

"Robin, you free?" he asked, eyeing me.

"Sort of. I'm going to be staying—" I elbowed him in the ribs. "—with other people," he said lamely. I didn't want everyone to know that he was going to be down at the lake.

"I put your stuff in the closet. Puke is staying in the room right now," Trojan told him. I knew Puke and could vouch for the fact that he'd come by his nickname honestly.

I followed Robin back to the closet. I'd been in the house a few times and was always surprised that it smelled as clean as it did, considering the people that were living there. Most of the residents looked like weekly baths were a burden to them.

Robin dug into the closet and pulled out a backpack that was large enough to hold a microwave oven. Tied to it were extra shoes, a raincoat and a sleeping bag. He opened it and took an inventory of his property before zipping it closed.

"Okay," he said, heading for the door. I stepped in front of him.

"This would be a good time to get rid of any alcohol or drugs," I advised.

Robin hesitated.

"Alcohol is one thing. Drugs are another. It's not fair to your mother to take drugs into her house," I said, staring him down.

He dropped the knapsack onto the floor and unzipped it, looking up at me. "You aren't going to see what I pull out of here, are you?"

"Yeah, I am, 'cause you're going to give them to me so I can dispose of them properly. You'll get a pass this time," I assured him.

Grudgingly, he pulled out a sandwich-size Ziplock bag containing a dozen jeweler's bags with a mix of pills.

"You know if you were found with this, you'd be charged with distributing drugs, not just possession?"

Robin shrugged. "They're for me... and sometimes I trade 'em."

"Like to Nat for... whatever." I shook my head and stuffed the bag into my pocket. "Let's go."

In the car, I told him that I expected him to stay sober for the next couple of days.

"I've already got the ants-in-my-pants thing going on now," he whined.

"Call me before you do anything stupid."

"I don't have a phone."

I sighed. "I'll fix that." I pulled into one of the three Dollar Generals in the county and bought him a pay-as-you-go phone.

"It's got thirty minutes on it," I said as I handed it to him. "Don't use them all up talking to Nat or trying to get a hit of something."

Just before we got to his mom's house, I pulled out my phone and showed him the notes I'd taken from his texts with Natalie.

"Where are those places?" I asked, handing him the phone while keeping my eyes on the road.

"Places?" he said, trying to evade the question.

"Come on, details. Nat texted you those locations like she knew you would know them. So tell me where they are."

Robin and I went back and forth until I was sure I knew where each one was. Once he explained, I understood the shorthand they'd used to describe each location. It all made perfect sense if you were a drug addict. Two were Fast Marts, one was a drug house that code enforcement had tried to have torn down a dozen times, the fourth was a vacant lot behind a strip mall and the last was the truck stop by the interstate.

"One more thing. If I find out that you've called and warned her that I'm looking for her, I will cut you loose," I said in my best drill sergeant voice. Robin nodded meekly.

Rose Walsh met us in the driveway.

"Robby, I need you to be on your best behavior," she told him.

"*He's* not here, right?"

"No. Still, if something should happen and he finds out that I let you stay here…"

"Don't worry," Robin said in an offhand manner that left me worrying.

"Call me before you do anything stupid," I warned him again, then left them standing awkwardly together.

On the way back to Calhoun, I decided to scope out Robin and Nat's meet-up spots, in the hopes of getting a lead on where she might be found.

The Fast Mart on the south side of town was the first location I came to.

"That woman's crazy! We have a trespass warning against her at all our stores," the clerk told me. He was part of the extended Indian family that owned the regional chain of stores.

"Have you seen her in the last week?"

"I would have called you all if I did. Honestly, man. She scares me. The tongue." He closed his eyes and shook his head in revulsion.

I didn't think he'd want to know that she'd used two of the stores as meeting places with Robin in the past week, though I figured she'd been hanging around the back. I thanked him and walked around the side of the store.

A pair of dumpsters, one for cardboard and the other for garbage, were behind the store. Scattered on the ground nearby, I found a number of indicators that addicts and drug dealers hung out there, which wasn't big news. Our drug unit had run more than one sting operation at the Fast Marts.

I stopped at the drug house next. It was about a block from the duplex where she'd been squatting. I caught sight of at least three people skulking in the area, but they scattered when I drove up. The rundown shotgun shack had been professionally boarded up. I assumed that the city must have finally managed to force the owner to take some responsibility for their property. I saw several new no-trespassing signs posted on the house as I walked around it, checking to see if anyone had tampered with any of the boards covering the windows or doorways. It was only a matter of time before the uglier elements would find their way back in.

As I came back to the front of the house, I saw a tall, lanky black man who looked to be in his fifties watching me from across the street. I waved to him and walked over.

"Can I ask you a few questions?"

He pulled his coat in around himself and scrutinized me for a minute before answering. "You a cop?"

I pulled out one of my cards and handed it to him.

"Investigator with the sheriff's office."

"Where are you all at three in the morning?" he asked.

"I guess it gets a little rough around here," I said sympathetically.

"Took us a year to get that place boarded up."

"And you are?"

"Jed Chamberlin. I'm the president of the homeowner association. We don't get much help." He looked down at the card I'd handed him. "You related to the sheriff?"

"I'm his son."

"He's not the worst we've had. He's come to our meetings and sends a deputy most of the time. Still, he's more talk than help."

I didn't see any point in trying to defend my father. Jed had every right to be angry and frustrated. Not that Dad wasn't equally angry and frustrated with the budget, and other restraints placed on him and on the department, that prevented him from enacting more proactive strategies.

"I'm looking for a woman who may hang out around here. She's white, thirty years old, with tattoos and a forked tongue."

At the mention of the tongue, Jed visibly flinched.

"I hope to high Heaven y'all are going to put that spawn of the devil in jail."

"When was the last time you saw her?"

"A week ago, right before they boarded up that crack house." He pointed across the street.

"Did you see who she was with?"

"That woman doesn't have no friends. Everyone around here, including the dealers and users, is afraid of her."

I asked a few more questions, then thanked Jed for his time and headed out to check the other locations. I found nothing. It had been a waste of time to try during the day. I knew I'd have to come back at night when the homeless, addicts and predators were out and about.

On my way back to the office, Marti in dispatch radioed to ask if I had time to take a call. He explained that they were shorthanded since a couple of deputies had called in with what he suspected were bad cases of springitis. With nothing better to do, I was routed to a homeowner with a report of vandalism.

"Mike Todd," said a middle-aged man with a thick New England accent as I got out of my car. He held out his hand and I shook it.

"See there?" He was pointing to a ten-inch gap in a chain-link fence that bordered his property.

His backyard was meticulously landscaped. The neighborhood, Pineland Trace, was only eight years old, but it had won the county's Best Neighborhood of the Year award for the past four. The years they'd won were even listed on the sign at the entrance to the neighborhood.

I walked over to the small gap in the fence.

"Looks like someone cut it with a pair of wire cutters." Whoever it was had only managed to cut five or six links of the fence.

"Yeah, I think my motion-detection light scared him away. Saw it come on around one and came out to look. Didn't seen no one then."

"This your fence?"

"Nope. Belongs to the Mathesons. They're going to build soon. Nice people. They just got married. We require each house to be at least three thousand square feet, so not everyone can afford that." He sounded very proud of his exclusive community.

"They put a chain-link fence all the way around their vacant lot?" I wasn't sure I could even afford to do that.

"I think their builder did it. He's supposed to break ground in a month or two."

"Why do you think someone would want to cut their way into a vacant lot?"

"Kids, maybe. Homeless." He shrugged.

I didn't bother pointing out that the homeless seldom carried around wire cutters big enough to cleanly snip through a chain-link fence. I looked around, but heavily mulched flowerbeds hid any footprints.

"Any cameras?" I asked.

"I don't have any back here. All the other sides of the property are caught by one or the other of my neighbor's security cameras."

Mr. Todd seemed very pleased with the level of surveillance in the area. I thought it seemed a little creepy. We walked over and talked to the neighbor across the street, whose camera would have caught anyone walking or parking in the street.

The neighbor, a black lawyer and apparent security nerd, had one of his bedrooms filled with monitors and equipment for his home's security system.

"We can pull up whatever you want. I've got a hundred terabytes of storage." He went on to explain what software he used and all the different functions associated with it. I tuned most of it out. "Here's last night. I can just scan and it will stop at any point where there's movement. What time parameters do you want me to set it for?"

"I know the light came on at around one in the morning, so do midnight to two," Mr. Todd suggested.

At first it didn't appear that the camera had caught anything near the Todd house, but just past one o'clock, there was movement across the screen. The lawyer leaned in toward the monitor and played it again.

"There!" He pointed to the lower right-hand corner of the screen. I could see what looked like someone's shoulder move across the corner of the image.

"Play it again," I instructed.

Watching the image again, I didn't like it. There was something oddly sophisticated in the criminal's effort to avoid the camera.

"It's like he knows the camera is there," said Mr. Todd, echoing my thoughts.

"Is there anything on that lot worth taking?" I asked. They looked at me with blank expressions. "Like maybe an exotic plant or animal?" I knew I was reaching. Then another thought occurred to me. "Have there been any robberies in this area?" I wondered if someone had thrown something valuable over the fence in a panic and now wanted to retrieve it.

"Never," said the lawyer.

I realized that I'd stretched a twenty-minute stop-and-go report into ninety minutes. I thought of the old gentleman living near the drug house and knew he wouldn't approve of the sheriff's office spending resources to protect a rich family's chain-link fence when he had violent crimes surrounding his home every weekend.

"If you can put up a camera to cover the blind spots, that

would be great," I told them. "Then let us know if you see anything else."

I handed them each my card and promised to email them a copy of the report, then I drove off.

CHAPTER EIGHT

I had just stepped foot in the office when I got a text from Dad wanting to know when I was coming for the van and dogs. The fact that the word "dog" was pluralized didn't register with me. I made a quick stop at my desk, then texted back that I was on my way.

After pulling into Dad's driveway, I started moving everything I would need for the weekend out of my car and into the passenger seat of Mauser's ratty old minivan. The van was the only option when I was on dog duty, as the big oaf wouldn't fit in my car.

I heard the front door of the house open behind me and turned, bracing myself for Mauser's patented kamikaze charge. What I saw then confused me. Instead of one giant dog running toward me, there were two, one brown and one black-and-white.

What is Cleo doing here? I had time to wonder, just before Mauser misjudged his stop and slammed into me with knee-crunching force. Cleo, much more polite, dropped her butt to the ground and gave me a wide doggie grin, her wagging tail making angels in the dirt.

"About time you got here," Dad said as he came down from the house.

I gestured at Cleo. "What? Why?"

"Bernadette called and asked if Cleo could stay with Mauser for the weekend. A cousin passed away, so she's going up to the funeral."

Bernadette Santos had become a great friend to all of us over the past couple of years, and normally I enjoyed spending time with her well-trained, gentle Great Dane. But nothing about this weekend was normal.

"Dad, Cara's out of town. I can't take care of both of them." I looked at Mauser, who was dancing like an idiot in circles around Cleo

"Of course you can. I already put Cleo's food, toys and bedding in the van along with Mauser's. I'd stop and talk, but we want to get down to the coast before it gets too late."

I stood with my mouth hanging open as Dad turned away and waved over his shoulder. Left without any recourse, I convinced my charges to get into the van. Before I could open the driver's door, Genie, Dad's wife as of a month ago, hurried up to me and put her hand on my shoulder.

"I'm sorry, Larry."

"It's no big deal." I couldn't blame her for how Dad chose to punish me.

"He's not muttering your name under his breath as much as he was a couple of weeks ago. I think that's a good sign." She smiled.

"That's great," I said with only a hint of sarcasm. "Is Jimmy going down to the coast with you?"

"No, he's going to a Greek food festival or something with the other folks from his place." Her son, Jimmy, had Down Syndrome and lived in a group home in Tallahassee.

"Genie, where's your bag?" Dad yelled from the house.

"I better go help him." She gave me a quick hug, then trotted back to the house.

As I drove toward home, the van literally rocked from side to side whenever the two dogs would see something out the window that interested them. Trying to keep the van on its own side of the road, my mind turned back to the King case and my efforts to find Natalie. That's when I thought of Eddie Thompson. Though he was now clean, sober and gainfully employed, he'd been my confidential informant when he'd been on the streets, and I thought he might still have some connections.

"Yo," he answered when I called.

"Are you at home?"

"Just closing up at the library."

"I've got some questions for you. I'll meet you in the library parking lot in ten minutes," I told him, slowing down to turn the van back toward town.

"Sure."

The temperature was falling as I waited in the parking lot for him. I rolled the windows down, bringing in cool air to help combat the humid dog breath being expelled by my two friends in the back.

"Cleo!" Eddie said when he came over to the van.

"I'm here too," I said.

"But Cleo is my buddy," he said, reaching through my window to try to pet her. "Bernadette brings her in to read with the kids, some sort of therapy thing."

"Get in if you're going to be petting the dogs while we talk," I said, tired of the dogs drooling all over me as they presented their large snouts to Eddie.

"I love you too, Mauser," Eddie said after he climbed into the passenger seat.

"Do you know Natalie of the forked tongue?" I asked him once he'd received his share of slobber.

"Avoid her like the plague. She's got a trespass warning from the library."

"Is there *any* place she can go without trespassing?" I frowned.

"People don't like to be spit on."

"That's a bit of wisdom. You heard about the murder?"

"I heard Rolling Robin killed some construction guy. Hard to believe. When I was on the street, I avoided Robin 'cause he was such a punk-as… I mean, a wimp. There was always someone looking to take advantage of him, so it didn't pay to be hanging too close. Oh… That's why you're asking about Nat the Snake. One of the guys at an AA meeting said they've been hanging out. Actually, he said Nat has turned Robin into her slave."

"How can I find her?"

"Normally I'd say find Robin and he'll know, but I guess that won't work."

"Obviously. Any better suggestions?"

"I think if you just listen to your radio, sooner or later someone is going to report her for something."

"I already thought of that and asked dispatch to notify me if any deputy comes into contact with her."

"It's only a matter of time," Eddie said matter-of-factly

"Time is of the essence. There's a body in the morgue." Mentioning the morgue made me wonder how the autopsy had gone. Since Pete hadn't texted or called, I assumed that nothing new had been revealed.

"I could give you some names and some streets to hang out at night. Sooner or later you'll see her."

"Trouble is, I got these two to take care of and Cara is out of town." I pointed toward the back of the van. Then a crazy thought took shape in my head. "Hey, what are you doing this weekend?"

"I was hoping to hang out with Jessie, but she's busy with the academy." He saw the look on my face. "Oh."

"Yeah, that's what I'm thinking. Would you be willing to come out to my place and moose-sit these two?"

Eddie looked at the dogs, who stared back at him with their tongues hanging out.

"Maybe."

"Whatever you want to eat, and we got a new TV."

"I guess."

"Good. Come out to my place as soon as you can." I was warming to the idea of doing some late-night reconnaissance in an effort to find the elusive Snake Tongue. Now that I thought about it, she seemed to have been lying low. Was this a sign of guilt, or just fear that if we'd picked up Robin, she'd be implicated too?

I took Cleo and Mauser home, apologizing to Ivy and Ghost as the beasts charged into the house. At least Alvin had gone south with Cara and would be spared the threat of being stomped to death.

As I grabbed a quick dinner, I thought about the fact that I'd invited Eddie to stay at my house for the weekend. What a difference a couple of years had made. It had taken a long time and a lot of work on himself, but he'd now become a dependable, if somewhat unpredictable, friend.

Finally, I heard his old clunker pull up outside. Once he'd brought his stuff inside and been properly greeted by the dogs, Eddie and I went over a list of the best hangouts for catching a glimpse of Natalie.

"How are you going to look less like a cop?" Eddie asked.

"Glad you asked. First off, I'm going to take your car rather than Dad's van." I saw the suspicious look on his face. "Don't worry. I'll bring it back with a full tank."

Eddie agreed and then began to describe all the eccentricities of his car, which almost made me rethink my plan.

I put on jeans, sneakers, a henley and a flannel overshirt, then called Pete to let him know what I was up to.

"I'm on call, so I'll be available if you need any assistance," he assured me.

"How'd the autopsy go?"

"Dr. Darzi didn't find any red flags. Drew was struck three times and Darzi confirmed our assumptions about how. Drew's blood showed a .04 alcohol level, which would only account for a couple of those beer cans."

"We should walk through the attack in the trailer when we have a chance."

"Agreed. What are you doing with Mauser while you're out looking for the spitter?"

I explained that I'd recruited Eddie to watch both Mauser

and Cleo, which Pete found very amusing.

I packed a few supplies for my stakeout, then headed back into town. It was fully dark by the time I parked at one of the spots I thought would give me the best chance of catching Natalie. I settled in to wait with a thermos of coffee and some music playing softly on my phone.

Hours passed and I witnessed a lot of aimless meandering by the denizens of one the county's more questionable areas. As the temperature inside the car dropped, I slipped on a heavy jacket. I wished I could put the hood of the jacket over my head and ears, but I didn't want to obstruct my peripheral vision or limit my hearing.

Eventually, someone approached the car, obviously checking it out to see if there was anything worth stealing. I opened my door to shoo him away, wishing I could flash my badge at him, but not wanting to blow my cover.

"Hey, hey, I didn't see you," the young man said, holding up his hands. "What you sitting here for?"

"Waiting on someone," I told him, wishing he would just go away.

"What you need? I'll get it for you," he asked, only using much more colorful language that involved the F-bomb every other word.

"Thanks, I'm good."

"Women, men, drugs. Whatever you want, man," he persisted.

I decided to throw the dice. "I'm waiting on Nat. You seen her?"

This caused him to look at me warily.

"Don't know who you're talking about."

"Sure you do. Snake Tongue," I pushed.

The look on his face and the fact that he started backing up told me he knew exactly who I was talking about and wanted nothing to do with her.

"No, man." He started to turn away.

I managed to pull a twenty-dollar bill out of my wallet quickly enough to stop his retreat.

"Man, that don't buy nothin'," he told me. I added another twenty. He looked left and right before moving back toward me. "I seen her about half an hour ago."

I pulled the money back before he could grab it. "Forty bucks buys more than that."

"You're a cop!" he yelped, sounding betrayed.

"I just want to talk to her."

"You don't know my name. So don't be, like, describing me to her or nothin'."

"She won't know where the information came from."

"That's good 'cause she crazy. Oh, man, I think she's, like, one of those devil worshipers."

I waved the money right and left, trying to get him to tell me what he knew before the information passed its sell-by date.

"She's one block over. They're having a party. Listen, man, you can hear them."

He was right. I could hear the sounds of hardcore, repetitive music blasting through the trees. I handed him the money and started the car while he was still fondling it.

I drove by the house first. There weren't a ton of people at the party, with only a few spilling out into the front yard. The music was loud, but under the decibel level that would prompt a neighbor to complain. Plus, it was only eleven-thirty, which was early for that part of town.

I parked down the street and watched the house, hoping Natalie would leave the party and also hoping that my informant's tip had been worth the money. All I could do was wait.

Forty-five minutes later, I saw her stumble out into the yard. There was a man trailing her who I instantly recognized. I let out a few F-bombs of my own. How could Robin have managed to screw things up that fast?

They were walking my way, so I just sat in the car and watched. Robin, underdressed for the cold weather in a T-shirt and jeans, stumbled along a few feet behind like a puppy while Natalie strolled down the middle of the street, pivoting her head right and left as though searching for someone to beat up.

I worked on a plan for a minute before acknowledging that all I could really do was play it by ear. I pinned my star to my jacket so it would be in clear view. I didn't want Natalie to be able to say she didn't know I was a deputy. And because I wasn't an idiot, I called dispatch and told them where I was and who I was about to confront.

Natalie and Robin strolled by without seeing me slumped down in the car. Once they were past me, I threw the door open and stepped out. Startled, they both turned. I was pleased to see the shocked look on her face.

"Don't run," I told them. I needn't have worried. Robin fell on his ass with his eyes as wide as saucers, while Natalie squared her shoulders as though she expected me to launch myself at her.

"I ain't running," she said and stuck her tongue out at me. In the glow of the streetlight, the effect was impressive.

"I have a few questions for you."

"Robin was with me the night that man was killed," she said in one of the most obvious and stupid lies I'd ever heard.

"He was found asleep in the trailer with his hand a foot from the murder weapon," I pointed out.

"He didn't kill anyone. Look at him." She pointed to Robin, who was still wallowing on the ground.

"You have a point," I admitted. "I want to find the person who *did* kill Drew King."

"You're that pig friend of Robin's," she said, letting her lips curl into a strange smile.

"If you can tell me where you all were Tuesday night, that would help."

"Partying."

"I'm sure. Partying where?"

"Some house."

"Where?"

"We just go where the party is." She was enjoying this.

"Where are you living right now?"

Her answer was to wave her arms around, indicating the neighborhood.

I opened my mouth to tell her she wasn't helping herself or Robin when I heard dispatch over my radio. I had put it on under my shirt and turned the volume up just enough that I could hear the calls. It's funny how your subconscious mind can still process the radio chatter while you're doing other things. In this case, I became aware that the dispatcher was directing a deputy to a body located in a ditch less than a block from where we were standing.

"I'm going to need you both to get in the car," I told them firmly.

I should have predicted Natalie's reaction. She leaned back and let a glob of spit fly toward my face before spinning around and running away at an impressive speed. By the time I dodged out of the way of her spittle, there wasn't any point in trying to pursue her.

I looked down at Robin, who was attempting to stand up. I pulled him up and half carried him to the car.

"I screwed up again, Larry."

"No shit," I said as I opened the door and unceremoniously tossed him inside.

By the time I got to the location where the body had been reported, there was already a patrol car parked with its blue lights flashing. Mattie Sanderson was standing by the car, talking into the radio attached to her shoulder.

"What's the story?" I asked.

"That was quick. Dispatch said Pete was on call."

"I was in the area," I said vaguely.

"Some old guy dead in the ditch. It's either a hit-and-run or a homicide. I'm guessing homicide." She pointed to the body with her flashlight. I could see by the amount of blood on the back of his head that she was right. Lying on the ground five feet away from the body was a four-foot length of two-by-four and a discarded jacket.

My gut was telling me this wasn't going to be good. I

looked back toward Eddie's car and wondered if the murderer was flopped over in the backseat. Or worse, if I'd let her run away without giving chase.

CHAPTER NINE

Pete showed up to the crime scene in twenty minutes. Sanderson and I had already strung up tape and called for backup to block off the street and deal with anyone attempting to use the road.

"I let you drive around town on a Friday night and the next thing I know there's a body involved." Pete shook his head like a disappointed parent.

We were waiting for Shantel or whoever was on call from the crime-scene unit to arrive before we started mucking around with the body or any evidence. Thanks to Sanderson, we knew that the victim was well and truly deceased. She'd checked for life signs when she arrived.

"The body was noticeably cool to the touch," she told us.

"What would you say the temperature was at sundown?" Pete asked me.

"Around sixty."

"And it's forty-nine now." He was looking at his phone.

"He's been dead for a couple of hours," I guessed. "Must have happened around eight or nine."

"We'll see when the experts get here." He looked around as if expecting his pronouncement to summon the coroner's van.

Eventually Marcus pulled up in the crime-scene van. Surprisingly, it was Lionel riding shotgun.

"What are you doing out of your electronic cave?" Pete asked before I got the chance.

"Marcus and I got permission to do some cross training. I'm spending time in the field, and he's helping me with some of the forensic tech stuff," Lionel explained.

"More power to you," I told Marcus, who was heading to the back of the van to fetch the camera and video equipment.

"I want to know enough that I don't screw anything up when we're collecting evidence, or so I don't miss something. Half the evidence we collect these days is off of electronic devices. Cameras, phones, computers, laptops, tablets, exercise monitors, you name it."

"You aren't wrong," I said, helping him lift out the larger camera case.

I directed them to the body and the murder weapon. My eyes fell on the jacket again. Something about it bothered me.

While we waited for Marcus and Lionel to document the scene, Pete and I walked the road with our flashlights, looking in the ditches for other possible evidence. They were filled with all types of trash, everything from used condoms to Bible tracts, though most of it was fast-food wrappers and cups. I hated having a crime scene at a place where we had to make judgment calls on what evidence to collect. It always left me feeling like I was leaving valuable information behind.

After walking both sides of the road and not finding anything that stood out, I went by Eddie's car and checked on Robin. I didn't need to worry. He was leaning against the door with his mouth hanging open, snoring. A voice in my head told me that I should wake him up and handcuff him, but I couldn't do it.

As I looked at him curled up in a fetal position against the door, I noticed again that he was wearing only jeans and a T-shirt. Was that his jacket back there in the ditch? If so, he was going to be spending a lot of time behind bars. Even if he wasn't guilty of either crime, no one was going to let him out while they waited for the trial to take place.

My phone buzzed. I looked at the name and saw that it was Robin's mother. I had entered her contact information when I'd dropped him off at her house.

"I can't find Robin," she said a little breathlessly.

"I'm with him," I told her.

"Oh, thank God." She paused and then sounded puzzled: "When did you pick him up?"

"I didn't. He managed to get to town, and now there's more trouble."

"What kind of trouble?"

"I'd rather not go into that right now. I can tell you that Robin is with me and is safe, but he won't be coming home tonight." *Or possibly for a while*, I thought.

"I tried… I…"

"Get some rest, Mrs. Walsh. I'll explain the situation tomorrow when I know more," I promised.

Marcus and Lionel were still busy taking photos and video. Darkness slows down and complicates the process.

"I'm not looking forward to canvassing this neighborhood," Pete said, looking around at the unkept yards and junk cars that suggested the transitory and often criminal nature of the residents. "You said you found the spitter?"

"I was talking to her and Robin when the call came in about the body."

"I'm pissed we didn't keep Robin in jail. This seems oddly familiar."

"We don't know what time he left his mother's or exactly when the murder took place," I reminded him.

At that moment, the coroner's van was waved past the patrol car blocking the end of the street. Linda jumped out of the passenger seat. In the past couple of months, she'd become Dr. Darzi's chief assistant.

"Another body. You all are the gift that keeps on giving." She gave us a wide smile. "My chauffer today is Moses Wallace. He's interning with us."

Moses looked like he'd already gotten used to Linda's barbed sense of humor. "Pleased to meet ya," he said, nodding to both of us.

"Marcus and Lionel are almost done with the area around the body," I said.

"Grab the kit out of the back," she told Moses. "I'll let you do the preliminary exam."

He didn't hesitate.

"I don't know where they find all these enthusiastic interns," Linda said. "What can you tell me?"

"All I know is that it was reported by a woman who lives over there." I pointed to a house across the street and several houses down from where we were standing. "She was walking her dog and saw the body in the ditch. Sandy told us that the body felt cool to the touch when she arrived."

"You can examine the coat and two-by-four," Marcus announced. "Lionel's almost done checking our footage of the body and the surrounding area. As soon as we're done, you can get to the body, Linda."

Pete and I approached the coat and piece of wood carefully, trying not to slip as we stepped down into the damp mud in the bottom of the ditch.

"Lift up the coat and let's see if anything is under it."

Pete shined his flashlight on the tan jacket, which was thicker than a windbreaker but wouldn't have been considered a heavy coat. I picked it up in my gloved hands, revealing a discolored candy bar wrapper and a pint bottle that had green stuff growing inside. It was a safe bet they'd both been there long before the body.

I searched the pockets of the coat while Pete continued to hold the light. Our breath was visible in the chill night air. I pulled a crumpled Fast Mart receipt from one pocket, along with a two-year-old electric bill with a past-due notice. I shook my head when I saw that the name on the bill was

Robin Hennessy.

Lionel joined us, carrying an evidence bag for the coat. I slipped it in and took out two smaller bags from my pocket for the receipt and the electric bill.

"This doesn't look too good for Robin," I muttered, stating the obvious.

"It will be interesting to find out who the victim is." Pete turned his focus to the piece of wood. "I can see hair and skin as well as blood."

We bagged the two-by-four. We weren't likely to find fingerprints on it, but there was a good chance that, if the killer hadn't worn gloves, we might find some DNA evidence. I remembered Robin's bare hands and wondered what we'd find.

Pete and I decided to knock on a few doors while we waited for Linda and Moses to examine the body. If this had been almost any other part of town, there would have been a dozen people standing around watching us. In some areas, we would have had to call in extra deputies to keep people back and answer their questions. But here, there were only a few silhouettes at windows. No one wanted to get involved and most had good reason to stay as far away from law enforcement as they could.

"I'll take those houses," I said, pointing to four homes across the street, "if you want to get the two on either side of our crime scene."

"Sure. I'm as likely to get shot knocking on those doors as the ones you're doing." He sighed. "Let's get our vests on."

Pete didn't have to remind me to put on Kevlar. These homes *probably* didn't house meth labs, but the odds weren't as long as I would have liked.

The first house I approached was concrete block with a dirt front yard and four vehicles parked in front. Two of the cars looked like they hadn't moved since Clinton was in office. There were lights on and the sound of a TV, but no one answered my knocks. I shouted to the occupants that I just wanted to ask a few questions, but got no response.

I moved on to the next home, which had a better-kept yard and no derelict automobiles.

My knock was answered by a frail voice from the other side.

"Who's there?"

"I'm an investigator with the sheriff's office. I just want to ask you a few questions," I said.

"I don't know anything." I couldn't be sure if the homeowner was male or female.

"If you could just give me a second of your time."

"I need to see your identification."

"Of course." There was a window three feet from the door. "I'll hold it up to the window."

I saw the curtain pulled aside as I held my ID up to the glass. A minute later, the occupant went back to the door and I heard the sound of the chain being unlatched.

"What's going on over there?" asked the hunched-over, elderly white man who opened the door.

"We got a call about a body in the ditch." I didn't see the point in mincing words. If he'd lived in this neighborhood for any length of time, he was familiar with bad things happening in the community.

"Oh my. Of course, that's why I keep my door locked. Would you like to come in?"

"That would be nice." I followed him into the tidy little house. "Do you live alone?"

"My daughter comes by every morning and evening to check on me. She works over at First Bank."

"Have you lived here long?"

He chuckled. "I've owned this house for sixty years. Didn't live in it all those years. Moved away and rented it until my wife kicked me out of our house twenty years ago. That's when I moved back here."

"I'm sorry. I didn't get your name." I had my notebook out.

"Chester Kelly. Eighty-eight years old and going…

well… maybe not strong, but I'm still going. Would you like a beer or maybe a Coke?"

"I'm fine. Have you been home all evening?"

"These days I only go out to the store and my doctor's appointments. Not that I'm complaining. I have my work."

"What's that?"

"Genealogy. I've traced my extended family back to the fifteen hundreds. Thousands of ancestors. That's why I stay up this late. I like to chat in real time with people all over the world." He pointed to a twenty-one-inch monitor and a computer set up on the dining-room table. The table had been pushed up against the wall and was covered in papers and charts.

"Aren't you uneasy living here?" I asked.

"I've got a four-ten Mossberg shotgun. My shoulder won't take a twelve gauge anymore. Used to shoot trap and skeet."

"Still…"

"Why don't y'all clean up the neighborhood instead of suggesting that the good guys move out?" There was some heat in his words.

"It's not that we don't try," I argued. "When I was on patrol, I was in this neighborhood almost every night."

"To clean up a mess, not to prevent one. I know the sheriff's office can't do it by themselves. You need to get the city in here to kick out and clean up the riffraff. Too many of the landlords are connected to the politicians. When my family lived here forty years ago, almost everyone owned their homes. Now most of the people living around me are renters. They don't care about their neighbors." He gave a dismissive wave. "Never mind me. I know you don't have much of a choice. It's like complaining to the cashier about the price of beer."

"Did you hear or see anything unusual tonight?" I asked, trying to get back on track. Getting an earful about how well, or not, the sheriff's department was doing happened a lot when I was canvassing an area for witnesses.

Mr. Kelly chuckled. "I always hear strange noises around here. People walking up and down the streets at all hours of the night. Like I said, I stay up late, and I'm always surprised when I see young people strolling down the road at three or four in the morning. Why don't they have jobs?"

"Were there any noises or people tonight? From sunset to, say, ten o'clock?"

"Let me think." He narrowed his eyes and pursed his lips. "Maybe."

"What?"

"I feed a couple of stray cats. Tonight, when I went out on the front porch to put their food out, I saw a car. Funny thing was, I got the impression it had been parked in the road, but there isn't a house there. It drove off right after I came out. I'm not absolutely sure it was parked. People these days drive so oddly. Always playing with their phones and whatnot. Another thing y'all should crack down on."

"Can you describe the car?"

The old man shrugged. "Just a car. The streetlight is busted so it's hard to see. I guess it was dark-colored. Blue, black, maybe. Not big, not small. Nothing to make it stand out."

"Did anyone get in or out of the car?"

"Don't you think I would have mentioned that?"

"I've learned to ask questions. You'd be surprised how many times someone won't mention a fact that could make a big difference unless you ask them directly."

"Yeah, I get that. People are funny."

Mr. Kelly wasn't able to give me any more helpful information, but he did manage to give me a few more items for the county and city to work on. I silently agreed with most of his suggestions.

The next house seemed to be genuinely empty, but at the last house the occupant colorfully expressed how upset she was that I woke her up. Once she'd inspected my credentials with half-shut eyes, she invited me to come in out of the cold.

"I've got to get my sleep. Bad enough those lights flashing all night," she grumbled. Even woken up out of a sound sleep, the woman was attractive. Her cheekbones were high and well-defined, and her eyes shone brightly out of her dark skin. "Let me guess, you want to know if I've seen or heard anything, right?"

"Between sunset and ten o'clock," I said with a smile.

"I'd move, but my grans lives a block over and there is nothing on this earth that can move that woman. My parents bought this house when the neighborhood was full of families just working and getting by. You know?" She looked at me and shook her head. "You talk to Mr. Kelly? He stays up all night doing his family charts or whatever. He was here when my parents bought this place."

"Where do I know you from?" I asked, realizing that her face was familiar.

"I work in the clerk's office. I've seen you up there," she said. "And I have to be at work by seven. I go in early so I can get off in time to watch my grandbaby until my son gets home."

"Sorry. Then I guess you didn't see anything?"

"See, no. Hear, maybe. Around here there's always some crazy person walking down the street. You get used to hearing stuff. But around ten I heard a... I don't know how to describe it... a squawk? It sounded like an animal, but there was a human quality to it. I think that's why I noticed it. If it had been a person screaming bloody murder, then I probably wouldn't have even noticed it. There was just a peculiar quality to the noise."

"Try and recall the sound. Did it sound like a male or female? Old or young?"

"It might have been someone trying to yell and they were cut off. Yeah, that might have been it. I couldn't say whether it was a man or woman. You know how it is with a scream or someone yelling."

"Was it close or far away?"

"Not too close. I would have looked outside if it had

sounded like it was in the yard."

"You said it was around ten o'clock. How sure are you of the time?"

"It was just before ten. Very sure, 'cause I'd turned off the TV to get ready for bed. You know, because I have to get up in the morning," she said, reminding me that it was time to get out of her house.

I thanked her for her time and headed back across the street in time to see Pete watching Linda and Moses climb up out of the ditch. I joined him and let him know that I had a couple of minor witnesses who could help us establish a timeline.

"You did better than me. One slammed the door in my face and another cursed me out for waking him up, while at the third house I heard someone run out the back door."

"You need to work on being more charming."

He just grunted.

"You can look at him *in situ* and then we'll cart him off," Linda said lightly.

"You have any preliminary thoughts?" Pete asked.

Linda turned to Moses, who looked shocked to be put in the spotlight.

"Umm… he was certainly dead for an hour or more. I'll have to work out a chart with the ambient temperature. His body temperature was eighty-seven degrees, so with the cool air, the skin would have felt even colder to the deputy."

"Cause of death?" Linda looked like she was enjoying putting him on the spot.

"He took a couple blows to the head. Without a more thorough examination, that would appear to have been a major factor in his death. If something else didn't kill him, the blows would have been enough to do it. The skull is fractured to the point that a three-to-four-inch indentation is present, with the depth of the depression being roughly two inches. It would be safe to assume that that level of trauma would cause internal damage and severe bleeding, which would have—"

"Stop!" Linda said. "He's like a textbook when you get him going."

Moses smiled, taking the comment as a compliment.

Pete and I took off our vests and put on protective gear to avoid any contamination of the body.

Down in the ditch, I searched the victim's pockets, finally finding a thin leather bifold wallet. Inside was a state-issued ID that identified our victim as Douglas Banks. The photo was not complimentary. I showed it to Pete. We'd both dealt with the man several times over the years. Older than Robin, they still had a lot in common.

"I always figured Banks would die of hypothermia," Pete said. "I can't tell you how many times he's been passed out in bad weather. Two years ago, I found him soaking wet after a front went through and the temperature dropped into the twenties. There he was, snoring away in the park."

"I think it's a safe bet that Robin knew him." I wasn't liking this at all.

"Yeah, I'm going to have to put him squarely in the crosshairs if he had the opportunity."

I was at a loss for words. Two bodies, both bludgeoned to death, and with Robin found in close proximity to each of them.

"I still wonder about Natalie. She's got the temperament for murder," I said.

"And you told me she was with Robin tonight. I'd sure like to know if she had an alibi for the night that Drew was killed."

"Her vague explanation was that she and Robin were partying. We were interrupted before I could press her for details."

"We need to talk to her." Pete pulled out his radio and called dispatch, requesting a pickup order for Natalie Owens as a material witness in two murders. "Are we agreed that Robin should go back to jail?"

"I wish we'd never let him out. Whether he had a part in the murders or not, we'd all have been better off if he'd stayed in jail and out of trouble. Now…" I looked toward Eddie's car.

By the time I put Robin back in jail and got home, it was almost four in the morning. I tried to open the front door as quietly as possible, hoping to get in without disturbing the dogs. I was so successful that I wondered if they were actually in the house. Looking around, I found Mauser and Cleo sleeping on the guest bed while Eddie was curled up on the floor with a pillow and a blanket.

I headed for my room, thinking about the hard time I was going to give Mauser for neglecting his responsibilities as a guard dog. Cleo would be allowed a pass since she was a guest.

CHAPTER TEN

"You look happy," I told Eddie when I shuffled into the kitchen at ten o'clock Saturday morning.

Eddie was at the table, phone in hand while he ate a bowl of cereal. Mauser had his head on the table, staring longingly at Eddie's bowl, while Cleo sat politely next to his chair. Ivy was lying on the table watching Eddie and the dogs, while Ghost batted at her tail from a chair.

"Jessie's coming over," Eddie said.

I almost said something snide about him asking guests over to *my* house, but I was grateful that Eddie was watching the dogs. Plus, I liked Jessie Gilmore. She'd overcome some rough patches in her life and, after a brief stint trying to replace Eddie as my confidential informant, she'd entered the law enforcement academy that winter. Eddie clearly had a crush on her, and I was curious to see where their relationship would end up.

"I thought she was working on academy stuff this weekend?" I said, getting a bowl down from the cupboard.

"I think she just wants to see Cleo and Mauser," Eddie admitted, grinning.

"I'm sure she likes cats too," I told Ghost, who'd jumped onto the counter to see what I was making for breakfast.

"We won't bother you," Eddie promised.

"I plan on going into the office for a while anyway."

"Did you have any luck finding Nat?"

"That's a long story and there's a big part of it I can't tell you."

"You know I can keep my mouth shut." Eddie took another spoonful of cereal under Mauser's watchful eye.

I'd already been contacted by several reporters and had referred them to Major Parks, who also served as our defacto communications officer. It would be safe to tell Eddie some of it, as it would be all over the news this morning anyway.

"Douglas Banks was found dead last night near the Ditch. The body was discovered about the same time I ran into Nat and Robin roaming around the neighborhood."

"I told you that's where you could find her. Wait a minute! Wasn't Robin supposed to be with his mother? And who did you say was found dead?" Eddie looked confused.

"I can't remember his street name. Older guy, always wears trousers and a button-down shirt like he's a businessman on a week-long bender."

"Sounds like Zero."

"I don't know. I dealt with him a few times, but it was never a big deal."

"He's, like, not all there," Eddie said, tapping his head. "He'll either not talk to you or go on and on about his bad luck. Begs money from a few people but doesn't do the whole 'homeless vet' routine. Most people just ignore him."

I took out my phone and pulled up a picture of Banks's state ID.

"Yeah, that's him." Eddie nodded.

"Where's he normally hang out?"

"When I was on the street, he lived in a blue pop-up tent in the camp out near the railroad tracks."

Every LEO knew about that camp. There had been high-level discussions between the city, county and sheriff's office about what to do about it. Everyone wanted it gone, but if you tore down the camp then all you did was displace the people living there. In turn, that just made the problem of policing them and keeping them safe even harder. In the end, the police and sheriff's office regularly did walk-throughs of the area, checking IDs, arresting anyone who was a suspect in an ongoing investigation, and getting medical attention or other help for those that needed it.

"Did he ever have any trouble with the other homeless people?" I asked Eddie.

"Zero. That's why we called him that. He minded his own business. Besides that, he was only a drunk, so no one was going to hassle him for drugs he didn't have or try to sell him drugs he didn't want. Just, like, he was there, but not there."

"Are you good to stay with Mauser and Cleo?"

"Jessie and I will look after them. You thinking about going out to the homeless camp?"

"I need to find out what he's been doing recently. Where he's been living. Anyone he's been associating with."

"You think Nat and Robin might have had something to do with his death?"

"We don't know anything at this point," I said evasively.

I texted Pete to let him know my plans for the day. He followed up with a note that he would check some of the nearest security cameras that might have picked up the vehicle that Chester Kelly had told me about.

I was getting ready to head into town when there was a knock at the door. I was almost run over by Eddie and the dogs as they rushed to open it. I waited my turn to greet Jessie, then listened to a few of her tales from the academy. She seemed to be having a lot more fun there than I'd had. After filling her in on a bit of the department gossip, I took my leave.

There were dark and ominous clouds moving across the sky as I drove toward Calhoun. Warm, moist air was pushing north from the Gulf and mixing unhappily with what was left of our winter weather. I parked up the road from the camp and called dispatch to let them know where I was and what I was doing.

I went to the back of the van and put on my Kevlar vest to guard against someone deciding that I looked like a pincushion. The homeless population had a concentrated mix of issues, with mental illness and addiction heading the list of problems they faced, neither of which was easily reasoned with. Before walking away from the van, I removed several ten- and twenty-dollar bills from my wallet for easy access to use as incentives.

The five-acre lot was an easy walk from downtown, the county health clinic, a Fast Mart and at least two churches that regularly served meals to the homeless, making it an ideal location for folks who wanted to keep a low profile while living off of the local resources. We'd tried to get the owner of the land to take some responsibility and fence it, but her response had been to post no-trespassing signs and then blame us for not being able to keep the homeless off her property. The end result was a stalemate that left the homeless with a semi-permanent tent city.

The path into the camp was easy to follow. A hundred feet into the woods, I came across the first of the tents. Some were neat and tidy, but most were dirty and stank of unwashed humans.

The first person to admit to knowing Douglas Banks was a woman sitting on a five-gallon bucket in front of a small fire.

"Sure, I knew Zero," she said, surprising me with the use of the past tense.

"He was found dead last night."

"That's the rumor going around." She flexed her arms and stood up. By my estimate, she was close to six feet tall. Her hair was bleached blonde and grey, clean and cut short. Her age could have been anywhere from thirty to fifty.

I gave her one of my cards. "Your name is?" I asked politely, in an effort to keep the conversation cordial.

"Tess," she said, and I decided not to press her for a last

name. If she came up with information that was important, then I'd cross that bridge when I got to it.

"How'd you know Banks?"

Tess laughed.

"What's funny?"

"You. 'How'd you know Banks?' You sound like somebody at a formal dinner. I knew Zero 'cause we're all a bunch of bums livin' in the woods. It'd be a lot weirder if I *didn't* know a guy who lived right over there." She pointed off toward the brush.

I thought of all the other times I'd come into homeless camps looking for suspects, witnesses or victims. There was an odd sameness to the experience, like going into a subdivision where all the houses look alike and all the yards are neat little postage stamps. Only here the tents were old and weather-beaten and the yards were heavily trampled suburban woods.

"Would you mind showing me where he lived?"

"Sure."

We walked through a thicket of wax myrtles and found a green two-person tent.

"That's his. Looks like the vultures have already gotten to it. There was always more stuff here when I came over to talk to him."

I wasn't surprised that the thieves had moved fast. In a way, I could understand the impulse. Was it any different than soldiers on a battlefield? What they had stolen wasn't money or jewels, only items that might make their barren lives a little more bearable.

"What did you talk to him about?"

"Life. He'd had a few hard knocks. His wife leaving him was the one that messed him up. Guess he loved her. Said he was blamed for her leaving… or something like that. I don't remember much. When we'd sit together, I did most of the talking. Zero was a better listener than a talker. Seemed to care too. Not many out here that think of anything but themselves."

"You were friends?"

Tess shrugged. "He helped me get my medicine and would remind me to take it, that kind of thing. I can't say we were really friends 'cause he didn't share much about himself, if you know what I mean." She paused and looked at his ransacked tent. "I guess he was the only guy I met out here that I liked. Sounds funny saying it out loud."

"How long have you been living here?"

"Here? I guess about a year. On the streets, more like ten years. Ever since I ruined my life." Her tone let me know that she would rather talk about Banks than about her own life.

I put on some gloves and crawled into the tent to see what the scavengers had left behind. There were several sets of clothes that had been pulled out of a garbage bag, along with a smaller plastic bag containing a few toiletry items. I was surprised to find three dog-eared romance novels.

"Are these his?" I held the books up so Tess could see them.

"I don't know about them, but I've seen him reading those types of books." She gave me a sad smile.

I pulled a plastic evidence bag from my pocket and put the books inside so I could go through them later. You never knew what a person might stick between the pages or write in the margins of a book.

There wasn't much else in the tent. I assumed he'd had a sleeping bag and other things, but they were gone and wouldn't be easily retrieved.

"Did he ever mention any relatives?" I asked.

"No. The wife. That's the only person he talked about."

"When did she leave him?"

"A long time ago. I know he's been hanging around here for as long as I can remember. I think he'd been on the streets for, like, twenty years?" She didn't sound sure.

"Was there anyone else he was friendly with?"

Tess responded with a bitter laugh. "I never saw him talk to anyone else."

"Never?"

"Like I said, he didn't talk much even to me. He listened, that's what he did."

"What about this guy?" I flipped through the pictures on my phone and showed her one of Robin. "Did you ever see them together?"

"I know that guy," she said, frowning at the picture. "He's not much different than Zero. Just begged for money and then used it to get high."

"Did you see them together?" I pushed.

"Yeah, sure, I guess. Didn't that guy, what's his name…?" She snapped her fingers. "Roller! Yeah, something like that. Funny guy. He talks more than Zero." She nodded at her own assessment.

"When was the last time you saw them together?"

"Buddy, I do my share of drinking. Truth is, if I was somewhere they were, then I was probably already blitzed."

"Where did you normally see them together?" I probed, knowing that I was probably digging for treasure that wasn't there.

"Fast Mart, behind the supermarket, by the library and… you know… on the street."

"So, think. When was the last time you saw them at one of these places?"

Tess frowned and looked back toward her camp. It was clear that she was getting tired of answering questions.

"Maybe last week near the library."

"Where do you all drink at the library?"

"At an old house behind it. There's a fence, but someone cut a hole in it. You can squeeze through. Great part for me is, I can use the library bathroom as long as I don't look too drunk. You got to pretend to be looking at books too."

I knew how much the library staff liked homeless people coming in and using their restrooms. We had issued hundreds of trespass warnings. Even Eddie, who had his own history on the streets, found it hard to deal with.

"Did you notice how Banks and Robin were getting

along?"

"They weren't getting along. I mean they weren't *not* getting along. We were just coming and going. Or I guess drinking and going." She licked her lips as though she were imagining the taste of alcohol.

"How many people were there that day?"

"See, I tell you I was drunk. I might have even slept there. How do I know how many people came and went? 'Sides, there are different areas around the house to sit. Not like all of us were cozying up together. It was a damn house party." Tess was getting irritated and snappy with her answers.

"What about this woman. Do you know her?" I showed her a picture of Natalie.

For a minute I thought Tess hissed when she saw the picture before I realized that she had just inhaled sharply. She gave me an angry look before taking off her jacket and pushing up the left arm of the thermal shirt she had on underneath.

"There's what that bitch did to me." She was pointing at a nasty-looking scar on her forearm that could have been used to make a dental cast of Natalie's teeth.

"Y'all got in a fight?"

"Fight! I reached for a beer and she bit me. I swear. *My* beer! Next thing I know, she's biting onto my arm and howling like an f'ing wolf. She had some creep with her run me off."

I could see the memory of the pain and fear in Tess's eyes.

"When was this?"

"Four months ago. I went to the clinic and they gave me drugs so it wouldn't get infected. I run when I see her. This place is safe 'cause no one here wants her around. A couple of the guys are big enough to run her off."

"Did you ever see her around Douglas Banks?"

"She wasn't interested in him. He wasn't young and didn't have money or drugs."

I thanked her, gave her ten dollars and headed back to the van. What would it be like to spend twenty years of your life just surviving? Not making friends or even enemies; just doing what you had to do to stay alive for another day.

I got a text from Phil Eccles as I was starting the engine. I told him where I was and that I'd meet him at the office in a few minutes. He was waiting for me in the parking lot.

"Why are you working on a Saturday?" I asked.

"I'm working overtime to pad my paycheck. Audrey has already figured the money from my questionable promotion into our household budget. You working the King case?"

I nodded. "There's a possibility that a murder last night is connected."

"That's what I heard. Look, I wanted to give you a heads-up. The rank and file aren't too happy with the way you and Pete are dealing with your main suspect."

"They can go hang." I bowed up, not in the mood to have the investigation criticized. Not yet.

"Calm down."

"Do *you* think we're screwing it up?" I was aware that I was talking to the man who would most likely be my supervisor in the next month or two.

"I think you need to be aware of what the other deputies are muttering about."

"I'm not going to change the way I'm investigating this case just to make people happy. I can promise you, Pete isn't either." I was still worked up at the suggestion that we were mishandling the case.

Phil put up his hand. "Cool down. I wouldn't respect you if you did. All I'm saying is, you might want to acknowledge that the case is not cut and dry."

"This is why I'm not sure I want the promotion. Last thing I want is to deal with office politics," I grumbled.

"I'm just warning you to watch your back. Specifically, I heard Klein and Lewis talking about it."

Mick Klein investigated burglaries while Lynn Lewis dealt with sex crimes. I wasn't sure, but I suspected that they'd both applied for the sergeant's position I was probably going to receive, though neither of them had even made it to the interview stage.

"I hear you." I chewed on the facts for a minute. "Robin is back in jail. Unless something breaks, I suspect he'll stay there. Though not for Drew's murder. At least not until more evidence comes forward." I let myself relax. "I can appreciate you not wanting to get hit by tomatoes the next time we do a presentation."

"I'll be glad when that particular punishment runs its course." He looked at the van, which everyone knew was Mauser's main mode of transportation. "I see he's still got you doggy-sitting. I guess I shouldn't complain." He snapped his fingers as if remembering something. "I did get assigned to your trespassing case."

"What case?" I wasn't sure what he was talking about.

"The one where some mysterious person cut the fence to rob a vacant lot."

"Parks assigned that to you?" I'd assumed it would be in my caseload, even though I'd just written the report as the responding deputy. Apparently, they were serious about clearing my calendar so I could assist Pete on the King case.

"I was surprised when I saw you'd signed the report. I have no idea what Parks expects me to do with it."

"Have you been out there?"

"It just showed up in my inbox."

"There's something weird about it."

"From what I read, there isn't anything out there to steal. Or, hell, even vandalize."

"That's true. So why would someone sneak around this guy's yard and cut the fence?" I thought of the house near the library that Tess had told me about. "Couldn't be homeless in a neighborhood like that."

"They wouldn't last five minutes with all the eyes watching. This is proof. According to what you wrote, whoever the vandal was didn't even get in."

"The hole wasn't big enough for a kid to crawl through.

Not without getting their clothes ripped to shreds."

"If it's quiet today, I might drive out there and take a look. Were there any pecan trees?"

I shook my head, knowing where he was going. "No. And, trust me, no one who lives in that neighborhood has to collect pecans off the ground."

"I'm betting it's a kid," Phil said. "In the higher-end communities, if there's trouble then it's usually local kids."

"Maybe." I shrugged.

Phil looked at his watch, then radioed dispatch that he was in service. "Stay safe," he said to me as he immediately got routed to a call.

I nodded and looked around at the nearly empty parking lot. It would be a good time to go inside and get some work done.

CHAPTER ELEVEN

The office always felt different on the weekend. A sense of nostalgia gripped me as I walked through the back door that opened into the hallway where the lockers and patrol breakroom were. When I was a kid, Dad would sometimes bring me to the office with him when he needed to pick something up or talk to someone, and it had always made me feel special. I'd known that the other kids at school treated me just a little bit differently because my dad was a deputy. When I'd walked the halls of the sheriff's office on a Saturday or Sunday with my dad, I'd felt a special pride in the job he did. Those feelings I'd had as a young boy had played no small part in my decision to become a deputy.

I heard sounds coming from the evidence room and, instead of heading for my desk, I turned to see who else was working on the weekend.

Shantel glanced up from her desk when I looked into her office.

"Are you on call?" I asked.

"No. Are you?"

"No."

"I wouldn't have to work on Saturday if you didn't find bodies on Friday night."

"That was not my intention," I assured her.

"I was looking at the pictures." She frowned.

"Which ones?" I moved in to look at her monitor, which she half turned toward me. I saw a picture of Banks's head wound.

"I'd say it's related to the King murder. I can't even tell you why I think that. Maybe it's the cold-bloodedness of the attack in both cases." Shantel wasn't an investigator, but I respected the number of cases she'd worked on, her intelligence and her knowledge.

"I know what you mean. There wasn't much hesitation in either attack," I agreed.

"Word is, you're friends with Robin Hennessy and are keeping Pete from arresting him."

I rolled my eyes. "How does the grapevine pick up on the fact that Robin and I were friends, but screw up the fact that it was the State Attorney who didn't want him held?"

"But you think he's innocent?" Shantel could come across as a fifth-grade teacher grilling a student when she wanted to.

"I'd word it more like: I'm not *sure* he's the killer," I said.

"Even though he was found in the trailer with Drew's body? The murder weapon less than a foot from his hand?"

"Yeah," I said tentatively.

"And then was seen, *by you*, not a block from this second body?" She waved toward the monitor.

"I think there are other possibilities." I settled into a defensive position.

"I agree with you." Her mocha-colored face broke into a mischievous grin.

"Really?" I wondered if this was a trick.

"I've been looking over other cases where a drunk killed the victim." She used her mouse to bring up and arrange a series of photos into a mosaic of carnage. "Not one of them was killed with less than five distinct injuries." She pointed to the graphic images.

"Exactly. It's that sort of thing that makes the King scene

feel hinky for me. A drunk isn't going to manage a perfect blow. Their coordination is off."

"And their judgment. See this one." Shantel pointed to a particularly gruesome image. "The murderer struck a glancing blow to the side of the head. The next two strikes were to the shoulder because he missed his mark, then one to the victim's jaw. Again, off from his target. The next one was to the head, which probably killed the victim. With the man mortally wounded, the murderer hit him three more times."

She pointed to an image of a different victim. "Ten hits and four were on non-vital parts of the victim's body." She went on to point out several others.

"If it had just been the King killing, then I might think it was just a one-off, or that Hennessy is a surprisingly efficient drunk. But now with a second murder…"

"We're assuming that they're connected," I reminded her.

"Blunt objects aren't the most common methods of murder. Guns, knives, strangulation are all more common."

"Feel free to share your thoughts with all the other deputies."

"You're on your own." Then she smiled at me. "Nah, I'll do my best to tamp down the rebellion."

"And I'm not even a sergeant yet. Truth is, I'm reconsidering the whole thing."

Shantel went from teacher to angry mom in a flash.

"Don't you go backing out now. You earned that promotion and CID needs you."

"I don't know about either of those things." I was surprised by her attitude.

"Shame on you! You're just turning chicken. Do you think it was easy for me to become a supervisor? I was scared to death."

"Come on, you're a natural boss."

"Bossy maybe," she admitted wryly. "But there's a difference between that and being the boss. I still feel funny every time I have to do Marcus's yearly evaluation. I think folks like you and I make the best supervisors. It's the ones that think they deserve it who are the worst."

"I'm just not sure I'm ready for the politics that go with the job."

Shantel waved my concerns away. "Office politics is just getting along with people. You'll be fine. Most folks like you."

"Most?"

"Most. Now get out of my office and go find Drew's murderer."

I wandered to my desk thinking about what Shantel had said about the murders. If Robin wasn't the murderer, then who was? He certainly seemed to be connected in some way to the killings. I thought about Nat. Was she the connection? She certainly came across as crazy, but was being crazy enough of a motive? It could be. I decided that interviewing her needed to be a top priority, but I was afraid it would be next to impossible to find her after our last encounter.

I called Pete.

"Our list of priorities is getting bigger," he reminded me. "I still haven't come up with a next of kin for Banks."

"I can talk to Mr. Griffin. Banks has been around long enough that he might have some information on him." Albert Griffin, my friend and Eddie's landlord, was the head of the local historical society and had become the custodian of the local newspaper's morgue when it had gone out of business.

"I'll leave that to you then. I'm still trying to pull as much security footage as I can. Being Saturday isn't making it easy."

"I'll also talk to Robin again and see if I can find out how he got into town from his mom's house."

Pete grunted, which I knew summed up his opinion of Robin's memory.

"I'll talk to some of the deputies and let them know how important Natalie is to the case. There's a lot of grumbling about us letting Robin go free," he said.

"Grumbling, muttering, bitching, I know," I said. "The good news for you is that most are blaming me."

"Well, you are his chief advocate." I could hear the smile in Pete's voice.

"Knock it off. You know it was the State Attorney. There's enough resentment about my promotion already."

"Potential promotion." He laughed.

"Your promotion isn't set in stone yet either," I shot back.

"Tell me about it. I'm hungry enough to eat dirt right now." He was dead serious.

"Hang in there, little kitten." I smiled, imagining his face super-imposed over the kitten hanging from a rope in the ubiquitous poster. His response as he hung up was predictably obscene.

Since the jail was across the street, I decided to go talk to Robin first.

"I'm recording this," I told him as he was brought into the interview room.

He looked horrible, even worse than the morning King's body had been found.

"Whatever." He dropped into the metal chair and put his head down on the table.

When I'd brought him in at three in the morning, I had requested that he be put on suicide watch. This meant that he was considered dangerous to himself and others, so he'd been transported in shackles. I asked the guard to remove his handcuffs and shackles before he left us alone.

After running through all of the information that was required for an official recording of an interview, I berated Robin for his attitude.

"You'd better start caring," I told him, feeling the anger rise inside me. Fighting for someone who wasn't willing to fight for themselves was unrewarding. "You left your mother feeling like hell."

"What happened last night?" he asked, finally looking at me.

"Ha! That's what I want you to tell me."

"What I remember is just bits and pieces. Was there really another body?"

"Do you know Douglas Banks?"

"No," he said, letting his head drop back to the table.

"Zero."

Robin lifted his head again. "Zero? You're telling me that Zero is dead?"

"Tell me about your relationship with him."

"Relationship?" He looked like he'd never heard the word before.

"How did you meet him? How often do you see him? Are you all friends? Everything," I said sternly.

"I don't remember when I met him. I think when I was in high school. He used to buy us beer."

"Are you friends?"

"He's… just like an old guy. Kinda. I wouldn't hurt him. Hey, I've even helped him out sometimes." He said this like it was proof that he couldn't have hurt Banks.

"You drank together?"

"What else are we going to do together?"

"How often?"

"I don't know. This is crazy. It's not like I keep a diary or something. My life is just drifting around drinking. If Zero is there, we drink together. Sometimes I give him some of my stash and sometimes he gives me some of his. That's all."

"What did you all talk about?"

"Did… Wait, you haven't told me. Is he really dead?" Robin was holding his head in his hands and rubbing his temples.

"He's dead. What did you all talk about?"

"Zero only had one channel. His life sucked 'cause his wife left him. Period, that's all. He was the worst kind of drunk. Boring. Okay, I listened to him 'cause he'd share his cheap-ass liquor with me. I didn't hurt him. Why would I hurt him?" Robin was clutching at the sides of his head. "This is a nightmare."

"When was the last time you saw or talked with him?"

"I don't know." He moaned and looked close to tears.

On the one hand, I was angry with him for leaving his mother's house, but I could also sympathize with him. For the first time in decades, someone was demanding that he account for his time. How long had it been since anyone had cared where he'd been the day before?

"I know this is a shock. But if you don't pull yourself together and start climbing out of the hole you're in, you're going to be buried alive by these murders." I took a deep breath. "Even if you *are* guilty, you can start to turn things around. Tell the truth now and it will be easier for you and your mother."

"My mother?"

"If there's a trial, how do you think that's going to make her feel?"

"I didn't do anything!" For the first time I saw a flash of real anger in his eyes. *Good*, I thought, *he needs to get angry*.

"Then let's see how we can prove that."

"I thought I was innocent until proven guilty?"

"When you're found in a trailer with a dead body and the murder weapon is almost in your hand, then you have some explaining to do."

"I told you, I don't know how I got in that man's trailer."

"Let's concentrate on Banks and last night."

"I… don't know. I just… after being locked up… I just went a little overboard."

"How did you get from your mother's house to where I found you?" I asked, ignoring his understatement.

Robin shrugged.

"I need more than that. Think. What's the last thing you remember?"

"I remember stuff from last night… or I think I do. It's all kind of a blur. Some of the things I think happened…" Another shrug.

"I dropped you off at your mother's house. Then what happened?"

Robin sighed heavily. "She was, like, too much. Asking me questions I couldn't answer, or that had answers she wouldn't want to hear. I couldn't take it and went back to my room. Not my room, but the room she was going to let me stay in. She made it a point of reminding me that her husband wouldn't like me staying there."

"Okay, so you're in your room. Then what?"

"I wanted to talk to Nat." He looked thoughtful.

"Did you?"

"Talk to Nat?"

"Yeah."

"I think so. I didn't want to use up the minutes on the phone you gave me, so I waited until Mom went back to her room before I snuck out and used the phone in the kitchen. Mom still has a landline."

"And?"

"I had to call a couple of times before Nat answered, then she made fun of me for being at my mom's. I asked her to come get me, but she just laughed. Told me to steal my mom's car. She can get real mean."

"So what did you do?" Like teeth, every answer had to be pulled out of Robin.

"I… don't know. Mom had to go somewhere. The store, I think. So I told her I'd be in my room. Yeah, that's it. I said I was tired and went to get some sleep."

"And?"

"I snuck out. That's right," he congratulated himself.

I just waited, tired of prompting him.

"I was going to walk to town if I had to. I did it once before when that asshole she's married to kicked me out of the house."

"So did you walk all the way?"

"Funny. I got a ride."

"What's funny about it?"

"I don't remember who gave me the ride."

Great, I thought. "Think about the car. What color was it?"

"I… Look, I could make stuff up, but I honestly don't remember much after that."

I sighed. "Any other details you can remember from last night would be helpful."

"We went to a house and got wasted." He shrugged.

"What'd you have?"

"X, I think," he said, mentioning one of the many street names for ecstasy. "Some nasty moonshine a guy had brought with him. Other stuff."

"Nat was with you?"

"Yeah, that was why I came into town, to see her, wasn't it?" He made it sound like I asked a dumb question.

"Who else was there?"

"I can't do that. I can't rat them out. No way I'm a narc."

"I'm not interested in arresting them. But for your sake, I need to ask them some questions."

"Man, these people are at red-level ten on the paranoia scale. A cop comes by and starts asking questions, they're gonna freak. Guess who they're gonna blame?"

I knew he was right. Anyone who abused street drugs usually ended up paranoid.

"I got bad news for you. I'm going to be asking questions whether you give me the names or not. If you don't give me the names, then I'll have to ask a lot more people a lot more questions. You got a chance here to narrow down your exposure."

Robin seemed to mull this over. Finally, he gave me half a dozen names of people he thought he'd seen the night before. It was hard to say if he was remembering the people and events correctly, but for my purposes it didn't really matter. Either way, they were people I needed to interview. Most of the names were regulars that I recognized from drug busts or overdoses.

"That's all I can think of," he said, and I saw his head start to fall back toward the table.

"Whoa!" I stopped him. "I want the big fish too."

"What are you talking about?" He looked puzzled.

"Natalie. She's top of my list."

"I don't know where she is," he whined.

I was prepared for this.

"Then I want you to give me the name of someone she'll respond to."

"What?"

"Someone who can call her and she'll answer the phone. Someone who can ask her where she is and get a straight answer."

"Me?"

"She knows that you're in jail, dumbass. Another person."

"I… Who…" he stammered.

"How long do you want to be behind bars?" I threatened.

"There's a guy." Robin stopped and I didn't know if he was going to continue or not. "Malik. He's always hanging around. Sucking up to her. He's pathetic." There was real anger in his voice. Jealousy, I assumed.

"What's his last name?"

"Jordan."

I thought the name rang a bell. "That's not his street name?"

"He doesn't even have a street name. He's just, like, there all the time. Drinks, pops whatever someone hands him and tries to rub up against Nat." Robin almost spat the words. I decided it would not be very nice to point out that his description of Malik's behavior was a spot-on description of his own.

"Where does he hang out?"

"If Nat isn't around, then Malik will be at Deshaun's house."

I got the address and, after giving Robin some additional advice on things he needed to do if he ever hoped to get out of jail, I left him and headed to my car.

CHAPTER TWELVE

My plan was to hunt down Malik Jordan and go from there. First, I pulled up Malik's priors. The list was long, but all of them were minor offenses such as possession, petty theft and trespassing. None of them rose to the level of a felony. When I saw his photos, I again had a vague recollection that I had dealt with him in the past, but he was so low down on the criminal hierarchy that he didn't stick out in my memory. Deshaun Williams was listed as a known associate along with Robin and Natalie. Douglas Banks was not.

At twenty-five, Deshaun was the youngest of the group. When I realized that his address was in an older, established neighborhood, I figured it was his parents' house. A search of the property appraiser's site confirmed that the house was owned by a Kendrick Williams, who also owned three other properties.

I drove to Deshaun's house. The neighborhood was made up of young families and retirees, with modest homes and yards filled with the toys of children or grandchildren. Deshaun's place had four cars parked in the driveway, none of which looked like they were safe to drive on the road. I parked so that the van blocked the others in. I didn't want to see my witness drive off.

Even with the cool weather, the windows of the house were open, allowing me to hear the TV and smell the pot smoke. As I walked up to the door, I could hear a sports announcer breathlessly reporting a game. The folks inside were not going to be happy to see me.

I rang the doorbell and heard grumbles from in front of the TV.

"The damn door's open!" someone yelled.

Not wanting to freak them out by walking in, I called back, "You might want to come to the door."

"Who the…" A string of expletives followed.

A young black man wearing only a pair of boxers answered the door. He sized me up in an instant and I could tell that he was thinking about slamming the door.

"I just want to talk to you." I did my best to sound nonthreatening. I must have done a good job because I saw his muscles relax, even though the suspicion in his eyes didn't go away. I showed him my star and ID.

"I didn't do anything."

"Are you Deshaun Williams?"

"Yeah," he said, drawing it out as though he didn't want to admit it.

"I'm looking for Malik Jordan."

"Yeah?" He visibly relaxed knowing that I wasn't there for him.

"Would you call him over to the door?" I didn't even ask to come in. No sense making them run around and hide stuff.

"Mal, he wants to talk to you."

I heard laughter and clapping from inside.

"He's trying to hide!" a voice shouted.

"Damn it!" someone else yelled from inside.

"I'll get him," Deshaun told me before he closed the door.

The sound of a struggle came through the windows before the door opened again and Deshaun and another man appeared, holding up Malik Jordan.

"Here's his stinking ass," Deshaun laughed. *If I had friends like him, I'd get new friends*, I thought.

"Malik, I just want to ask you a few questions. If you didn't have anything to do with a murder, you don't have to worry."

Of course, I should have known better than to use the word "murder." When he heard it, he renewed his struggles, but the two men held him fast.

"Don't make me take you to jail as a material witness," I said; not that I had any plans to do so.

"Why me?" he whined.

"You were partying last night. I just want to ask you a few questions." I didn't want to say more in front of the other two men.

"I don't know nothin'," he mumbled.

"Just come out and sit in my van so we can talk."

Malik looked everywhere but at me as he considered this. "You aren't going to arrest me?"

"No."

"Okay."

"He's going to run." Deshaun smiled. "You really want us to let him go?"

"Malik, I can put cuffs on you. Is that what you want?"

He looked like the answer to this question was the Final Jeopardy category. Finally, he said, "I won't run."

"Let him go."

"He's going to run, man," the other guy warned.

Slowly, they released him. Malik stood there for a moment before I saw his muscles tense. Sure enough, he tried to run past me. I stuck my foot out and, to the amusement of his faux friends, he went sprawling onto the walkway. I dropped down and placed my knee on his back.

"Come on. There's no need for this," I told him while I pulled my handcuffs out. I had him cuffed in a second.

"I knew you was lying," Malik huffed.

"I wasn't lying. Come on." I pulled him up. "I can come up with a charge if you want. Would you like that?"

"No!"

"Then let me lead you over to my van and we can talk."

I took the sulking Malik over to the van as the door to the house closed behind us.

"Those are some friends," I said, opening the door and pushing him into the passenger seat. I left the cuffs on.

"You really just want to talk to me?" he asked after I was seated beside him.

"Isn't that what I said?"

"Yeah, but…"

"You know Robin Hennessy?"

"Yeah…"

"Was he with you last night?"

"I saw him."

"When did you see him?"

"Last night," he said and saw the look on my face. "I don't know the time. My phone got rained on and doesn't work."

"Was it dark?"

"Yeah, sure."

"Where did you see him?"

Malik described an old house a couple of blocks from where Banks's body had been found.

"Do you know Douglas Banks?"

He gave me a blank look.

"Zero."

"That old man? He's just an old drunk."

I almost asked Malik what he saw in his own future. Instead, I said, "Did you see him last night?"

"I don't know."

"What do you mean, you don't know?"

"He's around, but I never talk to him or anything."

"Have you ever seen Robin argue with Zero?"

"Oh shit, he's dead!" Malik tried to turn and open his door, but the cuffs slowed him down. I grabbed his arm and pulled him back into his seat.

"Have you ever seen anyone argue or get in a fight with

Zero?"

"I mean, he's disgusting. People shove him away when he comes around begging for a drink or somethin'."

"Have you ever heard anyone threaten him?"

"I'm telling you, nobody talks to that old man." He screwed his face up in disgust.

"Was Natalie Owens with you last night?"

Malik again turned and tried to get out of the van.

"Are you scared of her?" My hand was firmly on his shoulder.

He looked down, not meeting my eyes and not answering the question, though the answer was obvious.

"Was she with you last night?"

"Yeah," he said so softly that I almost didn't hear him.

"I need to talk to her."

"I don't know where she is." He blurted the answer too quickly to be believable.

"We can do this the hard way or the easy way."

"What's the easy way?"

"You tell me where I can find her."

"What's the hard way?"

"I find a way to force you to tell me."

"You can't do that!" he protested.

"I can't physically make you tell me anything. However, I can find ways to put pressure on you until you decide that telling me is better than not telling me."

"I don't know where she is… really."

"What's that mean?"

"She told me she was going to be lying low for a couple of days, maybe a week."

"When did she tell you this?"

"Last night."

His inability to be specific about times and places was maxing out my frustration level. "Was Robin with her?"

"No. Which was weird 'cause he'd left with her."

"You're sure?"

Malik looked down and shuffled a little in the seat. With

his arms cuffed behind him, I knew he was uncomfortable, but his demeanor was that of a teenage boy being asked about his first crush.

"I don't like him being with her."

Jealousy again.

"Had she left earlier in the evening?"

"I don't know. After I took a couple of hits a guy gave me, I was out of it for a while."

"If you called her, would she answer?"

"Maybe. But like I told you, my phone is fried."

"But you have her number?"

"No." He rocked back and forth in the seat. "Pisses me off." His frustration was poignant.

"So how can you reach her?"

"I can't. She won't answer a call from a number she doesn't know," he said, and I wondered why she'd answered when Robin had called from his mother's landline. Had he called Natalie from that house in the past? Maybe.

"Can you use someone else's phone?"

"If they'd let me. There aren't too many people she'll take calls from. Mostly just dealers or players. They ain't goin' to let me use their phones."

They wouldn't be interested in *me* using their phones either. I was feeling his frustration.

"Do you still have your phone?"

"It's in my pocket, but I'm telling you, it's fried."

"I might be able to get it working again."

He looked at me and tried to raise his hands up from behind his back.

"If I let you loose, are you going to try and run?"

"Can you fix my phone?"

"I don't know," I said honestly.

"I need it, bad."

Figuring we had a deal, I unlocked his cuffs. He squirmed around to take his phone out of his back pocket.

I thought about trying to turn it on, but remembered that Lionel had told me ages ago that it was better to leave a phone off if there was a chance that it was damaged. Instead, I pulled out my own phone and called Lionel.

"I know it's Saturday," I said, apologizing from the start.

"What's up?"

I explained the situation.

"I can make a clone. We've got a bunch of burner phones." He paused. "You want it done now." I heard someone groan in the background.

"I'll make it up to you."

"Sure. I'll meet you at the office in half an hour." Another groan came from his end of the line.

I felt a little bad because I could hear the gears in Lionel's head turning. He'd told me in the past that he wanted to stay at the sheriff's office and become more involved with cases. I was sure that he was thinking that doing a favor for the boss's son wouldn't hurt his chances. Being the sheriff's son came with its share of disadvantages, so this time I only felt a little guilty for taking advantage of the occasional perk as long as it was for the common good.

"I'll get a new phone?" Malik asked after I'd hung up.

"Yep," I told him, without pointing out the obvious fact that we could make ourselves a copy of his phone too. I'd have to make sure he agreed to it before Lionel made the copy, but with him being so anxious to have his contacts back, I didn't think it would be a very hard sell.

Once at the office, I led Malik back to the evidence room. The lights were off and Shantel had gone home.

"I've never been back here," he said, looking around wide-eyed.

Lionel showed up a few minutes later and unlocked his office. He looked Malik up and down with raised eyebrows.

"This will take a minute," he said, popping the SIM card out of Malik's phone. "The SIM card has most, but not all, of the data on it. I'll copy everything after I find out how fried this phone is."

"Malik, we're going to copy your phone. Do we have your permission?" I asked him.

"You'll give me a new phone that's like my busted one?"

"Yes," I assured him.

"Okay."

I took a deep breath while I decided how to push forward. I didn't want to spook Malik, but I wanted to be clear what I expected in return for the new phone. As desperate as he was to get his phone back, now was the time to ask for what I wanted.

"I need to talk to Natalie. Once we've fixed your phone, I want you to call her and find out where she is."

I watched him process this.

"I can't screw her over. No way." He shook his head adamantly.

"You'll be helping her out. Right now, there is an order out for her to be picked up as a material witness. If I can talk to her, I'll cancel the order," I explained.

He scrunched up his face in thought.

"Yeah, but she'll think I'm, like, working with you."

"To help her," I argued.

"I don't know."

It was time to quit being nice. "I'll make her think you're working with us whether you are or not," I said, doing my best to sound like an asshole.

Malik looked like a fish dangling from a hook.

"That's fucked up!"

I wasn't surprised that he didn't have any true friends. He was too naïve for the bad guys and too messed up for the good guys. While I felt sorry for him, I wasn't going to let him off the hook.

"Your choice. You can get your phone back and help Natalie out, or you can *not* get your phone back and I'll spread the word that you're an informant for us."

"You can't keep my phone!"

"You can have this piece of trash back anytime," Lionel chimed in at just the right time, holding Malik's ruined phone out to him.

Malik looked from the phone to our faces.

"This is messed up," he mumbled.

"The deal is, you get to keep the phone when I've made contact with her."

"You just want to talk to her?"

"If she's not involved in the murder then, yes, that's all."

"She didn't kill him," he said, not sounding convinced.

"Then she doesn't have anything to worry about. And neither do you. Do we have a deal?"

Malik looked at the new phone that Lionel was putting together. The longing in his expression told me that I had won this battle.

"Yeah, okay. But this better not screw me up," he said as though his threat held any weight.

Lionel cloned Malik's phone and handed it to me.

"I want you to call her," I told Malik as I held the phone out to him. "And set up a place to talk to her. Tell her the police questioned you and you're freaking out. Put it in your own words and make it believable."

"She doesn't always answer or call me back," he muttered.

"Make the call and we'll go from there."

Reluctantly, he opened his phone and called Natalie.

I could hear the phone ringing as sweat dripped down Malik's face. He wasn't sweating from the temperature. He looked at me when it went to voicemail. I shook my head and he ended the call.

"Let me have the phone."

He held it out to me.

I typed a message to Natalie that read: *Police came by. What should I tell them?* If she thought about it, she'd probably know it wasn't from him, but she had no reason to be suspicious of a text from his phone.

Sure enough, in ten seconds the phone rang. I wish we could have had the phone on speaker or recorded the call. Unfortunately, it's impossible to hide that a phone is on speaker and, in Florida, both parties had to agree to have the conversation recorded if there wasn't a warrant.

"I'm freakin' out," Malik told her. His tone was believable, and he used it to good effect. After a little back and forth with Natalie, he hung up and said, "She's going to meet me in thirty minutes near the Calvary Mission Church. There's a house across the street that a woman sells out of."

"I'll need you."

"No!" He jumped out of his chair and paced around the room, shaking his head. "No, no."

"Do you want your phone?"

"Keep it." He dropped it on Lionel's table. "I'm not gonna trap her for nothin'."

It was clear he was telling the truth. Natalie had obviously instilled enough fear in him and enough…love? … that he wasn't willing to be there and see the look on her face when she figured out that he'd betrayed her.

"Okay. I'll just go and sweep her up."

"Wait, wait! I got something you could do." He was almost begging me.

"What?" Now I was the suspicious one.

"Have me handcuffed in the back of a cop car. Let her see that." His eyes were pleading with me. "Please."

"I guess." I began to warm to the idea. If we needed him later as an informant or for another trap, he'd still have some street cred. I wondered why I hadn't thought of it. "Sure, we can do that."

I called Pete to tell him what was up, and took him up on his offer of help. Next, I checked with dispatch to see who was working patrol. The two best choices were Phil Eccles and Julio Ortiz who, while now a full investigator in CID, still needed the occasional overtime and had volunteered for the weekend. Marti told me Eccles had just arrived at a multi-car accident involving serious injury, but that Julio had just finished a burglary call. I got him released by the watch commander to help out.

With the operation set up, I texted Eddie and told him I was running later than I'd planned.

We're good, he sent back, adding a thumbs-up and a dog

head emoji.

A text from Cara came in at the same time. She had managed to convince her mother to go to a doctor on Monday and would be staying over until then. I texted her the most loving and supportive words I could think of and told her that I'd talk to her later.

"What's the plan, Stan?" Pete asked as he joined us in the parking lot of the office.

"Here's the satellite view of the area." I had it pulled up on my laptop, which was sitting on the trunk of Julio's patrol car. We'd already locked Malik in the back of the car.

"Julio can hang back with the patrol car and be ready to give chase if she runs. You and I can park back here," I said to Pete, pointing to a spot on the screen, "which will give us plenty of cover to walk up to the house."

"You said the owner deals?" Pete asked.

"Low level, according to our friend." I nodded toward Malik. "I checked the woman's history. She's been pulled in repeatedly for possession, but only twice for dealing, and each time she was able to convince the State Attorney to drop the more serious charges because the amount in her possession was just over the limit to be considered a dealer. No resisting arrest or assault charges in her history."

"What about an SO?"

"According to our informant, she lives with another woman. Her priors are along the same lines as Gia's, the leaseholder."

"So you and I are going up against three women," Pete said with a crooked grin. "I say we need a few more troops on the ground."

"We've got Julio for backup," I pointed out. Julio rolled his eyes.

"What's the worst that can happen?" Pete laughed. "I'm wearing my vest."

"10-4."

It was four o'clock on a Saturday, and there were plenty of people moving around the neighborhood where we were going to corner Natalie. The area was only four blocks from the courthouse square. The homes were modest and most dated from the mid to late 1800s. About half had been renovated, while the other half needed some work. Even though it was a dreary day in March, I could smell someone grilling out nearby as Pete and I rendezvoused on the street and tried not to look suspicious.

"Back door or front door?" I asked.

"On three," Pete said, holding out his fist.

I had scissors; he had paper.

"I'll take the front," I said.

"Good, I wanted the back anyway."

We were lucky that there was an old workshop nearby where we could watch the house. When the meeting time came, I looked at Pete, who shrugged. We hadn't seen Natalie or anyone else come out of the house. The same two cars were in the driveway and a light was on in one of the rooms.

"I say we give her ten more minutes before we go for it," I said. Pete nodded and I radioed Julio and informed him of our current timetable.

I walked toward the front of the house, trying to look casual while feeling very exposed. Even though the neighborhood wasn't known for a high crime rate, it still attracted some nefarious types due to its proximity to downtown and the mix of people with money versus the ones who were just getting by.

Nothing rang any alarm bells as I walked up the concrete steps to the front porch of the single-story clapboard house. It was painted pale blue with pink shutters and a pot-leaf-shaped doorknocker. I gave the door a confident but not aggressive rap.

I heard footsteps and a female voice asked who I was.

"I'm from the county," I said honestly.

"What?"

"I just have a few questions." I tried to keep my voice light and nonthreatening.

"I don't understand. Can I see some ID?" asked the voice on the other side of the door.

I sighed and held up my ID, folded so the star didn't show.

"It's the damn cops!" the voice shouted.

"I just want to talk to you," I said clearly. "Just talk. No one's in trouble."

I heard a noise from the back that included Pete yelling: "Stop!"

I radioed for Julio to join us as I started around to the back of the house. If anyone came out the front, Julio would be there to catch them. I was halfway around the house when Natalie came flying through a window, even though it was more than six feet off the ground.

I had to duck to keep from getting glass in my face. Startled, I hesitated long enough that she had a good ten-yard head-start on me. I heard Pete yell for me to run faster. She was fast. Very fast.

I did my best to keep Natalie in sight as I breathlessly radioed Julio.

Julio's car passed me as I followed Natalie into a wooded drainage area. As soon as we got into the woods, I knew she was going to get away. The greenway backed up to a ten-acre park that was adjacent to the old city cemetery. If she'd been an armed robber, we could have called in the highway patrol and pulled in some of our own off-duty officers. None of that was going to happen for a witness.

I radioed again for Julio, who was circling around behind in case she came out the other side of the cemetery or the park. Meanwhile, Pete came huffing down the road toward me.

"I'm behind you," he radioed.

"She's going to be hard to pick up now," I responded.

"Haven't lost enough weight to be chasing down featherweight suspects," he complained.

"What happened?" I asked as he caught up with me.

"I was standing on the landing at the back door when she

threw it open. I thought she would stop, or at least I'd have a moment where she paused. Instead, she slugged me in the stomach and ran back into the house. If I'd been wearing steel plates instead of Kevlar, she'd have broken her hand."

"You're lucky she didn't kick you between your legs."

"You aren't kidding! Anyway, since she'd assaulted me, I had cause to chase her into the house." He paused and shook his head. "Never in my career have I seen a suspect throw themselves through a closed window."

"What are you thinking?"

"Maybe she's more than a witness."

We were walking through the greenway on the one-in-a-million chance we'd catch a glimpse of Natalie, or a clue as to where she'd gone.

"I've been considering that. She's tied in with Robin tight enough that she could have gotten him drunk and in Drew's trailer. But what's the motive?" I asked.

"There are plenty of murders where the person doing the killing is just evil. I mean, we hadn't even come up with a solid motive for Robin. Maybe she just took offense to comments or looks from King and Banks. Maybe she's just playing a crazy game. The woman I saw at the door was nuts," he assured me.

"We're going to have a time finding her now," I said, mentally kicking myself. "I should have laid a better trap. I just didn't think she'd object that much to answering questions."

"Maybe she's afraid we have more answers than we do." Pete turned to me. "I'm going to put out a BOLO that includes her assault on me. That will get a bit more attention."

"And it gives us the charges to put her in jail until we can figure out what her role in the murders is."

We spent another half hour walking around until we ended up back at our cars, where Julio met up with us.

"Here's your phone." I handed Malik his phone after letting him out of Julio's car and uncuffing him. "I'd offer to drive you home, but you probably want to put some distance between us."

"What happened?" Malik looked confused.

"Your girlfriend assaulted a deputy, so now she's wanted. I'd advise you to contact us if you talk to her. You don't want to find yourself charged for aiding and abetting," Pete told him.

"What do I do now?"

"If you remember anything else from last night or hear from Natalie, call me." I gave him my card.

"She's going to be pissed."

"From what I saw, she already wasn't in a very good mood," Pete quipped.

CHAPTER THIRTEEN

By six o'clock I was headed home and trying to figure out if I'd made any progress. In my mind, the focus of the investigation had shifted from Robin to Natalie, if for no other reason than her extreme desire not to be caught.

I wouldn't be able to do much tomorrow, but on Monday I wanted to dig into Natalie's past. I knew she'd had run-ins with the law, including a stint in jail. She'd also had a probation officer for six months, who might potentially prove to be a fount of information. Probation officers were supposed to keep close tabs on their charges during the probation period, including home and work visits. They were also often privy to psychological and medical backgrounds, if the information applied to the conditions of the inmate's probation.

There was much barking and bouncing up and down when I got home. Mauser performed his traditional bump-and-slobber routine while Cleo took a more refined approach to the greeting.

Eddie was in the kitchen and the smell of pasta was thick in the air.

"Did you talk to Natalie?" he asked, taking plates out of

the cupboard.

"You didn't have to make dinner," I told him, but thinking how good the food smelled.

"I've gotten into the habit with Albert. Besides, I kinda owe you for a pillow." He pointed toward a Mausered throw pillow sitting on the counter with its guts ripped out.

I chuckled. "I don't think there's ever been a time he stayed here that he didn't tear something up. Where were you and Jessie while he was wreaking havoc?"

I asked the question casually, not thinking about the possible answers. When I saw Eddie blush and glance away, I regretted asking. "Never mind."

"Did you find Natalie?" Eddie asked, desperate to change the subject.

"No. She flew out a window to avoid talking to us."

His eyes widened, then he tapped his head. "She ain't right."

"She punched Pete, so we've got a pick-up order out on her for that."

"If she was a normal person, I'd say she'd go to ground someplace and lay low, but Snake Tongue is a little... odd."

"I know what you mean. She appears to be wired differently."

I called Cara and told her about my adventures. I could hear loud music in the background as we talked.

"It was nice of Eddie to make dinner," she said. "I'm envious. The co-op is having an Ostara celebration."

"A what?"

"It's a pagan celebration of the spring equinox. They're a little early, but... there's been a lot of smoking, dancing and less clothes than the weather would suggest."

"Is your mother up to that?"

Cara laughed. "Think who we're talking about. If there's going to be half-nude dancing around a bonfire anywhere within a hundred miles, she'll be there."

We shared a few mutual endearments, then I hung up and joined Eddie at the table.

"Cara is really nice," Eddie said as we filled up our plates.

"I'm a lucky guy," I agreed. "What about you and Jessie? Can I assume that your relationship is back on track?" I was honestly interested, but I hoped the conversation wouldn't devolve into a discussion of their recent activities.

"I don't know," he said, sounding like every guy ever. "She seems to want to be in a relationship, but she also kinda doesn't."

"Give her time. I'm sure she needs to get through the academy before she can think about personal commitments."

"I get that."

Eddie was surprisingly good company. After dinner, he settled in to watch a movie with the dogs while I worked on reports under the close supervision of Ivy and Ghost.

"When do Mauser and Cleo go home?" Eddie asked the next morning at breakfast.

"Dad's going to text me when they get back from the beach. You don't need to stay. I'm just going to hang around the house today."

"Cool, 'cause I want to help Albert clean out one of the rooms upstairs."

"That reminds me. I wanted to talk to him about Douglas Banks."

"He knows everyone," Eddie said, sharing my conviction about Mr. Griffin.

"I'd be curious if Banks was ever a productive member of society," I mused.

"That's hard to imagine."

"Maybe I'll come over with you and talk with him today." I looked at the dogs, who were both staring at my cereal bowl with desire. "Though I don't know about leaving these two alone in my house together."

"Bring them. You can't take them into the house because of Brutus," Eddie said, referring to one of Mr. Griffin's many cats, a big black bruiser with a strong dislike of dogs.

"But we can let them play in the backyard. I've patched the privacy fence."

At this, I put my spoon down and looked at him.

"Eddie, I really have to tell you how impressed I am with everything you've done for Mr. Griffin. And… well, just with how much you've changed."

For the second time in twelve hours, I saw Eddie blush.

"What you and Albert have done for me…" He was quiet for a moment, then resumed: "You know what a bunch of scumbags my family is. Having friends like y'all has made up for a lot of shit in my life. I like paying it back."

An hour later, I followed Eddie over to Mr. Griffin's house.

Once we'd set the dogs loose in the backyard and Eddie had headed upstairs to start his cleaning project, Mr. Griffin and I stood for a while and watched Mauser and Cleo frolic in the grass.

"Every time I see Mauser, I'm astonished again at how big he is," Mr. Griffin said.

"He makes Cleo look small in comparison," I agreed.

"Eddie said you wanted to ask me about someone?"

"Douglas Banks. You might not know anything. He's the homeless guy that got killed on Friday night."

"The name sounds familiar." He tapped his head. "But my mind isn't as good as it used to be. Come inside. I'll check the index I've been working on for the back issues of the *Adams County Times*. There's a non-profit that's trying to digitize small-town papers from the last century. I've put in a request to have it done with the *Times*."

I followed him in through the kitchen. In the room where the newspapers were stored, a computer was set up in one corner.

"Eddie and a couple of the ladies from the library have been helping me."

Mr. Griffin sat down at the computer and started going through folders on the monitor.

"This is quite a project." I couldn't imagine spending hours upon hours in there, digging through old editions of the paper and creating an index, let alone the work it was going to take to digitize whole editions.

"I've dedicated my retirement to everything in this room. I'm just glad that there's the possibility of preserving it in a way that others might find useful."

"Douglas Banks isn't the rarest name in the world," I said, trying to lower my expectations of what Mr. Griffin would find. But in less than twenty minutes, he'd found a reference to Banks in the index.

"It might not be him. Let's see."

Mr. Griffin got up and went back into the stacks that filled the room. Boxes and boxes sat on metal racks from floor to ceiling. Each box had the edition numbers and dates of publication for the neatly folded newspapers inside. I followed him and took the box he pointed to off the shelf.

He opened the box, flipped through the contents to find the edition he was looking for, then carefully folded back the front page. "There." He laid the paper on his desk and pointed to a small article on the inside of the first page.

"Man Claims Wife Kidnapped" read the headline. The story itself was made up of quotes from Douglas Banks claiming that his wife was missing and the police weren't doing anything about it. I'd run his name through our records and nothing had come up, so I looked at the date on the paper. August of 1998, which explained it. Our electronic database didn't go back that far.

"I can read between the lines," Mr. Griffin said. "Seems like Douglas was just upset that his wife had left him. See that quote from a neighbor that they'd been having some marital problems? 'Marital problems,'" he made air quotes, "equals someone was having an affair. And the line: *Sheriff says he's keeping an eye on the case.* That was Sheriff Montfort. He was no-nonsense. If there had been anything there, he'd have looked into it."

"I knew that Banks's wife had left him," I said.

"Apparently that's what sent him into the tailspin that landed him in the gutter."

"Looks like he worked for the state department of motor vehicles," he observed.

"Not sure that helps much after twenty years. Anyone who knew him is probably long gone."

"Sorry."

"It doesn't sound like he was very persistent. Poor guy has his wife run out on him and tries to get the sheriff's department to help him find her—that happens more than you'd think. We've even had wife beaters try to get us to find their spouses for them. But we have to take every missing person report seriously, and I'm sure Montfort did."

I glanced at the article again, making a mental note of Banks's wife's name, Georgia. The article didn't mention any other relatives, his or hers. Figuring that Mr. Griffin had helped me all he could, I thanked him, collected the dogs and headed home.

The next couple of days passed quickly enough. Mauser and Cleo went back to Dad on Sunday evening, and I spent most of Monday working on reports and following up on other cases. Robin was arraigned on several minor charges and failed to meet bail. I knew that his mother had refused to help him out, which was a good thing. The best place for him right now was in jail.

Cara returned home late that night with news that her mother needed a fairly routine hysterectomy, which had been scheduled for early in April.

On Tuesday, I drove straight to Tallahassee in the morning to attend the autopsy for Douglas Banks. Pete met me at the door of the morgue.

"Don't think we're going to learn any great secrets from this one," he said, shaking his head. "But on the positive side, I've been going through the video footage I picked up Saturday. I may have a lead on who drove Robin into town."

"Any leads on where our snake is hiding?"

"Nothing. I stretched the BOLO out to a two-hundred-mile radius. Of course, by now she could be all the way to California or New York."

"I have an appointment this afternoon with her last parole officer," I told him.

"At this point, any information on her is going to help. I hate working cases that involve homeless people. There's no starting point. From the witnesses that I've interviewed, she couch-surfed most of the time. The few times she's had a car, she lived out of it."

Once we'd been allowed into Dr. Darzi's lair, I noticed that he had another in a regular rotation of interns working with him.

"Gentlemen, come in. This is Devon." He pointed a scalpel at his assistant. "Devon, these are two of our best customers. Investigators Macklin and Henley."

"Are we late?" Pete asked, looking at Banks's splayed-open chest.

"We wanted to get a jump on the day. There were two accidents on I-10 last night and we are trying to keep our workload from getting ahead of us. I promise, you have not missed anything. There were two blows to the victim's head." He pointed out the lacerations to Banks's scalp. "The piece of wood found near the victim could certainly have inflicted the wounds as presented."

"Which one killed him?" I asked.

"Either or both. They came too close together to leave any clues about the order. Though I would suggest that the one that is slightly off center was the first, simply based on the fact that it was the lighter of the two hits."

"Would it have been enough to kill him?"

"Eventually. Brain swelling and internal bleeding would have resulted even if the victim had not been struck a second time. That one was delivered with slightly more force. It caved in this area of the skull." He was indicating a sunken area about four inches wide. "Either blow would have killed him. The combination simply killed him sooner."

"How long did he live after the attack?" Pete asked.

"A couple of minutes." Darzi shrugged. "Not long. There are no signs that he was trying to rally to save himself."

"Anything else?"

"We had just gotten to the heart of the matter." Darzi smiled at his own joke, indicating the heart sitting in a pan near the scale. His assistant looked like he wasn't sure whether he should laugh or not.

"The only thing unusual I've noticed," Darzi continued, "is that he was reasonably well kept for someone living on the streets. I have observed this in other deceased victims without severe mental illness who have been on the street for extended periods of time. I would call them the professional homeless. Ones who have developed routines that allow them to remain reasonably healthy considering their lifestyle."

Darzi cut out the liver and pointed to the damage caused by a life of heavy drinking. This merely confirmed my opinion that I could never be a doctor. I couldn't distinguish the difference between the healthy parts of the liver and the unhealthy spots that he pointed out. To humor him, I nodded sagely and thought it all just looked disgusting.

"Not *so* healthy then," Pete clucked. I'd noticed that since he'd started his strict weight-loss program, he had become more judgmental toward people who didn't take care of themselves—the reformed hooker syndrome.

"I'll send over the toxicology report when I get it back from the lab. Is there anything of special interest that you would like them to look for?" Darzi asked as he finished packaging up the samples.

Standard toxicology tests looked at a very narrow range of substances. If there was reason to think that a particular type of poison was a contributing cause, it was a good idea to ask the technicians to test for that substance. Of course, every additional test was an additional cost and took more time.

"If you didn't see any indications, then I don't think we have reason to suspect he died of anything other than wood to head," Pete said.

As we were walking out of the hospital, I asked Pete if he wanted to go talk to Natalie's parole officer with me.

"No, I've got to go over to FDLE and talk to them about another case. I'll meet you back at the office and show you the footage of the car that probably drove Robin into town."

I grabbed a quick lunch, then headed back to the courthouse annex in Calhoun to talk with Natalie's parole officer, Patti Tygart.

The woman had country good looks and appeared to be in her mid-forties. Her blonde hair was cut short, and her eyes were steady and piercing. When I saw her, I remembered an earlier encounter when I was on patrol.

"We've worked together once before," I said.

"Yes, Terrance Major. He'd locked himself in his apartment and was threatening to commit suicide."

"You did a good job talking him into surrendering."

"And I was impressed with your patience. Once he'd made the threat to harm himself, I didn't have any choice but to call for backup. Most of the time I hate to do it because I usually get an officer who just wants to handle the situation by the LEO book. He or she doesn't understand that I know these people and can probably guide the situation to a better ending."

"Knowing your clients is why I'm here."

"Natalie Owens. Let me just say, I was glad when she finished up her probation. Wowsers! She's one for the record books." Patti reached across her desk and picked up a thick folder. "I kept copies of all the reports."

"Can you give me your impressions?" I asked, taking the folder.

"She was scary and sad all in one. Her background was a little unusual. According to medical and psychological reports, she had—and likely still has—reactive attachment disorder. An inability to form strong emotional bonds. This is almost always caused by childhood trauma or being shuffled from one set of caretakers to another. There is some disagreement in Natalie's case. Her parents claimed she was non-emotional from the time they brought her home. She was even tested for autism several times because of her responses. Eventually, the state removed her from her mother because she'd had a few too many trips to the emergency room, though it was always blamed on Natalie's own behavior."

"What did the investigation show?"

"Inconclusive. But I'll tell you that the behavior continued with each set of foster parents."

"If it was inconclusive, then why didn't her parents get her back?"

"To be blunt, her mother didn't want her back. By this time, she'd divorced Natalie's father and remarried. I think she was a little afraid of Natalie and simply couldn't cope with her behavior."

"That's cold," I said, almost feeling sorry for Natalie. "I suppose Natalie acted out when she was in the foster system."

"I've known plenty of kids that were acting out. What she did was different. You have to understand, she is very smart and very narcissistic. She seemed to get off on manipulating her foster parents into fighting amongst themselves. In one case, she got one of the parents arrested and in another they assaulted each other."

"Wow. Is she an addict?"

Patti looked thoughtful. "I'd say no. A user, certainly. But she surrounds herself with addicts. I figure she does it because she can control them."

"And she managed to meet the terms of her probation?"

"I can only document what I can prove. She made sure I couldn't prove she had crossed any lines."

"What's your personal opinion of her?"

"I'm not paid to give my personal opinions." Patti smiled.

"I haven't had a chance to really talk to Natalie since she became wrapped up in our investigation. It would help me, and it would help her, if I can get an understanding of who she is at her core. Is she dangerous?"

"I'd have to say that she could be. I'm not a psychologist, so I can't say if she's a psychopath or not. What I will say is that I've seen her take advantage of others and never look back. I've also heard from some other clients that she did cruel things to people while she was in prison."

"Like what?"

"One woman said Natalie talked her into stealing some cigarettes from another prisoner, just so she could then rat her out to the person she stole the cigarettes from. Apparently to Natalie, it was an elaborate scheme that she'd cooked up. Ultimately, Natalie wound up in charge of the cigarette trade in their wing while the other two were punished."

"Did anyone retaliate against Natalie?"

"That's where the violence comes out. As soon as the other two were back in the general population, they were beaten up by half a dozen prisoners. No one admitted seeing anything, but it was clearly a warning from Natalie. Another time, she stabbed a girl's hand with a plastic spork for looking at her food. Not taking, mind you, just looking."

"Was she punished?"

"Never. Always managed to keep herself in the background or terrify anyone who might complain. The woman whose hand got stabbed begged for and got a transfer into another wing."

"Do you know when she had her tongue split?" This question was pure curiosity. I didn't think for a minute that the answer would help me find her.

"She was nineteen and the 'lead singer,'" Patti said, making air quotes, "for a band called Medusa. Lasted all of two months, but she really bought into the theme. Once she figured out that her tongue freaks people out, she's used every opportunity to flaunt it."

"It certainly freaks me out," I admitted.

"I'd worry about anyone that it didn't."

"That covers background. Can you give me any idea where she might hide out?"

"You're welcome to look through that folder. There are plenty of addresses. Some might be useful, though most won't be."

"Family?"

"Her biological father is dead. Her mother is in New Mexico, or at least she was when I was supervising Natalie. There's no other family that I know of."

We talked for a few more minutes before she directed me to an empty office where I could read through Natalie's file.

The reports were carefully worded so as to mute the bias of the responding officer or social worker. Even still, from the time that Natalie was ten years old, I didn't see a single word that suggested anyone saw a light at the end of the tunnel for her.

I made notes. Her mother was Elizabeth Case and her father was Harlen Owens. Even though the address and phone number for her mother were several years old, I had reason to hope they would still be current. The good news was that I was sure all of Natalie's known associates were already in the sheriff's department's database.

I returned the file to Patti and thanked her.

"Let me know what happens when you find her. I imagine it will put the most exciting episodes of *COPS* to shame."

"Let's hope not," I said with a droll smile.

CHAPTER FOURTEEN

On the way back to the office, I got the feeling that there was something in Natalie's probation file that was important. But the harder I tried to figure it out, the more the thought seemed to slip away. Eventually I gave it up and hoped that it would come to me at some point.

I found Pete at his desk working on reports.

"So you think you know how Robin got to town?" I asked.

"Sit," he commanded.

I dropped into my chair and wheeled it over to his desk. "I'm going to miss being able to do this."

"Soon you'll be sitting in the big office." He pointed to an office down the hall that had been vacant since the last CID sergeant had moved on.

"The jury is still out on that," I reminded him. "And I get the feeling from the masses that if we screw up the investigation into Drew's murder, we might *both* be sitting in patrol cars for the next ten years."

"Then we better solve it."

Pete turned his monitor so I had a better view, then clicked through some videos on the screen. The first was of Robin walking down a street. The next showed a dark-colored, four-door sedan going in the opposite direction on the same street. A third video, time-stamped just a couple of minutes after the first shot of the car, showed it coming back in the same direction as Robin. After that, there was no more sign of Robin on the street.

"I think it's a safe bet that the driver of that car took Robin into town," Pete said.

"I agree." I watched the videos a few more times. "The car looks high-end, probably foreign. BMW maybe?"

Pete nodded. "Good eyes. The rear lights are the clue. I could pretend like I figured this all out myself, but the truth is, I took a screenshot and showed it to FDLE's car guy. He nailed it in one. It's a 2018 BMW M3."

"Nice." It was rare to have security footage that wasn't too grainy, too dark, at the wrong angle or too brief to give us the information we needed. This was even better since Adams County didn't have a ton of BMWs clogging its streets.

"Play the footage of Robin again."

Pete pulled it up and I watched Robin walking quickly away from his mom's house. I stared hard at the coat he was wearing. The image was too grainy to be certain, but it looked like a close match for the one I'd found by Douglas Banks's body.

"You looking at the jacket?" Pete asked.

I nodded. "I'd like to find the BMW."

"The DMV told me their system is down and it's gonna take a few days to pull the registrations of all the BMWs in the county. I'm thinking I just might take a ride through the neighborhood and see if I spot it."

"I was hoping you'd say that. Let's go."

Pete was up out of his chair before the words had left my mouth.

"You're sparky today," I observed.

"It's the damn diet. Makes me restless. I'll drive."

"Is it my imagination, or are people avoiding eye contact with us?" I asked as we crossed the parking lot. In the last couple of days, I'd been noticing brief glances and even briefer acknowledgements from the other deputies and civilian employees.

"I've seen it too. A few days ago, we were getting disgruntled glares 'cause we weren't moving fast enough. Now, with a second murder and a second suspect, I think they're confused," Pete said, taking out his phone as we reached his car to respond to its insistent text tone. "The girls," he explained, referring to his wife and two daughters.

"Even at your heaviest, your fingers could always move like lightning." I was watching him tap out messages at the speed of a twelve-year-old.

"It's a superpower," he answered, putting the phone in the holder on the dash.

"If the owner of the car is at work, we might be wasting our time," I said.

"Or they could keep the car in a garage, or they might live somewhere else. However, I'd say a trip down to the lake is never a waste of time."

"You have a point." I leaned back and enjoyed the view of longleaf pines and palmettos as he drove.

Once we got to the lake, Pete pulled off the road near Rose Walsh's house.

"That's the house with the doorbell camera that got the footage of the car," he said, pointing to a small log cabin about two blocks from the Walsh house.

"The question is: Where does the BMW's owner live?"

"I say we start from here and just drive along the lake and keep our eyes out for it," Pete suggested.

"A mile in each direction, then we can get out and knock on a few doors. The car is distinct enough that someone might know who owns it. This is all assuming that the car is from this neighborhood," I reminded him.

"At least we're doing real policework."

He drove slowly, watching the driveways on the left while I checked out the ones on the right. After more than a mile, he turned around.

"Why don't we talk to Robin's mother?" I suggested after we'd covered both directions.

Pete nodded and headed to Rose's house.

I felt guilty for not calling ahead when she met us at the door, her hand clutching nervously at the cross around her neck.

"I was scared something had happened to Robin," she said after I assured her that her son's situation had not gotten any worse than it already was.

"We just want to ask you about a car that was in the neighborhood Friday," I explained.

"A car?"

Pete pulled up the image of the car on his phone, turning the screen so that she could see it. "It's a BMW."

She leaned in and peered at the image.

"I'm not very good with cars. They all look alike to me." She shifted from foot to foot. "Is this important?"

"We're just trying to get as much information as we can," I told her.

"The one you should ask it Chris. He lives just over there." She pointed to a cedar-sided, two-story house across the street and down a ways. "He restores cars. I can call him if you like?"

"We'll just go knock on his door."

Rose nodded. "He's retired, so he should be home."

A few minutes later, we were talking with a tall, dark-skinned man with twinkling eyes who looked like he had been waiting all day for someone to come by and talk about cars.

"Come on in," he said, backing away from the door and ushering us inside.

"We're looking for a BMW that was seen in the neighborhood on Friday," Pete said.

"Willie Samuels has a beautifully restored 1978 BMW. He lives about three miles north of here."

"This is a newer car." Pete pulled up the image again.

"Ah. That's Alan Wells's car," Chris said, giving it a single glance.

"Where does Mr. Wells live?" Pete asked.

"A quarter mile south of here. It's a two-story brick house on the lakeside. Come on back and I'll show you the 1965 Mustang I'm working on."

Obediently, we followed him through the kitchen and out into an oversized garage. The walls were painted white and hung with vintage signs and the cleanest tools I'd ever seen.

"Wow!" Pete exclaimed, looking at the four antique cars parked in the garage. Chris's eyes beamed with pride, and it took us another thirty minutes to get out of there.

"You know, if we were rude, we'd get a lot more work done," I said as we walked back to Pete's car.

"It's not in our blood," Pete said, leaning into his natural Southern drawl.

Alan Wells's house looked like the perfect retirement home. Behind the large brick structure was a generous backyard that sloped down to the lake. The house had a two-car garage with a single widow on the side. A curtain prevented us from seeing if there was a BMW lurking inside.

We knocked on the front door and waited, then knocked again and waited some more.

"We could walk around back," I suggested, looking at the gate in the four-foot-high white picket fence that blocked access to the yard. A gate was always problematic. Without permission, anything we saw or witnessed on the other side that wasn't in public view could be considered tainted evidence in a trial.

"If you're looking for Alan, he's down on his boat," a woman's voice called to us.

Pete and I looked around to see an attractive older woman watching us from the house next door.

"Thanks," I told her.

"Y'all are cops, right," she said, making it a statement and not a question.

"We're investigators with the sheriff's office." Pete gave her his best disarming smile.

"What's the trouble?" she asked.

"We just want to talk to Mr. Wells about an event he might have witnessed," I said.

"You two are a regular Starsky and Hutch," she said, walking toward us. "I'm Tyler Diaz. I'm retired from the Tallahassee Police Department."

The air between the three of us changed. There is an instant camaraderie that comes from sharing an occupation, especially one that demands, when necessary, that you put your life on the line. We quickly established connections by discussing mutual friends.

"You said that Wells is on his boat?" Pete asked as a way to get our day back on track.

"He's working on it. Fishes most mornings, then cleans fish and works on the boat in the afternoon. What did he witness?"

"Well…"

"I get it," she said. "I just wanted to make sure there's not something going on that I need to be aware of." She smiled a little to show that she was half joking, but only half.

"Would you be surprised if he was involved in illegal activity?" I asked.

"Nope. After twenty-five years in law enforcement, I wouldn't be surprised if a ten-year-old dressed up like Shirley Temple tried to kill me with a hatchet."

"You've got me there," I agreed. "Okay, try this. Have you ever seen Mr. Wells do anything that would lead you to believe he was involved in anything illegal?"

"If I did, then I'd get to the bottom of it." She seemed to love verbal sparring.

"That's good enough for me," Pete said. "We'll go talk to him."

"I like living in Adams County. Your dad's a good man," she told me, then gave us a wave as she headed back to her house.

Pete and I went through the gate and followed a path down to the boathouse where a man in his sixties was working on a bass boat. The engine cowling was off, and parts and tools were strewn around the dock. Wells was wearing shorts and a polo and looked almost too healthy. His legs and arms were muscled, and I judged him to be the kind of sixty-year-old who did triathlons in his spare time. I wasn't sure I could outrun him.

"Mr. Wells?" Pete called out to get the man's attention.

Obviously lost in his work, he looked startled to see us. "Hi." He looked around as though searching for a clue to tell him who we were and why we were walking toward his dock. "Can I help you?" There was a light challenge in his tone.

Pete and I showed our stars at the same time.

"We're investigators with the sheriff's office and we'd like to ask you a few questions," I said, beating Pete to it.

"I..." He looked closer at the IDs as though he wasn't sure they were real. "I'm in the middle of a two-week project but, sure, what can I do for you?"

"Do you own a 2018 BMW M3?" Pete asked.

"Yes," he said as though longing to ask his own questions.

"Were you driving it on Friday afternoon?"

"Let me think." He took a moment, looking at the ground, then back at us. "Yes. I went down to the fish camp and then into town."

"Was anyone with you?"

Wells shook his head as though he'd finally received the answers he'd been seeking. "I see. This is about Robin. I should have known. His poor mother."

"Was Robin with you on Friday?" I asked, trying not to let him know what we did and didn't know.

"Yes. I saw him walking along the side of the road. So I stopped and offered him a ride."

"You knew him?"

"I've known him and his mother for years. I think she'd just gotten a divorce from his father when I met her. I had a house near town close hers. Robin was... oh, I guess around ten or twelve years old at the time."

"What did he say when you asked him if he wanted a ride?"

"He seemed surprised to see me. Last time I ran into him was… I guess… two years ago. At one of the Fast Marts in town. At that time, he was pretty much out of it, and seeing a friend of his mother's, I think, embarrassed him. Anyway, Friday he just climbed into my car and told me he needed to get to town."

"Did he say where he wanted to go?"

"The Supersave."

"And that's where you took him?"

"Yep. Dropped him off right out front. Then I went to the auto store to pick up some parts."

"Did anyone meet him there?"

"Not that I saw." Wells shook his head.

"What did you talk about on your way to town?" Pete asked.

"I don't think he said more than 'yes' and 'no' to the few questions I asked."

"Questions?"

"I asked if his mother was doing okay. It's been almost a month since I've seen her. Then I asked how he was doing and he just shrugged. Honestly, I could look at him and see that things haven't been going great for him." Wells looked down at the ground and shook his head sadly.

"What did you do after you dropped him off?"

"Like I said, I went to the auto store." He paused, then added, "Oh, yeah, I stopped for gas at the Fast Mart."

We asked a few more questions, then thanked him for his time.

"Come back and we'll go fishing," he offered. "Though maybe after I get this motor back together. Right now, it's the canoe or the kayak." Wells grinned and went back to his work.

"Let's go see if we can get Friday's security footage from the Supersave," Pete said as we got back into the car, beating me to the suggestion.

Back at the office, I ran into Phil Eccles near my desk.

"The promotion committee is going to meet first thing in the morning. Word is that they've made a decision." He sounded nervous.

"You're golden," I reassured him.

"I think we both are, but…" He frowned.

"I'll try not to do anything stupid between now and when they meet." I smiled, trying to feel like it didn't matter to me.

"I just wanted to tell you… what you did for my wife and me…"

"I thought we'd gotten past all that. I know you've got my six," I said, embarrassed. Then, feeling the need to take on the role of peacekeeper, I added, "And you know Pete has yours."

I saw him tense at the mention of Pete's name. There was a clear struggle behind his dark eyes as his emotions warred with his good nature.

"I'm still not ready to let that one go. Give me a little more time." The look in his eyes told me that his grudge might take more than a little time.

"Have you solved the Great Empty Lot Caper?" I joked, trying to lighten the mood.

"I helped the guy install a couple more cameras on the side of his house, so if anyone tries it again, we'll have better video."

"More video of a person in a hoodie?"

"Maybe not. We mounted one at eye level and hidden under the roof of his little trashcan shed."

"Nice working with someone who has the money and time to throw at a problem," I said.

"Unfortunately, it's a silly first-world problem we're trying to solve. Though I still don't get why someone was trying to get into a vacant lot." Phil shook his head. "That's the only reason I'm wasting time on it. The lack of motive bugs me."

"Criminals don't need motives."

"Is that what you're dealing with in the King and Banks murders?"

"Maybe."

Phil headed for his own desk, and I settled in to go back over all my notes and reports about the two cases. I couldn't help thinking there was some connection between Natalie and the victims. Then I remembered a trick Darlene had shown me when we were working cases together. She would write down the names of everyone involved, and any of their friends or relatives, looking for connections.

I was bogged down in this project when I looked at my watch and saw that it was already six o'clock. *I'll fiddle with it at home*, I told myself, gathering up my laptop and heading for the door.

Cara was on the phone when I opened the front door. She rolled her eyes and mouthed: *Mom*. I nodded, greeted Alvin and the cats, then headed to the bedroom to change clothes.

"She's driving me crazy," Cara said, running her hands through her red hair as I came into the kitchen.

"I'm sure she's just nervous." Her mother had been calling constantly since Cara had returned from Gainesville.

"She's trying to back out of the operation and wants me to say it's okay."

"That's odd. She's never struck me as someone who needs anyone's approval." I was staring into the refrigerator, trying to find something I wanted to eat.

"She knows she has to have it. And I know she's nervous, and it frustrates her that her herbal remedies aren't taking care of her problems. But it won't do her any good to drive me over the edge."

"It won't be that much longer."

Cara looked at the calendar. "I'll be gone the whole first week of April."

"I'll be good as long as Dad doesn't make me babysit all

the dogs in Adams County again." I picked out some leftover meatloaf and green beans to heat up in the microwave.

"I think it's hilarious that you got Eddie to help you." Cara shook her head.

"I wouldn't have imagined it two years ago."

We watched an old episode of *Grimm* as we ate our leftovers together on the couch. Afterward, Cara worked on her side business, ordering supplies for both her own clinic and the county's equine vet, while I sat at the kitchen table and worked on my list of names and relationships.

It was on the second trip through my notes that I saw what I'd been missing. In Natalie's parole file, her mother's name had been listed as Elizabeth Case. That hadn't meant anything until I started charting Drew King's family and focused on his third wife, who now went by the name Betty Bostitch. A public records search revealed her third marriage to a Frank Bostitch, which had been preceded by marriages to Harlan Owens and Drew King. Which meant that King had been Natalie's stepfather for exactly eighty-three days in 2000.

I leaned back in my chair and thought about the implications of this revelation. It was now more than a possibility that Natalie could have had a motive for Drew King's murder. On the flipside, if Natalie had a motive, then it meant that Robin, who seemed oddly devoted to her, did too. Had something happened back in 2000 between Drew King, Natalie and her mother? Had she held a grudge for two decades? Or had Robin heard her complain about him and decided to do her a favor?

I texted Pete about what I'd learned. We spent the better part of an hour swapping theories back and forth before calling it a night. As I sat in the kitchen, I could hear the wind howling around the trailer and I couldn't help thinking about the old Irish superstitions of banshees foretelling death in a family. I looked at the weather on my phone and saw that a cold front was moving through North Florida.

It's just the weather, I told myself, trying to shake off my sense of foreboding.

The temperature had dropped into the thirties by the time I left the house the next morning. As I drove, I tried to map out my day and listened with half an ear to the calls coming in over my radio.

Five minutes into the trip, I got a phone call from Pete.

"They found Natalie. Julio has eyes on her." I could hear the excitement in his voice. "I'm en route."

"Where?"

"She's at a drug house they've been watching."

As we talked, I heard the chatter on the radio escalate. Julio's voice came through loud and clear, asking for backup and stating that a suspect had resisted arrest, stolen a 2015 white Ford Flex and was heading south toward town.

Pete quit talking to me and informed dispatch that he was in the area and would try to intercept.

My heart was racing as I turned toward the area of pursuit, with the radio issuing a constant staccato of updates. From what I could piece together, the drug house was about four miles outside of town and Natalie was now on a two-lane road that led to Calhoun. I hit my siren and grill lights, racing in their direction.

Pete radioed that he'd missed his chance to intercept Natalie and was now behind her. He reported that she was driving over ninety miles an hour. Other deputies were on their way to intercept her, but they wouldn't reach her before she crossed the city limits.

"She's headed for Adams Elementary," I heard Pete say, and my stomach tightened. At this hour the road in front of the school would be crowded with buses, parents in the drop-off lane and children... lots of children.

Dispatch reported they were alerting the school, but what good would that do with only a few minutes' warning?

"I'm going to overtake." Pete's voice was cold as ice. His

daughters had gone to that school years earlier.

I knew exactly what Pete was planning to do.

"Get life flight en route!" I yelled into my radio, sensing hesitation on the other end. You didn't order life flight until it was needed.

"Say again?" Marti, one of our most seasoned dispatchers, asked.

"Marti, do it!" I ordered. "I'll take full responsibility. I'll pay for the damn thing out of my own pocket if I have to."

The radio was silent for a second before Marti came back with, "Life flight en route."

I was barreling toward what I knew would be a scene of mangled wreckage, but I was still three or four minutes out, even with my speedometer edging toward eighty.

Then Julio's voice came over the radio, reporting an officer-involved accident near the school with multiple injuries. My blood ran cold.

CHAPTER FIFTEEN

It was worse than I'd imagined. The Ford Flex was crumpled against a tree on the other side of a ditch, while Pete's unmarked Dodge Charger was leaning on top of a guardrail fifty feet past the Flex. Pete's car had flipped end over end after forcing Natalie off the road at more than eighty miles an hour.

I felt like throwing up as I skidded to a stop on the side of the road and ran to Pete's car. The driver's side had slammed down onto one of the concrete posts of the guardrail, pushing the driver's door inward almost past the steering wheel. Matti Sanderson was half inside the car, talking to Pete, though he wasn't making much sense. She climbed out and came over to me

"Looks like he's got a lot of broken bones," Sanderson told me, "but I didn't see much blood."

I just stood there listening to the wail of sirens coming from all directions, frustrated that I couldn't do anything to help Pete. Finally, I shook myself out of my stupor and hurried over to where Julio was tending to Natalie. There was a gaping wound in her thigh. He had applied a tourniquet, but there was still a life-threatening amount of blood pooling inside the car.

"She needs help now," Julio told me as he worked to keep pressure on a second wound in Natalie's side.

We looked up at the sound of the helicopter approaching. I glanced around and saw that Phil Eccles was making room on the road for it to land.

Almost before the skids touched the tarmac, two EMTs jumped down and one ran toward Pete's car while the other headed for Natalie. I followed the one who went to help Pete and watched as he spent a few minutes assessing Pete's condition.

"It'll be okay for him to wait for the ambulance," he told me.

"Why?" I demanded as the other EMT came rushing toward us.

"He's got broken bones and we can't be sure of his back… He'll be better off in an ambulance. They can take the time to brace his back and get him out of the car slowly."

"She's lost a lot of blood and needs to go now!" the second EMT told us.

"Hondo's on his way," the first EMT assured me as he waved to the third member of their team, who was pushing a stretcher toward the wrecked cars. Within minutes, they had Natalie on board the helicopter and were headed for the trauma center in Tallahassee.

Dad called as I walked back toward Pete's car.

"Talk to me," he said.

After I'd filled him in, he asked, "You ordered the life flight?" Not much got by him.

"I wasn't going to waste a minute when I knew—" I started to argue.

"Stop. I'm giving you a slap on the wrist and telling you that I would have done the same thing. Understand?"

"Thanks."

"I'll call Sarah and talk to her, then I'm going to the hospital. Parks is putting Eccles in charge of the investigation."

I knew that Dad had approved the decision, which was

certainly the right one. Phil had hundreds of car accidents and dozens of vehicular death investigations under his belt. He understood the math and physics involved in car accident investigations much better than I did.

Before I did anything else, I called Cara to let her know I was okay. Knowing the speed at which information traveled in our community, I didn't want her to hear about the accident not knowing if I was involved. While she was relieved to know I was safe, the news about Pete hit her hard.

I waited for the ambulance with Pete, who seemed to fade in and out of consciousness. I was relieved when Alejandro Valdez, whom we all called Hondo, appeared over my shoulder. He was the best EMT I knew.

"His left leg and arm are bad," he said as he lay inside the overturned car and assessed Pete's injuries. "The good news is, his back doesn't seem damaged."

It took four of us to ease Pete out of the car and onto a stretcher. I wanted to go to the hospital with him, but I knew I had other work to do.

"Major Parks has made me primary on this," Phil said as we watched the ambulance drive off, not knowing I'd talked with Dad. "I owe Pete an apology."

"I hope you'll be able to deliver it to him soon," I told him.

"This was a hell of a wreck." He was already getting his measuring wheel out of the back of his trunk. "Took a lot of guts to cause a collision at that speed."

"Do you want me to secure the dashcam?"

"Thanks," he said, setting a binder on the hood of his car and beginning to draw the scene so he would have a template on which to add his measurements. "I've called Shantel. She's sending Marcus out to document the scene."

I spent an hour helping at the scene before heading to the office. I needed to push forward with the murder investigations so we'd be ready if there was an opportunity to question Natalie. Assuming she survived her injuries, it could still be days or weeks, but I wanted to be ready to interview her at the first opportunity.

The air in the office held a mix of fear and forced optimism. Pete had such a big personality that just knowing he wouldn't be walking through the door and making a joke darkened the day. All we could do was wait for word from the hospital.

I called Art King to ask him what he remembered about his father's relationship with Natalie and her mother.

"Wow. I haven't thought about Natalie in years. She was one of the reasons that the marriage was so short. Not that it wouldn't have ended like all the rest. Still, Dad usually managed to get a few years out of them."

"Can you remember the last time your father mentioned her?"

"Not really. I'd guess it was back when he was married to her mother."

"You weren't living with him then?"

"No, I lived with Mom. That was my choice. Not that I had anything against Dad. He just wasn't around much and… well, I resented the other women he dated. I would have been about eleven when he married Natalie's mom."

"What do you remember about Natalie?"

"I only met her a couple of times. We were close to the same age and Dad thought we could entertain each other. That didn't go so well. She was… odd. I'd say she was a tomboy, but that's not quite right. Tried to boss me around. It was mostly kid stuff, you know, taking my toys, that sort of thing. But there was a meanness to her. At one point she kicked me hard enough to leave a lump on my shin. That was the end of us spending time together. Hey, you don't think she's involved in Dad's murder, do you?"

"We're looking into everyone who had the means and opportunity," I told him. "You're going to hear in the news eventually, but she was involved in a serious accident this morning."

"That was her? The one where the deputy ran her off the

road to keep her from plowing through a school zone?" His voice was incredulous.

"Where did you hear about it?" I hadn't thought about how fast the news would get out.

"It's all over Facebook, Twitter. The deputy is being lauded as a hero."

"At least they got that part right."

"What happened?"

"We were trying to question her."

"And she stole a car? You think she killed Dad?"

"People can run from the cops for lots of reasons. We need more hard evidence before we can tie her to your dad's murder, but it's safe to say that she's a person of interest."

"What about the guy who was found in the trailer with Dad?"

"He was very intoxicated. It's possible that he slept through the murder. But nothing's off the table. We have him in custody on unrelated charges."

"I hope the deputy's okay."

I thanked him and told him we'd be in touch. I looked at my phone, trying to make it ring with an update about Pete. I debated calling Dad but knew that it would be a while before the doctors would be able to tell anyone anything.

I tried to kill time by digging back into Natalie's list of relationships. Since I'd managed to find a connection to Drew King that could possibly provide a motive for murder, maybe she'd had some connection to Douglas Banks as well.

It was noon when Phil came over to my desk. He was wearing an odd look on his face.

"What's wrong?" I asked, concerned that he'd heard news of Pete's condition.

"This is weird and not the way I wanted to get the news," he started, and my heart dropped. Then he said, "The committee confirmed both of our promotions. I'm trying to be happy about it, but I can't find it in myself to be in a good mood right now."

I sighed. "I'm with—" My phone rang with a call from

Major Parks to deliver the same news.

"Phil just told me."

"Sorry I didn't deliver the news first. Congratulations. We'll have the pinning ceremony at a later date. One more thing." He paused. "God willing, Pete will be okay, but from what I've heard he is certainly going to be out of service for quite a while. I want Eccles to take over the King investigation. Fill him in soon as you can."

"Of course," I told him, and he hung up.

"The committee also retroactively promoted Pete to sergeant," Phil told me, "dating it from the day they told him that he would be made a sergeant if he met the requirements of the tactical team. He'll get some back pay."

I nodded, knowing that Dad would have had a major hand in that decision. If Pete were to be put on disability, at least it would be at a sergeant's salary.

I spent an hour bringing Phil up to speed on where the investigation into the King and Banks murders currently stood.

"I'll read all the reports tonight. Let's plan on a strategy meeting tomorrow morning," Phil said when I was done.

I agreed and was turning back to my desk when I got a call from Dad.

"He's not in any immediate danger," Dad told me.

"But?"

"His left leg and arm were crushed. They're going to have to put plates and screws in both. They operated on the arm today, but there may be more surgeries. As for the leg, the doctors want to wait until Pete stabilizes. And they're not willing to say how much mobility Pete might recover."

"It's a small mercy, but I guess it's a good thing it wasn't his right arm." I knew that Pete loved being the department's firearms instructor and I hoped that was something he'd be able to keep.

"At this point, all we can do is pray and hope for the best."

"I heard that the committee promoted him."

There was silence on the other end of the phone. I knew how much Dad hated to admit when he did something nice. Finally, he said, "I would have done it for any deputy under these circumstances."

"I'm glad you did it. It's going to be tough enough on Sarah and the girls."

"They're holding up pretty well." He paused. "Natalie will live. I got that call about half an hour ago. Though it may be a while before she can be questioned."

"I can imagine. I guess everyone knows she should be restrained."

"I've got Sanderson on duty outside of ICU. I also talked to the hospital's director and explained the situation. Currently she's under heavy sedation."

"I guess you know that Parks assigned the cases to Phil."

"We discussed it. Is that a problem?"

"No."

"Is Natalie Owens responsible for Drew King's murder?" It almost sounded like Dad was begging for a reason for Pete's condition.

"I don't know," I said honestly, "but I'd be surprised if she's not involved." I went on to explain the link between King and Natalie.

"That's interesting," he said noncommittally. We both knew that coincidences happened, and a good investigator shouldn't take a plausible coincidence and turn it into a firm belief in someone's guilt. Evidence was what put a suspect in the spotlight, not unlikely connections.

After we hung up, I called Cara and told her what I knew about Pete.

"Can he have visitors?"

"I imagine they have him pretty drugged up right now."

"You said that the woman in the other car was your suspect for Drew King's murder?"

"Is. She's still alive. Everything is up in the air right now. Chances are I'll be working late. Oh yeah… I got the promotion."

"It doesn't feel right to go out and celebrate after what's happened," Cara said sadly.

"That's what Phil said when he told me." I also told her about Pete's promotion.

"Your dad's a big softy," she said.

"He takes care of the people that work for him. Everyone except me."

"Liar."

"I'll see you when I see you," I said. Before we hung up, she made me promise to be extra careful.

A few hours later, I smelled chicken and looked up to see Darlene standing in front of my desk, holding a greasy bag from the taco truck.

"Chicken ranch tacos." She held out the bag. "I figured you'd have your nose to the grindstone."

"You get some for yourself?"

"Hell yeah!" She smiled and pulled a chair over to my desk. Her duty belt squeaked as she sat down. "I talked to your dad. Sounds like Pete's banged up pretty bad, but at least he's going to live."

"He's lucky."

"Agreed. I drove by the scene and saw his car. Took a lot of guts to do that. It's one thing to run a car off the road at thirty or forty miles an hour, but at eighty you're in a whole 'nother realm of test-pilot crazy."

"I'd like to know what she thought she was doing," I said between bites of taco. It was good and reminded me how hungry I was.

"She's one of the lost ones," Darlene said. "There are folks on the street—addicts, petty criminals—who can be helped. Most don't mean any real harm except to themselves. Then there are the people who are so damaged that…" She shrugged and took a bite of taco.

"Makes you wonder how bad it would have been if Pete hadn't stopped her before she got to the school zone."

"Don't even joke about that. I've seen enough dead children for a lifetime." She took another bite and was quiet for a minute. "Pete's not going to be happy with his spreading internet fame."

"What?" I was in the small minority of people who didn't pay much attention to social media. I used it when necessary to work a case, but that was about it. Cara was a little more active, using Facebook and Instagram, but I was grateful that she wasn't obsessed.

"He's trending. Hashtag hero cop, hashtag Florida crash, hashtag kids saved, plus a bunch more tagging both him and the Adams County Sheriff's Office. I saw where someone has already set up a GoFundMe to pay for any medical expenses or other costs he might incur because he's a hero."

I grimaced. Pete liked to be the loudest guy in the room, but he didn't like people making a fuss over him. A few years earlier, Sarah had put on a surprise party for his birthday, and I thought his face would never lose the bright red blush.

"These days you can't head off a wave like this. A deputy throwing himself in harm's way to save kids at an elementary school is a feel-good share that people can't resist."

"At least it's good press," I said.

"It starts out as good press…" she said ominously.

"What's that mean?" I asked, though I had an idea where she was going.

"A little sheriff's office like this gets put under a microscope, people are going to find blemishes. Even if there aren't any."

"Thank you, Little Miss Sunshine."

"Yeah, sorry. There's enough bad stuff already without borrowing trouble."

Her phone rang. She looked at it, rolled her eyes and answered. "Speak to me." After listening for a minute, she said, "Move the car. If he abandoned it in the middle of the street, you have every right to tow it." There was another pause. "Then smash the window."

After a little more back and forth, she hung up. "Wayne's a good officer, but he overthinks things. I don't care if the guy is going to be mad if we break his window so we can tow his car. I'll tell him to go pound sand."

"That's why they call you the Iron Chief," I kidded her.

"Thanks. And they call you Son of Big Dog."

"Sergeant Son of Big Dog," I said and filled her in on the recent promotions.

"Congratulations. Why didn't I know about this?"

"Too much other stuff going on today."

"Too true."

CHAPTER SIXTEEN

I spent the rest of the day and Thursday morning working on cases, both mine and Pete's, while I tried to get used to the idea of being a supervisor. A meeting with Major Parks and Phil had ended with an agreement that Phil and I would continue to work our current caseload while slowly transitioning to our new positions. At the moment, CID was overwhelmed with Pete's cases, the two murders and the investigation into the accident.

That afternoon, I went to the hospital to see Pete.

"The hero," I said, trying not to react to the sad sight of him in a hospital bed. His arm was in a cast up to his shoulder and he looked like he'd been lost at the bottom of a mine for two weeks, pale and drawn.

"Don't even go there." His voice was hoarse and dry. He waved toward the flowers and cards that filled most of the room. "Only good thing about it is the hospital gave me a private room so no one else would be falling over all this stuff."

"What's the news?"

He sighed. "They're going to operate on my leg Monday. If all goes well, I should be at ninety-five percent by fall."

"That's great."

He held up a finger on his right hand. "If things don't bind together, then they'll have to try something else. The bad news is that the surgeon warned me there isn't much solid bone to work with in some places. If this doesn't work, we might not get a second chance, in which case they'll have to amputate."

Pete was trying to look tough, but who can stare down that possibility and keep their chin up?

"A bunch of schoolkids appreciate what you did." I wondered if I could have made the same choice he had.

"It wasn't an option." He forced a smile. "Hey, look at us sergeants! I can't tell you what it meant to Sarah and me that your dad did that for us." He started to choke up.

"He just didn't want you getting headhunted by your admirers," I said, pointing to some of the floral arrangements that had come from other law enforcement agencies.

Pete really smiled for the first time. "Yeah, offers are pouring in. What I wish your father would let me do is get back to work. I can still make phone calls and write reports."

"Give it some time. Believe me, we need you."

"Sorry about leaving you with all my cases. What do you have on our prime suspect? By the way, she's in stable condition now."

"I heard. The doctor said if she continues to make progress, he might let me talk to her as early as Monday."

"I'd like to kick her ass." Pete frowned, then shook his head and grimaced. "Positive attitude. That's what Sarah keeps telling me."

"There's a bunch of us that wouldn't mind giving her a little kick. Right now, I'm trying to find out if she killed King and Banks or had a part in it. While we wait to talk to her, I've been digging into her past. Her father's been dead for years."

"What happened to her mother after she divorced Drew?"

"She's living in New Mexico. I talked to her yesterday.

Let's just say there isn't much parental love left for Natalie. Betty blames Natalie for her failed marriages."

"How many?"

"Three counting Natalie's father, Drew and another one years later."

"I'd say it's harsh of her to blame her daughter, but considering that it's Natalie we're talking about…"

"I don't want to be too touchy-feely about a woman who was prepared to run down little kids, but her life was rough from the beginning. After talking to her, I was sure that I wouldn't have wanted Betty for my mother."

"Which came first, the chicken or the egg?" Pete asked.

"Nurture is fifty percent."

"As you get older, you start thinking that nature accounts for eighty or ninety percent."

"Either way, it's not our call," I said. "I asked Betty if she knew of any other connections between Natalie and our victims, but she couldn't think of any. Then again, she hasn't talked with her daughter in years."

"At least we don't have to worry that she's protecting Natalie."

"No. Quite the opposite. I'd say she was eager to see her spend the rest of her days in jail."

"So what's next?"

"I want to see if there's any evidence to link Natalie to either of our two crime scenes. And I'm going to keep digging for a connection between Natalie and Douglas Banks. My gut tells me that Natalie could kill, but not without a motive."

"Anger or fear are motives," Pete observed. "She was roaring down that highway fueled by one or the other."

"Julio rounded up the other people who were with her when she stole the Ford. I talked to them and the impression I got was that she's been freaking out ever since she learned that Robin was found with Drew's body."

"Was she worried about Robin?"

"I doubt it. My guess is that she just didn't want to have

to talk to the police and everything she's done since backs that up."

"She's been arrested more than once. It's possible she's had some bad experiences," Pete suggested

"And some of her arrests were in other jurisdictions. I thought the same thing and looked at the reports I got from her parole officer, and also requested her sealed juvenile records."

"I don't want to feel bad for her."

"I know what you mean. Still, we need to know what makes her tick."

"What about Robin?" Pete asked.

"I haven't ruled out Natalie using him as a tool to kill King and Banks."

"Robin as the murder weapon?"

"Wouldn't be the first time."

"I wish I could do more to help."

As soon as the words came out of his mouth, I saw his mood drop and decided that I should stop talking about work. Instead, we spent the next hour gossiping about our friends and families.

"Let me know if there's anything Cara and I can do for you," I said as I stood up and headed for the door.

"There *is* one thing." He smiled.

I didn't like that smile. "What?"

"You remember what you did for your dad when *he* was in the hospital?"

My mind went blank for a minute, then it dawned on me what he was talking about. "You don't really want me to bring that monster in here?"

"A pet therapy dog, a little dachshund, came by this morning. Then I got to talking with the nurse about Mauser. She said she's heard rumors about him."

"He's still got his vest." When we'd snuck him into the hospital the last time, Mack Burrows, one of our K-9 officers, had fashioned a service dog vest for Mauser. "I'll talk to Dad. He'll probably love the idea."

"I've got ten bucks riding on it." Pete smiled, a genuine ear-to-ear grin that made me determined to make it happen.

"I get five."

"Maybe."

As soon as I was out of the hospital, I called Dad with Pete's request.

"Consider it a done deal." It's good to be sheriff.

"Cara and I want to be there."

"Might have to be after hours like last time."

"We can do that," I assured him.

Drew King's funeral was held at eleven o'clock Saturday morning at the First Baptist Church, as it was the largest church in town. Cara came with me, even though I'd told her she didn't have to.

"Funerals hold a strange fascination for me. Maybe it's because I never went to a traditional one growing up," Cara said in the car on the way to the church.

"Let me guess. Viking funeral pyres?"

"There was one of those."

"Seriously?"

"And one of the communes had a sacred burial ground back in the woods on their property… at least until the health department forced them to dispose of the bodies in some way other than leaving them on wooden scaffolds. Not that the birds and insects ever left much."

I looked at her to see if she was pulling my leg. She wasn't. Knowing her parents, I wasn't that surprised.

"I'm going to get a certain amount of looks from people who know I'm working the murder case." I knew that most of the mourners would be wondering why a suspect hadn't yet been named.

"On TV the murderer is always at the funeral," Cara pointed out.

"That thought has crossed my mind. But there will be too much chaff to find any wheat today." I knew there would be too many people in attendance today to allow me to notice anyone unusual.

As I had expected, every pew in the church was full. The service was long with half a dozen eulogies, including one from Dad. In true Southern tradition, the service was followed by a large spread of food in the church's dining hall. Untraditionally, Art had decided to keep the burial private, saving everyone a trip to the graveside.

Afterward, I dropped Cara off at the house and spent the afternoon working. I had a dozen cases that needed attention. Several had witnesses that it would be easier to talk to on a weekend, so I scheduled the interviews as close together as I could and managed to resolve two of my cases. One was an assault where the suspect thought there wasn't a witness. I'd found one and, after getting the witness's statement, I was sure that the State Attorney would be able to get the suspect to take a plea deal. The other case was a physical altercation where both parties had been screaming for the arrest of the other, while neither of them had any serious injuries and they'd both been at fault. A sit-down meeting and an explanation of what would happen if we moved forward convinced both of them that it might be best to shake hands and let the matter drop.

I got home in time for a late dinner, then we headed for the hospital to meet Dad, Genie and Mauser. At ten o'clock we rendezvoused in the parking garage looking like a misfit gang of cat burglars.

"We aren't crawling through the roof vent," I said, looking at Dad's black sweater, knit cap and black BDUs.

"So why did you dress all in black?" he asked.

"Brings out the color of my eyes," I smirked.

"Come on, boys." Cara was playing with Mauser, who looked way too excited for an unobtrusive visit to the hospital.

"She's right," Genie said, coming around the back of the van looking like the villain in a *Pink Panther* movie.

"Another *Mission Impossible* extra." I shook my head.

"If I wanted to go through the skylight, I could," Genie said with a laugh.

"Don't encourage her," Dad told us.

"I just wish Jimmy could be here. He'd love all the cloak-and-dagger stuff." At the mention of Jimmy's name, Mauser turned to Genie. "Sorry, big guy. Your buddy couldn't get off work," she told him.

Getting to Pete's room was anticlimactic, with only a few people intercepting us. As soon as they learned our mission, they petted and scratched Mauser and let us go on our way. Dad didn't even have to drop any names or show his star.

"I knew you guys wouldn't let me down," Pete said, turning off the TV. Mauser lunged over to the bed and proceeded to lap Pete's hand and arm with his Jurassic slug of a tongue.

Pete did his best to round up every nurse working the floor to come in and meet Mauser.

"We're supposed to be keeping a low profile," I told him, to no avail.

"I've never been kicked out of a hospital," Pete said.

On Sunday, Cara and I lounged around the house for a while, took Alvin for a long walk in the woods, then spent the beautiful, cool spring afternoon clearing up the yard, stacking deadfall and burning it.

Staring at the fire, Cara told me, "We have hot dogs, and I wouldn't mind running up to the store for s'mores makings."

"Sounds like a meal fit for a king." I pulled her in for a hug and a quick kiss.

After we'd had our fill of campfire food, we sat in our chairs and watched the sun go down as sparks from the fire drifted up into the trees.

"Days like this make it all worthwhile." I reached out and took Cara's hand, keeping my head back to watch the stars.

"What do you think is going to happen to Pete?"

"He'll have a job with us for as long as he wants it. I just hope it's not a desk job."

"Surgeons can do some amazing things these days." Cara made it sound like she was whistling in the dark and I didn't blame her. With all my heart, I wanted to believe that everything would work out for the best, but the odds were long.

"We just have to wait and see."

I didn't tell her that I'd seen fear in Pete's eyes when he'd talked about the surgery. Ever since I'd known him, he'd put on a slothful persona that was far from the truth. He often put in ten hours as an investigator before going out to the department's range and instructing and qualifying officers for three more hours. On top of that, he was with his family every minute he wasn't working. Having his mobility and coordination restricted would take a heavy toll on him.

CHAPTER SEVENTEEN

Monday's first order of business was to set up an interview with Natalie. It took an hour of back and forth with nurses before I was finally able to talk with her doctor.

"I don't have any objection to the interview, but is it possible we could remove the restraints?" he asked.

"I'll let you know after I talk to her," I said, though I couldn't imagine feeling comfortable enough with her attitude to leave her unrestrained as long as she was in the hospital.

"I'm going to have a nurse monitoring Natalie's condition," the doctor told me. "If she says the interview is over, then it's over. Do we agree?"

"Of course."

We settled on eleven o'clock, so I called Phil and asked him to come with me to the hospital. I wanted a witness for this interview, and a second opinion when it came to her answers.

"I feel like I'm spending a lot of time here," I said when we walked into the hospital lobby.

"All Pete could talk about was y'all bringing Mauser up to his room."

"You visited him?"

"Audrey and I came by yesterday. I had a few things to settle with him," Phil said without elaborating. "Since you've been working the case, I'll let you take the lead with Natalie."

We got directions to Natalie's room. After nodding to the deputy standing guard outside, I knocked on the door. Natalie cursed in response, which I took as an invitation to come in. I opened the door to see her lying back with her arms strapped to the bed. She reminded me of Regan from *The Exorcist*. The impression was cemented into my head when Natalie flicked her forked tongue at us.

"Untie me, you bastards!" she yelled, followed by a string of curse words that had me wondering if she'd read my mind.

"We're here to talk to you about the murders of Drew King and Douglas Banks," I told her. "Which was all we were trying to do before you pulled the stunt that ended up with you strapped to that bed." I didn't see any reason to play good cop with her.

She cursed some more.

"Your attitude is just going to land you in jail for a very long time."

"I have a right to an attorney."

"Correct. If you hadn't spent the last two minutes yelling at us, I would have told you that." I went through her Miranda rights, then told her she was being charged with the physical assault on Pete from when she'd punched him, and also for reckless driving and endangerment. I didn't bother to tell her that there was also the possibility of car theft and various other charges.

A little surprisingly, she waived her right to have an attorney present.

"You won't believe me, but I just want to get to the truth of what happened," I told her.

"Bullshit!" She spat at us.

"Since you've been charged in the past for spitting at an officer, I shouldn't have to remind you that that is also a form of assault."

She spat again.

"I know that Drew King was your stepfather for a few months."

This sent her into a rage that had her pulling at the restraints. There was no way in hell I'd be telling her doctor that it was okay to remove them before she was released from the hospital.

"I knew it." She barred her teeth.

"What did you know?"

"That as soon as you figured out I was his stepdaughter, you'd try and stick his murder on me." Her words were laced with profanity, making it hard to follow her thoughts, like listening to a song on the radio that is all but drowned out by static.

"You're related to Drew King and a friend of yours was found with his body. This gives us every reason to want to talk to you. Now, where were you when Drew King and Douglas Banks were killed?"

"How would I know? I was getting buzzed somewhere. That's what I do."

"Did you hate Drew King?"

"I hate everyone," she hissed. This was oddly unconvincing and came across sounding like a scared young teenager in the principal's office.

"Did you have a particular grudge against Drew King?"

Natalie ground her teeth. For a minute I didn't know if she was going to answer, then she said, "He was a dick, but so was everyone in my life back then."

I took this for a "no."

"Do you think Robin Hennessy killed Drew King?"

She almost laughed. "He's nothing. I tell him to do something and he does it." Her eyes narrowed. "That's not what I meant. What I meant was, he doesn't do anything on his own. I've never even seen him talk back to no one."

"When was the last time you saw Drew King?"

"I don't know." She looked like she was actually thinking about her answer. "I ran into him at a Fast Mart maybe a year ago. We didn't say nothin' to each other."

"He knew it was you?"

"Hell yeah. I should have spit in his face."

"Why?"

"'Cause he thinks…" She realized she'd used the present tense. "Screw you. I didn't kill him."

"Who did?"

"Not my job."

"Did you know anyone else who didn't like him?"

"He hasn't been a cop in years. Nobody on the streets cares about a retired cop."

"No one he arrested was angry about it?"

She glared at me. "You know who has time for revenge? Rich people. People on the streets are too busy lookin' for their next fix. Kill him for twenty bucks, yeah, that's possible. Kill him because he arrested them, nah. If these guys went around killing people who arrested them, it would be a full-time job. That would be like you arresting people who think you're an ass." At least she was engaged in the conversation.

"We need to find the killer."

"Don't look here."

"You just stole a car and tried to run down a bunch of kids 'cause you didn't want to talk to us. What do you expect us to think?"

"What damn kids?" she asked, looking honestly puzzled.

"No one told you that you were heading for a school zone when you were run off the road?"

"I wouldn't hurt a kid," she pouted.

"Evidence speaks to the contrary, but we'll let that drop for now. Why did you steal that car and run?"

"I already told you. When that cop showed up and said he was taking me in so you could ask me questions, I figured it was a trap. You knew my mom was married to King and that was it. You'd lock me up forever."

"The night King was killed, where were you?"

"I guess I was at the green house."

"What green house?"

"That's what it's called, 'cause it's green. Always a steady supply and sometimes a party."

"We need to know anyone else who might have seen you there."

With a little more convincing she gave us the names of five people other than Robin and Malik. I didn't bother to ask her where we could find them. I could just check in with our vice squad.

"What about Douglas Banks?" I asked.

"I barely knew him. No reason to kill him."

I figured I'd learned everything I could from her today. "The good news is, according to your doctor, we should be able to move you to the jail by Wednesday."

Natalie glared at us and cursed.

"It means you won't have to be strapped to a bed," Phil told her, "so count your blessings. It also means you can be arraigned."

She glared at us.

"I can't do anything about the charges around the car crash," I said, "but if you aren't guilty of the murders then I'll do my best to clear you of any suspicion."

For a millisecond I saw a slight softening of her eyes and took that as our cue to leave.

We headed up to Pete's room, where a nurse told us he was in surgery so we detoured to the waiting area.

"He's been in there about three hours," Sarah told us in a voice that wanted to be strong.

Pete's daughters, Jenny and Kim, gave us weak waves when they looked up from their phones.

"Let us know if we can do anything."

"Thanks. Your dad called before they took Pete into surgery." She turned to Phil. "And it meant a lot to Pete that you came to visit him yesterday."

"I needed to clear the air." Phil looked embarrassed.

I said a silent prayer for Pete as Phil and I walked to the elevator.

When we were in the car headed back to Adams County, Phil turned to me and asked, "Thoughts on your prime suspect?"

"I think she's capable of murder, but I can't see a solid motive for killing either King or Banks."

"I agree. Plus, why leave Robin at the scene of King's murder?"

"That could have been an accident. Maybe he was supposed to have left, but instead he passed out," I suggested.

"And why did she panic when Julio showed up? She should have known that she'd be questioned."

"That bugs me too." I paused, then asked, "Does she look like an addict who's been in the hospital for days without her drug of choice?"

"You noticed that too? I think she uses, but I don't think she has a full-blown addiction."

"Her parole officer said that too. Which would help her to be able to manipulate Robin and Malik."

"It all comes back to: What's her motive? Especially for Douglas Banks," Phil said.

"I'm not even sure she has a motive for killing Drew. Yeah, she has a connection to him, but then so does half the town." I thought about the number of people at his funeral.

"You aren't wrong."

"I think maybe we've become too fixated on Robin and Natalie."

"Then start over," Phil said. "Look for connections between the two murders."

"It's possible they aren't even connected," I said morosely.

"Let's assume they are for the moment. Banks and Drew don't have any obvious ties to each other, which is good."

"They probably met when Drew was on patrol."

"I'm sure, but were any of those meetings significant? Dig deep into the records. Pull all reports that mention Banks and see if Drew was on the scene."

"I need to talk to Robin again. If he's not the perp then he's a witness, and somewhere locked inside that drug-addled brain of his is information. Even if all he can tell us is what time he arrived at the trailer, that would help us narrow down the time of Drew's murder."

"You'll be lucky to get anything useful. Still, it's worth a shot. I wish I believed in hypnotists."

"Hypnotists are real enough," I said, "but it's impossible to say if the information you get from the subject is real, part of a dream or subliminally implanted."

"We'll have some bargaining power over Natalie when I get done charging her for the damage she did with her little stunt. She should thank Pete twice. Once for preventing her from running through that school zone, and second for not dying. If he'd died, I'd be working up a murder charge against her for that. As it is, there are going to be some charges that carry heavy penalties."

"I hate it when we negotiate with a criminal."

"It's part of the job. We need to do the most good with what we have. If we need her to talk, we might have to give her a small break on the charges she'll face."

"I'm not going to feel very charitable if Pete's leg doesn't heal right."

"Yep."

At the office, I headed for my desk to check and respond to emails and to see what additional cases I'd been assigned. One of the emails was from Major Parks, wanting to schedule a meeting with Phil and me to discuss the responsibilities of our new positions. I sighed and thought, *I'm not doing a very good job of handling the responsibilities I currently have.* But it was too late to turn down the promotion now.

After handling my paperwork, I walked across the street to the jail to see Robin. He was jittery and showing all the signs of withdrawal that Natalie wasn't.

"You okay?" I asked.

"I'm going out of my mind. It's like my skin is trying to crawl off my body."

"Think of it as free rehab." From the look on his face, he didn't seem to appreciate the joke.

"How's Natalie doing?" he asked me.

"I talked to her this morning. She'll be shipped over here to the jail in the next day or two."

"Good," he said, drumming his fingers on the table.

"Do you know Alan Wells?" I asked him.

"Mr. Wells? Sure, yeah. Nice old guy. I knew him when I was just a kid. He lives near my…" He looked puzzled for a moment, then snapped his fingers. "Hey! He drove me to town the other day."

"That's right."

"I'd forgotten," he said obviously. "Yeah, he dropped me off at the Supersave."

"Where did you go from there?"

"I… think I walked over to the camp behind the Supersave."

"Why?"

"I guess to find Loops."

I recognized the name. Loops was a notorious all-around bad guy, but very savvy. At forty-three, he was old for a dealer and a little creepy-looking, with red hair and multiple skull tattoos. While not homeless, he hung out around the homeless camps where he had a ready supply of desperate people who would do anything for a little money or a quick high.

"Did you find him?"

"No," Robin said, and I thought he was going to leave it there, but a bit of his memory seemed to be coming back. "I called Nat."

"Did she answer?"

"No. So I called dick face." I saw a mix of emotions on Robin's face, including anger and disgust.

"Who?" I asked, though I thought I knew who he was talking about.

"Malik."

"You thought he'd know where she was?"

"He told me she was at the green house."

"Was he there?"

"No. He was high and not making much sense." This time Robin smiled. "He was acting crazier than usual, and Nat didn't want him around."

"What did you do then?" I asked and he looked at me like I was dense.

"I went to the green house to find her."

"And?"

"That's where things get fuzzy. I…" Robin looked down and seemed puzzled. "No. I think I was feeling a little… floaty. Like I'd had a sweet downer or something."

"So you took something at the house. Did Nat give it to you?"

"No. At least I don't think so. Funny, I don't remember taking anything, just getting… loose." He looked confused.

"What do you remember after that?"

He laughed. "Nothin'. Blank from there on."

"You remember when we met?"

"No."

"Being put in the back of the car?"

"No. I just remember waking up here." He waved his arms around.

"Do you normally black out?"

"Sometimes yeah, sometimes no. I like to remember the trippy times, not so much the bad. I could use a little downer now." He held his hand out like he expected me to put a magic pill in his palm.

"You can have whatever the doctor will let you have," I told him.

"They don't have no doctor, just a nurse, and she's a witch." He called her a witch with the conviction of Cotton Mather.

"She hasn't given you anything for your withdrawal symptoms?"

"Just crap I could buy at a drugstore." He waved his hand dismissively.

I thought about asking him what he expected, but let it drop. I asked a dozen more questions without getting any useful answers, then sent Robin back to his cell.

As I was walking back to the office, I got a group text from Sarah letting everyone know that Pete had come through the operation. Now it was just a waiting game before we would know if all the screws and plates in his leg would hold.

I looked at my watch and saw that it was after one. I called Cara.

"Have you had lunch?"

"We've been crazy all morning. I'm just now getting a chance to come up for air," she said. Mondays were always busy days at the vet.

"Want me to grab something and meet you at the park near the clinic?"

"That would be great. I need to stretch my legs."

"I'll text you when I'm leaving Deep Pit."

"Would you pick up a pulled pork sandwich for Terry? I'm going to get him to fill in for me when I'm gone for Mom's operation."

Thirty minutes later we were sitting in the sun, enjoying the dry cool air of a lovely spring day. We talked about Pete in worried and hopeful tones, then opened our bags of bar-be-que.

"Where are you on the cases?" Cara asked, knowing that I could only discuss so much with her.

"I'm going back to square one and working up victim profiles," I said, unwrapping my sandwich.

"Like the killer profiles that the FBI do?"

I nodded. "Understanding the victim is as important as understanding the killer. It can lead to motive. Also opportunity, like a victim who keeps to the same routine."

"Do you still think it was Robin or Natalie?"

I shrugged. "I told Phil that I thought we'd gotten off on the wrong foot. Now we need to do all the work we should have been doing already. I'm convinced we're missing important clues."

"It shouldn't be hard to fill in Drew King's profile since so many people knew him."

"Just means I have more information to sift through. I'm going to have to go over all the major cases where he played a large role. That will mean the last fifteen years of his career, and a lot of those are still on microfiche."

"On the bright side, you'll get plenty of sweet treats," she said with a grin.

Beth Miller, our head records clerk, was famous for her baking and frequently brought cookies, brownies, cakes and more into the office. Her desk was a popular stop for both deputies and civilian employees, and I'd been known to show up in records myself just to see what she'd brought in.

We ate in silence for a while, then Cara asked, "When is your promotion official?" She had been careful not to make a big deal about it, knowing all of my mixed feelings.

"Friday. I've already been told that I need to see HR and get my ID updated."

"Will you get a new star?"

"Yep. One with 'sergeant' on it." I saw her pride in my promotion and admitted, "It will be kinda cool."

Cara smiled and gave me a kiss.

Back at my desk I started individual profiles for Drew King and Douglas Banks, then carried my laptop down to records. All that was left of the morning's cinnamon rolls were two empty trays that still gave off a mouthwatering aroma.

Beth set me up at a desk where I made notes from the microfiche index. In 2006 the department had started inputting all reports electronically, but before that it was hit or miss on what would be found in the computer records and what could only be found the old-fashioned way, as photos of written reports on microfiche. When Dad became sheriff, he had organized a team of employees and interns to develop the index for all the old cases going back to 1985, so that would at least help my search.

Four hours later I had a list of all of the cases I needed to dig up on microfiche. They included all the ones where Drew King had played a major role, and any that mentioned Douglas Banks as either a witness, victim or suspect. Banks had only been mentioned in twenty-two reports, which was pretty low for a person who had been living and panhandling on the streets for as long as he had.

"Done?" Beth asked.

"My eyes are actually burning," I told her.

"Wait until you've searched through all that microfiche." She was looking over my shoulder at the list I'd drawn up. "When you come in tomorrow, I'll let Shenika help you. We'll put two machines side by side and she can look for the reports while you read them."

"That would be great," I said, hoping I sounded as grateful as I felt.

"I'll even hold back a couple of peach tarts for you. I'm making them from peaches I canned last summer."

"You're making me hungry."

"Get out of here. We need to lock up." She shooed me out the door. "Do you think Pete would like me to send something to the hospital? I know he's trying to lose weight, but I want to do something for him."

I turned around. "I think a little comfort food would hit the spot right now."

"I'll make up a special treat." She smiled like she'd won the lottery. I could only imagine the amount of calories and fat she was going to pack into that special treat. I made up my mind to be at the hospital when he got it.

On the way home, I swung into a Fast Mart on a whim. I picked the one closest to the homeless camp where Douglas Banks had stayed.

It was the Adams County version of rush hour, which meant that the gas pumps were full and there was a line at the counter. Two of the four people in line were buying beer. There were two people working behind the counter and one of them was the owner's son. We were well acquainted, and I waved to let him know that I wanted to have a word.

"What can I do for you?" he asked, coming out from behind the counter to meet me with a smile. I'd always gotten the impression that he liked working with law enforcement.

"I know y'all are busy…"

"Don't worry about it. Our other register is broken, so we can't both check out the customers anyway. Besides, Divya is faster than I am. Come back here." He waved me to a small office at the back of the store.

"Do you know this man?" I showed him the photo of Douglas Banks that I had on my phone.

"The Old Man and the Street. That's what I called him. My high school English teacher made me read that Hemingway book about that old guy going out alone and catching a huge sailfish. Whenever I saw this one, he reminded me of the old man in the story. I heard he got killed. It's crazy out there."

"How did he remind you of *The Old Man and the Sea*?"

"You know, kind of sad all the time. Quiet, but there was a way he had of standing that made me feel like there was more… there. A lot of these guys on the street, they only have eyes for money and their poison of choice. Not him. He always seemed to be looking for something." He shrugged. "What else are you going to do working retail except make up romantic backgrounds about your customers? Doesn't help that my *naani* made me watch Bollywood movies when I stayed with her."

"Did you ever talk with him?"

"Sure, he loved to talk. Problem was, he only had one subject—his messed-up life."

"His wife left him," I said, remembering the report.

"I guess he was really in love with her. He didn't like your lot. Claimed you all didn't even look for her."

"We don't look for healthy adults who decide to leave their families," I said a little defensively.

"He talked about losing his job too. Wife gone, job gone, family gone, hope gone. Sometimes, when these guys tell me their sad stories and how it led to them drinking and doing drugs, I think the truth is that's the *reason* they lost their wife, family and job. Not the other way around."

I thought about that. Had Banks been a drinker before his marriage broke up? It would help to find someone who had known him before he ended up on the street.

"Did he ever mention any enemies?"

"No, but he had a little bit of the street paranoia about him."

"Did he hang out with anyone in particular?"

"The regular gang of misfits. But he was by himself most of the time. Maybe that was the paranoia, or people just didn't want to hang with him. Like I said, he had this poor-poor-pitiful-me thing going on. Just seeing him could make me question the point of living."

"So you could understand why others didn't want to hang around with him?"

"Yep. I got the feeling he wasn't a sharer either. Some of the guys act like Rockefeller at the bar on Saturday night, sharing their bottle or the crystals in their baggie. Not Banks. I've seen him come into the store and, if a fellow traveler was in here or came in right after him, Banks would pretend to look around until the other person left before buying his beer."

"Making sure he wouldn't be asked to share," I said, getting a better idea of the type of guy Banks had been.

"I don't think he was mean, like nasty, but he was mean, like not wanting to share the little bit he had."

"He never mentioned any threats made against him or any particular fears he had?" I asked.

"Nope. Sorry. I'll keep my ears open and let you know if I hear anything," he said in true film-noir tradition.

I thanked him and we made our way to the front of the

store. I made the mistake of glancing at the lotto sign on the counter and saw that the Powerball was up to half-a-billion dollars. Cursing myself for being an idiot, I bought two tickets and headed home.

When I showed Cara the tickets, she laughed and told me she'd bought one herself.

"I hope you'll share with me."

"It's a community property state. I don't have a choice," I said, handing her my tickets and giving her a kiss.

CHAPTER EIGHTEEN

We didn't win the Powerball jackpot, but there was a very rich person in Kentucky on Tuesday morning. Without a new found fortune as an excuse, I headed for the office and spent most of the day sitting in front of the microfilm machine.

On Wednesday afternoon, I drove into Tallahassee. Officially, it was to talk to Dr. Darzi, who had done a detailed report comparing the attacks on Drew King and Douglas Banks. Unofficially, I wanted to see Pete, who was just starting his physical therapy and would be going home soon.

I went to see Darzi first.

"You caught me between cadavers." He always seemed to get a lot of amusement out of his job. He'd once told me that part of the fun of being a pathologist was making people squirm.

"You do a healthy business," I said.

"Ha! I'll make a pathologist of you yet." He waved me down the hall to his small office. It wasn't my favorite place due to the wide array of specimen jars he kept on the shelves behind his desk.

"I don't know that I came up with much. My analysis was

of the physics involved, and a detailed examination of the wounds on the two victims to see if there was any foreign matter in them. As you know, the physical interaction between the killer and the victim is of utmost importance." He had a tendency to slip into professor-speak when explaining his work.

"I appreciate you taking the time to do a thorough job."

"No problem. I made sure to bill your account." He gave me another big smile, and when he saw my face, he laughed. "Don't worry, I did this pro bono. I've published more than one article thanks to all the work you've given me."

"Our budget needs all the pro bono it can get."

"I hear they are going to be paying you a little more. Congratulations, Sergeant Macklin. Very impressive-sounding." He shuffled through the papers on his desk. "I'll send you all the slides and the report in the next day or two. Now, first I examined the bat from the King murder and the board from the Banks murder."

"Shantel let you have them?" I asked, amazed.

"Don't worry. We preserved the chain of custody. You can return them, if you'd like."

"I'd rather let your people return them to our people." I didn't want to add more names to the custody register.

"Fine. Now, let's consider the weapons. The size and weight of the two objects varied, but not by as much as one would think. The bat used in the murder was a standard adult baseball bat. It weights thirty-two ounces, which is within the normal range for a bat of its size. I called the company that made the bat and its length of thirty-four inches and diameter of two-point-six-one means that it has not been altered in any way. Did the killer bring the bat with him?"

"No. Drew played baseball in high school and college and always had a bat around his home and office. He even coached little league for a few years."

"That's interesting."

"Why?"

"Assuming the murder of Douglas Banks was committed by the same person, and since he or she chose a weapon that mimicked the size and weight of a baseball bat for the second murder, you would assume that the bat had been his choice of a weapon."

Shaking his head, Darzi continued his analysis.

"There are two ends to each of the weapons. One end came into contact with the killer as he held the weapon, and the other end came into contact with the victim. On the victim's end, we found all the biological material that we'd expect to find. The victim's blood, hair and skin. No surprises there. But like the man said, there's more. When I examined the end held by the killer, I found microscopic fibers on both the bat and the two-by-four, which were most likely left by the same fabric. The color, shape and size of the fibers are a match. At least they are a match to the human eye. I collected some from each and they can be examined by a fiber expert with more sophisticated equipment. My guess would be that they come from gloves, possibly wool gloves."

"Nice. Having the two murders linked like that saves us going down a few rabbit holes. You might just be worth the exorbitant amount of money we pay you."

Darzi gave a little bow. "I wasn't able to determine much by comparing the injuries on the victims to the weapons. In my judgment, the attacker was right-handed. As I said earlier, almost any normal-size adult could have delivered the blows that killed both men. And nothing I saw argues against the theory that the same person inflicted the wounds on both victims."

After thanking Dr. Darzi and telling him I'd try not to send him another body for a couple of months, I headed up to see Pete. He was clearly done with being in the hospital.

"I want to go home," he groaned.

"You're getting out tomorrow?" I asked.

"And it's going to be weeks before I can really get around. Weeks with a physical therapist."

"If you have any problems with the insurance, Dad said

to give HR a call."

"Sarah is already stressing out about the bills. I told her it would all be taken care." He shook his head. "Most of it *will* be taken care of. She wants us to use some of the GoFundMe money that people sent in. I'm not going to do that. If we can't give it back, I'll donate it to a charity."

"People were impressed with your heroism," I told him, and watched his face flush.

"Don't start with that hero crap. There's not a deputy in the department that wouldn't have done the same thing I did to prevent that woman from running right into a school zone." His voice had risen as he talked until he was almost yelling. "Sorry. I'm just tired of everyone making a big deal about it, when the one thing I wish is that I hadn't had to do it." He tapped the cast on his leg and waved his cast-bound arm. "Ouch."

"We'll get you through this. Sergeant," I added, earning another look of irritation from him.

"I appreciate what your father and the committee did, but I didn't earn it. I still have about twenty-five pounds to lose, which is going to be damn near impossible if I can't even walk."

"How long do you have to wear the cast?"

"At least six weeks."

"Ugh."

"It already itches." He grimaced.

"My grandmother always said to try and think about something else." He gave me a look. "Yeah, that never works."

"Let's talk about my cases," he begged.

We went over the half dozen cases that he'd had on his desk. It was the first time I'd assigned cases to other investigators, and Pete wasn't happy that I'd allocated one each to Mick Klein and Lynn Lewis.

"Lynn's okay," I told him when he grumbled about them. "Now Mick is a pain in the ass. Still, they'll do a good job on your cases."

"Who did you give the rest to?"

"Phil and I took a couple, and the rest went to Julio, who was excited to get them."

"If we aren't careful, we'll all be working for *him* one day." Pete smiled, but it quickly faded. "If I'm still working as a deputy."

"You thinking of quitting?" I joked.

"Sarah and the girls spent the last two days telling me about all the other jobs I'd be great at. I know that they're worried I won't be able to do the job." He tapped his leg. "But there's another side of it too. I scared them. I can see it in their eyes. There was never any real worry in Sarah's eyes until now."

"You scared all of us. They'll get through it. Just like you."

"The sooner I can get back on the job, the easier it's going to be." Pete visibly shook himself, like a bear coming out of hibernation. "Let's talk about the King and Banks murders. What evidence do you have against Natalie Owens?"

"None." I explained that I'd gone back to square one. He listened, frowned and nodded.

"I hate to admit it, but you're doing the right thing. Still, it's hard to look for other trails when the fox seems to be right in front of you."

"Even if it *is* Natalie or Robin, we'll be in a better position to charge them if we've gone down all the side roads."

"Tell me how I can help."

"You know we need to get Dad's approval to put you on light duty before I can let you work on the cases."

"I can help you go through Drew's old cases." There was just a hint of pleading in his voice.

"Yeah, you can do that. Just no contact with anyone associated with the case."

"I know, I know."

"You can look up all his newer cases, and I'll get you

copies of all the older reports that seem relevant."

"Hell, send me the irrelevant ones too. You never know."

I headed back to Adams County with my mind racing, trying to find something useful in all the information I'd gathered. The only progress I felt like we'd made was the work done by Dr. Darzi, which provided physical evidence that the two cases were linked.

"Why a blunt object?" Cara asked me while we were eating the roast and vegetables she'd cooked in the Crockpot. I'd told her about Dr. Darzi's findings.

"What do you mean?"

"I mean, why use a piece of wood? Isn't a knife or a gun more efficient?"

"A piece of wood has advantages. Especially if you found it on-site. And attacking a person with a knife isn't that easy. Often the attacker themselves ends up with injuries from using a knife, which of course leaves DNA at the scene."

"And a gun leaves all kinds of stuff that can be identified and possibly tracked back to the murderer."

"Right. Now the question is: Did the killer know that there was going to be a bat in the office? We know that Drew King's friends and family knew that he kept a baseball bat around. All of his workers would be familiar with the office. Who else? Tomorrow I'm going to re-question the men and women working at the site. If Robin or Natalie were seen there prior to the murder, that would be a red flag."

"You've already asked them about strangers hanging around the construction site, haven't you?"

"Witnesses don't always remember a person who might have seemed to have a legitimate reason for being there. Like if Drew had brought someone to the site, everyone would have assumed that that person belonged there because Drew was with them. We asked about strangers, and we showed Robin's picture around. We haven't shown Natalie's photo to any of them."

"Where did the piece of wood used to kill Banks come

from?"

"We're still working on that. The day after the murder, Shantel had three patrol officers drive all the streets within a mile of the crime scene, looking for a place of origin for the two-by-four. They found a couple of possibilities, but nothing concrete."

"So the killer might have carried it with them or found it when they confronted Banks."

"Banks wasn't confronted. No one heard anything and it didn't look like he tried to defend himself."

"You have means and opportunity for both Robin and Natalie, but no solid motive for murder?" Cara was sounding like a defense attorney.

"Lots of people had the means and opportunity for killing both of them. And going back through the reports, there are any number of criminals who didn't like Drew. On top of that, I talked to his foreman, and he said that Drew had customers who weren't thrilled with him."

"You have customers and criminals that might have held a grudge against Drew, but what motive would they have had for killing Banks?"

"Exactly."

"Maybe Banks saw the killer at the construction site."

"That's an idea. I wish Banks had been a normal adult with a cell phone and a schedule; then we'd be able to see where he'd been the night Drew was killed, or ask his family where he was that night."

"I'm beginning to see your problem."

"Dealing with suspects and victims who are homeless and addicts is driving me crazy. Most of the witnesses can't even tell me what day it is, let alone what they were doing last week. I need to talk to Malik again."

"Who's that?"

"He's Natalie's other toady. He's younger and hangs around people who are a little higher up the food chain. The type of folks who might have a doorbell cam or phones that work."

We changed the topic to Cara's work as we cleared the table and did the dishes. Another local vet had approached her about doing their ordering and record-keeping.

"I'm thinking about taking some accounting courses at Tallahassee Community College," she said. "I've been winging a lot of this. If I could learn to be more professional, it would help my business, my work at the clinic and help with our finances."

"You sound like you think I'm going to try and talk you out of it." I smiled.

"Or I'm not sure myself if I should do it."

"I think it's a great idea."

"For six months or so, I would have even less time at home."

"We'll survive." I nodded toward the living room, where the two cats and Alvin were all in their usual after-dinner spots. "Not that we won't miss you." I leaned in and gave her a kiss. "With my new responsibilities, I'll be busier too."

I cursed when my phone rang at two in the morning. I wasn't on call that night and kicked myself for not turning off the ringer. Grabbing the phone, I looked at the caller ID and had no recollection of who Mike Todd was. Figuring it was a victim I'd given my card to, I reluctantly answered it.

"Macklin," I said.

"I know it's late, but my neighbor called and a guy shot paintballs at his cameras."

None of that made any sense to my sleep-addled mind.

"First, I just woke up, so you need to tell me what this is in reference to." I felt Cara roll over and cover her head with a pillow.

"I'm sorry. I… This is crazy, I know. I'm the guy who called about the fence being cut. Now my neighbor called me. He lives on the other side of the vacant lot. Someone just shot paintballs at his security cameras." Now I recognized the Northern accent.

I sighed. "I think Lieutenant Eccles is going to be handling that case," I said, trying to keep the irritation out of my voice.

"I tried calling him, but all I got was his voicemail. And you *did* give me your card."

More the fool me, I thought.

"Did your neighbor call 911 and report a prowler?"

"He didn't know what had happened. When he went to look, he saw the paint and called me 'cause he knew I'd had some trouble on my side of the lot."

Wide awake now and knowing I wouldn't be able to get back to sleep, I grumbled, "I'll come over and talk to him."

"I'll let him know you're on the way."

"It'll be about an hour. I have to get out of bed and get dressed." I added the last bit hoping he'd feel at least a little guilty for waking me up.

"His name is Samson Jordan. I'll let him know." He didn't sound like he cared about my lost sleep.

I disconnected the call and swung my feet out of bed.

"What was that all about?" Cara asked from under her pillow.

"Vandalism, cut fence, paintballed cameras, a bunch of nonsense."

"You're a sucker."

"Tell me about it." I headed for the bathroom.

The air was bracing as I walked to my car. *What are you doing?* I asked myself. *Going above and beyond.* I would never admit it, but a part of me liked it. I'd always enjoyed being on patrol after midnight. In our county, the businesses were closed and only a few people drove around late at night. The only bad thing about the midnight shift had been the drunks and the domestic disputes, which were often the same calls.

These days, the only time I got called out at night was when there was a dead body. And while I sometimes enjoyed driving around at night, I didn't like going out to deal with bodies. At least I wouldn't be looking at cold, dead eyes tonight. Hopefully.

Halfway there, I remembered who Samson Jordan was. He'd played baseball for Florida State and then for a major league team. I thought it was Cincinnati, but I wasn't sure. Samson had grown up in Adams County and come back after he retired from major league ball.

I pulled into his driveway and the six-foot-five Samson stood up and came down off the porch to meet me. His baseball-glove-size hand enveloped mine.

"Thanks for coming over," he said in a deep, rich baritone. His charisma was almost palpable.

"I'm Larry Macklin."

"I like your dad," he said with a smile. "This is the damnedest thing. I probably shouldn't be making a big deal about it. Still… it's creepy." He looked toward the upper floor of the substantial home, where a few lights were on. "I made the mistake of telling my wife and now she's all freaked out."

"Why didn't you call 911?"

"At first I thought my cameras had just messed up. When I went to look, I saw the paint and… it's just weird. That's when I called Mike, 'cause we'd talked about keeping an eye on the vacant lot." He waved toward the lightly wooded lot next door.

"Let's take a look at these cameras." I already had my Maglite in hand.

I followed Samson to the side of the house, where he pointed up to his eaves. Mounted twenty feet up were several security lights and cameras. Shining my light on the cameras, I could clearly see the blotches of paint. The camera lenses had been hit, and there were a couple of misses around each of them.

"How did you notice the cameras were out?" I asked while trying to figure out where the shooter had stood.

"I don't know if it was the sound or the lights that woke me up."

"You heard the pellets hitting the house?"

"Yeah, that's right, and I guess they were setting off the

lights. They're motion-activated. When I noticed the lights were on, I went to check the cameras and that's when I saw they weren't on. At least, I didn't think they were on. I messed with the computer a bit, and when I still couldn't get a picture, I came outside. Stupid, now that I look back. I should have called you all right away."

"We're guys. We solve problems," I said sympathetically.

"Yep." He let out a little laugh.

By backtracking and looking at all the angles, I eventually found a spot in a tea olive hedge where the shooter might have been kneeling. I gauged the distance as a hundred feet.

"He's a pretty good shot," I commented.

"Why would he be shooting at my cameras? Mike thinks it has something to do with that lot." Samson pointed next door. I wondered about Mike's obsession with the lot. It seemed to me more likely that someone was planning a burglary, or maybe it had just been kids causing trouble for the fun of it.

"I'm thinking it might have more to do with vandalizing the neighborhood," I said. "Have you heard about anyone else having trouble?"

"A house a couple doors down is always having their trashcans overturned. Everyone thinks that's just raccoons. They're an older couple and leave cat food out for a stray."

"That'll attract raccoons, all right. One thing I'm sure of is that it wasn't a raccoon shooting paintballs at your house."

"Why would they want to paint over my cameras?"

"I don't mean to pry, but do you have a lot of valuables in your house? Something that a thief might be willing to work hard for?"

"Not like a bunch of money. I've got my trophy case, but they're only valuable to me. It's not like I have a World Series ring." He laughed.

"Let's walk around the house and check all the windows and doors," I offered.

The house and yard were immaculate. I didn't see where anyone had tried to get in or damage any of Samson's property.

"I'm sorry, but there isn't much else I can do. If you see any trash in the yard or near the bushes, let me know and I'll come by and bag it up in case it was left by the vandal. The truth is, we won't test it unless a more serious crime occurs. Let's hope that doesn't happen."

"I got you. No sweat," he said and once again clutched my hand in his.

Like a fool who never learns, I took out a card and handed it to him.

CHAPTER NINETEEN

Having decided it was too late to drive home and get any more sleep, I headed for the office, where I found three deputies in the breakroom.

"Larry, do you ever miss being a deputy?" Andy Martel quipped in his Wisconsin accent that had never faded, even though he'd spent the majority of his life in Adams County. I gave him an appropriate hand signal.

"I'm sure all the bad guys are shaking in their boots, knowing you three are sitting in the breakroom drinking coffee," I said.

"How's Pete doing?" asked Teresa Pelham.

"Better. He should be going home today."

I grabbed some of the black sludge out of the coffee pot and joined them at the table. Andy slid a box containing two leftover donuts over to me.

"Who died?" Derick Jacobs asked. "I didn't hear anything on the radio."

"Nobody has been shot, stabbed, clubbed, electrocuted or run over. Can't I just come in and see you guys?"

"Sure, but then you should have brought some fresh donuts." Andy smiled.

"And maybe some coffee." I looked at the cup I'd just

drunk out of and wondered if I'd been poisoned.

"That pot has been here since I came in," Derick said, just as dispatch called his number and told him to head for a robbery at the southside Fast Mart. "Roger that," he said into his radio, heading out the door as he asked for more details.

"You all seen any uptick in vandalism?" I asked Andy and Teresa.

"I took a report from some guy whose car was seriously keyed. He had every four-letter word in the dictionary written on his Kia." Teresa shook her head in amusement. "Of course, it was his ex-girlfriend. A little talking and she agreed to pay him for the damage."

"I had a woman get her mailbox bashed in. She couldn't think of anyone that would target her. My guess was kids from the high school. She only lives a mile away from the school and her mailbox was this fancy birdhouse thing. Really nice before some idiot turned it into splinters."

"Heard of anyone going crazy with a paintball gun?"

"This have anything to do with Drew's murder?" Andy asked.

"No, just a vandalism case in Pineland Trace."

"First-world problems." Teresa smiled and shook her head.

"High strangeness is more like it," I said, and went on to explain what had been going on.

"My family lived over there when there were just a few older houses. That drunk who got bludgeoned was one of our neighbors," Andy said.

"When was this?"

"I was just a kid. Maybe ten," he said. I knew he was a little younger than me, so it would have been around twenty years ago. "We used to play all through those woods."

"What was Banks like?"

"Just a guy. I thought he was old 'cause he was the same age as my dad. Now that I think back, I guess he was roughly the same age I am now, and that just feels weird."

I should have followed up with more questions, but it was five in the morning and I was tired, especially when I thought about the full day of work ahead of me.

Andy and Teresa were called out, so I wandered back to my desk to get a head-start on the day. I wrote a report on the paintball incident and sent a copy over to Phil. I looked at my desk, then over at the small office set aside for the sergeant. Inside the office were a desk, two chairs and a couple of filing cabinets. With a look to the future, I started moving the stuff from my desk into the office.

By the time the office filled up, I was almost completely moved in. There was still my desktop computer, but since I also had my laptop, I wasn't in a rush for it and wouldn't press Lionel about moving it.

"Nice!" Julio said, poking his head inside. He turned around and looked out on the low-walled cubicles where the other desks were. "So this is the view from the mount."

"Knock it off." I gritted my teeth, feeling awkward about the physical separation from my colleagues.

"I'm just kidding you. I think it's great. No matter what everyone else says," he said with an ear-to-ear grin.

"The cool thing is, I can now kick people who annoy me out of my office."

Julio dropped down into the other chair. "Kick me out? You and what army?"

"How are the cases you picked up from Pete going?"

"Sorry, gotta run!" He pretended to get up.

"See, there's more than one way to get someone out of your office."

Julio settled back into the chair. "I've cleared half of them. If there's any work on the King or Banks case I can help with, let me know and I can squeeze it in."

"I read your report on the incident with Natalie Owens."

He looked down at his feet. "I hate that I let her get away. When I think about what might have happened to Pete…"

"It doesn't sound like she gave you any time to react. Did

you mention anything about why you were there before she took off?"

"Like I said in the report, I'd only said that we wanted to talk to her. I didn't even mention the murder or King's name."

"Have you had any dealings with her in the past?"

Julio hesitated. "That's where I feel guilty." He paused to gather his thoughts. "I should have put this in the report. Yes, I've had run-ins with her in the past. That tongue… And I saw her spit at Sanderson a couple of months ago when we stopped her 'cause she and a couple of other people were walking down the street drinking out of a bottle that was in a paper bag." He paused again. "So I didn't get as close to her as I would have with another person. I stopped about three feet away and told her I wanted to talk to her. If I'd gotten closer to her before I spoke…"

"You can't second-guess yourself. If I was a training officer, I would tell a recruit to maintain their distance in that situation because the most likely issue to come up is what you were concerned about. You didn't have any reason to think she was going to steal a car and go on a rampage."

"Maybe. I still think I could have done better."

"Which is why you're a good investigator who's going to get better. I promise you, Pete doesn't blame you for what happened."

After Julio went to work and I fielded another dozen jokes from my colleagues about my new office, I headed down to records. There I found a large group of folks standing around several trays of green-iced cupcakes that Beth had made in recognition of St. Patrick's Day. Half of the cupcakes were already gone by the time I grabbed one.

"Can you print these reports out of microfiche?" I asked Beth. "I'm going to let Pete read through them for me."

"Good idea." Beth winked. "Give a person a job if you want to take their minds off their troubles. I'll have Shenika work on them and let you know when she has a pile."

Phil was looking at my office as I walked back into CID.

"This just puts pressure on me to move into mine," he said.

"I'll help you. That way everyone can spend the rest of the day making fun of you instead of me."

"Maybe later," he said. "I got the report from last night. You should have called me." I wasn't sure if he was serious or not.

"I figured I was doing you a favor."

"Truthfully, I didn't mind having the sleep, but I'm getting the itch to catch this jackass. Maybe I'll check out a pair of night-vision goggles from the equipment room."

"The case feels like a UFO or Bigfoot incident. Any possibility that the other property owners are messing with us for some reason?"

"Funny you should say that. When I read your report, that was the first thought that popped into my head. About six years ago, I kept getting called to this woman's house about a prowler. Eventually it turned out that she had some mental issues and was just craving attention. But she went to extremes. One time she was on the phone with the dispatcher pretending like someone was trying to break in. You could actually hear the banging on the door over the phone. It was like a radio play."

"But why would they want to gaslight us?"

Phil shook his head. "Honestly, I don't really think it's them. All I know is that something weird is going on."

"Have you talked to the Mathesons, the owners of the lot?"

"Hey!" He snapped his fingers. "Thanks for reminding me. When I tried calling them, I talked to a relative who was housesitting for the couple while they were on their honeymoon. They were supposed to get back yesterday. You want to go with me?"

"Where do they live?"

"Deer Run or Deer Creek, deer-something. It's a small subdivision just over the Leon County line. Half an hour over there, tops."

"Sure. I can make the time this afternoon."

"I'll try and set it up."

After he left, I wondered why we were wasting our time on a vandalism case. *Because it's odd*, I thought. Someone was playing games and I didn't like it. Besides, it would only take an hour to go talk to the owners and rule out anything hinky on their end.

I was walking down the hall when I saw Dad come out of his office.

"I want to talk to you," he said, making me cringe a little. His tone of voice was the same one he'd used when I was a kid and he'd wanted me to do my homework or perform some chore around the house.

"Sure." I followed him back into his office. "Where's the big guy?" I asked, surprised that Mauser didn't come over and bounce into me.

"Jamie is watching him today. I've got to go to a homeowners' meeting in the Crestwood neighborhood tonight. The president always brings his bulldog, who doesn't like Mauser."

"I thought everyone in the county was enrolled in the Mauser Fan Club," I joked.

"Not all dogs. Anyway, I was wondering if you could watch Mauser tomorrow night." He held up his hand. "This isn't part of your punishment. I guess if the committee can promote you, then I'll have to let you off the hook. So I'm asking. Jimmy has been made employee-of-the-month at Publix, so Genie and I are taking him out to dinner."

"Cara and I would be glad to watch Mauser," I said graciously.

"Thanks. And congratulations again on your promotion." His tone changed. "Any updates on the King or Banks murders?"

"We're running down leads without knowing which direction is the right one."

"That's all you can do until you catch the scent of your prey." Dad looked like he wanted to ask more questions but restrained himself. Instead, he started guiding me toward the door.

"I need to go talk to the owner of the truck stop. He wants to put in an area for our deputies to take breaks. He's going to create a little desk space off to the side in their restaurant. Of course, he's really looking to get a little free security, but it's in a good place for our troops to hang while waiting for calls."

"We all use the truck stop's restrooms anyway," I said, walking with him down the hall.

"Exactly. It could be a win-win."

We parted at my office and I watched as he headed for the lobby. His walk was purposeful and strong, and recent days had proved to me that his mind was sharp as ever. It had seemed to take a very long time for him to recover from the head trauma he'd suffered back in December, and I was glad to see him back to his old self.

I worked for a few hours, then decided to sneak out to my car and take a short nap lest I fall asleep at my desk. Once outside, I moved my car far enough away from the building so that none of my fellow law enforcement officers would be tempted to play a prank on me while I slept.

The nice weather was perfect for napping. I dozed off and, after a series of dreams which involved people swinging baseball bats at each other, I was awakened by the ringing of my phone.

"Yep?" I said.

"You sound like you were asleep," Phil answered.

"Yep."

"Is that all you can say?"

"Yep."

"I got ahold of our newlyweds. They'll see us at their house at two o'clock."

"Yep." I had closed my eyes again.

"Yep," Phil said and disconnected the call.

After a few more minutes, I pulled myself out of the car. I could have easily slept for two hours instead of the forty-five minutes I'd gotten. *I remember when I could go two days without sleep*, I thought. Then an old man's voice in my head mocked me: *You ain't getting any younger, sonny.*

I went back inside and worked on one of the cases I'd taken over for Pete. This was one that Pete had taken on personally, an older woman who was being harassed by her adult son. Apparently, he was trying to control more of her finances than she wanted. At some point, he'd grabbed her arms hard enough to leave bruises, but she'd only reported it at the urging of a friend. While we had pictures and witness statements from the neighbors, the woman was hesitating to press charges. We could have moved forward without her, but I knew the State Attorney would be reluctant to do so without the victim's support. Pete's notes indicated that he'd called her half a dozen times.

When I spoke to her, she was clearly conflicted over whether to prosecute her son or not. I arranged to meet with her the next day. I knew it would take a while to build up the trust that she had in Pete. When I told her why I was taking over her case, she was genuinely upset that Pete had been injured. It just reminded me of how well Pete connected with people.

I got to the Mathesons' house before Phil and waited in my car.

"I'm on time," Phil said when he arrived.

"For me, ten minutes early is on time and five minutes early is late," I said, using my best schoolmarm voice.

"You're a freak," he chided me with a laugh.

The house was a classic brick-fronted starter home, small and well-kept. The freshly minted Mrs. Matheson was beaming when she opened the door.

"Come in!" she welcomed us before Phil or I could introduce ourselves.

"Sorry to bother you when you're just back from your honeymoon," Phil said as we followed her to the living room, where her husband was standing by the couch. They were both older than I'd envisioned when Phil had told me they'd just been married. CiCi and Damon Matheson both looked to be in their mid-thirties. He had blond hair that covered his ears and almost touched his shoulders, while she had black hair cut slightly shorter than his. Each carried an extra twenty pounds around their middles, and they kept touching each other affectionately.

"No bother. We were concerned when we heard there was trouble going on around our lot," Damon said.

"We want to start building as soon as possible," CiCi added.

"We aren't sure if the trouble has to do with your lot or if it's centered more on your neighbors," I said.

Both of them frowned.

"That's disappointing. I mean, that anything is going on. The neighbors seemed really nice," Damon said. "We've met most of them when we've been over there planning our new house."

"Did any of the folks you met seem hostile to you?" Phil asked.

"No…" Damon said, but he sounded unsure.

"But?"

"It's just that Mike made it sound like he wished he'd bought the lot. He didn't come across like he was mad at us, just disappointed that he didn't buy it," Damon said, glancing at his wife for support. She nodded and looked back and forth between us.

"What exactly did he say?" Phil asked.

"Gosh, I don't know if I can remember. Honey?" Damon looked at his wife.

"It was something like, 'I always planned on buying that lot. Guess I should have jumped on it sooner.' Something like that." CiCi looked at her husband and rubbed his leg affectionately.

"That sounds close," he acknowledged.

"Who did you buy the lot from?" Phil asked.

"The realty company that developed the subdivision. There is also a homeowner association that has to approve the house designs and the builder. Mike's on the board," Damon told us.

"It has us up in the air right now, because they only allow a couple of construction companies to build houses there," CiCi piped in.

"Just our luck our builder got murdered," Damon said. When he saw the look on our faces, he obviously thought we were shocked at his callous comment and added, "That sounds awful. Of course we feel horrible about Mr. King's murder. Stupid of me to act like we're the victims."

"Drew King was going to build your house?" I asked, trying to digest this new information.

"That's right. We met with him a dozen times, talking about the materials, his timetable and the financing."

"Where did you all meet?" I asked.

"A few different places. At his office, in his house and a couple of times at his construction sites," Damon said, exchanging more looks with his wife.

"He was a very nice man," she added.

"When was the last time you met with him?" Phil leaned forward and looked at them closely.

They glanced at each other before Damon said, "A week before we left for our trip. He wanted to get a little further along with his current project, but then as soon as they had the ground prepared and the foundation poured, he was going to start on our place. He explained that he had a few different crews that did different types of work. One was dedicated to ground preparation and pouring the foundation." Damon seemed unsure about the intensity with which we were now asking questions.

"Was he acting any different the last time you met with him?" Phil asked.

Damon and CiCi looked at each other again.

"I don't know. What do you think?" Damon asked his wife, who was now holding his hand.

"Not really. He seemed in a bit of a hurry, I guess."

"That's true. He was kind of rushing us out. We got to his office late, and he acted like he had someone else coming over."

"He did say one thing I thought was odd," CiCi said, tilting her head to the side.

"What was that?" I prodded.

"He said he'd be willing to buy the lot from us."

"He wanted the lot?"

"No… It was more like he knew someone else who wanted it."

"Mike Todd?"

"Maybe. He wasn't specific. Just said he could give us a good return on our investment if we wanted to sell," Damon said.

"I didn't feel like he was being pushy," CiCi added.

"What did you say?" I asked.

"CiCi loves that lot." Damon clutched her hand and brought it up to his lips and kissed it. "We couldn't sell it. We've picked out the perfect spot for the house."

"How did King take that?"

"Kind of no big deal. Like CiCi said, he wasn't pushy. We were just surprised by the offer."

"But you didn't ask him any more questions, like how much he was willing to offer?" Phil asked.

"No. Like I said, we weren't interested."

"You had no contact with Mr. King after that?" I asked them.

"No. We were planning to get together with him as soon as we got back from our honeymoon," Damon said.

"When did you leave for your trip?"

"We left two weeks ago and did a tour of Mexican resorts."

"When did you buy the lot?" Phil asked.

"Two years ago, right after we got engaged. It was sort of a present from my dad." Damon sounded slightly embarrassed by the admission that the lot was a gift.

"Not that Damon needed his dad's help. He makes plenty of money as a game developer." CiCi must have picked up on Damon's embarrassment. He kissed her.

"Would you mind if we walked around the lot?" I asked.

"No. Let me get the extra key to the lock," Damon offered.

"Whose idea was it to put the fence up?"

"Mr. King said he usually puts up a fence around his construction sites to keep people from stealing his material. I asked Mike and he said it was a good idea. We have just six months to finish construction."

"Which, without Mr. King, could be a problem," CiCi added.

"And Drew's men put the fence up?" I asked.

"It's part of his site prep. That's what he said. I got the feeling that he liked to have several projects going at the same time, each at a different stage of construction. He came across as very professional."

After a few more questions, we thanked them and left the two lovebirds to do whatever lovebirds do when no one is watching.

CHAPTER TWENTY

"That was too much sugar for me," Phil said.

"Weren't you ever in love?" I joked.

"Still am, but my wife and I don't paw at each other like teenagers." He grinned. "What did you think of the bombshell?"

"Just a coincidence? Or is it significant?"

"I asked you first." We were standing beside our cars outside the love nest.

"It's the first hint we have of Drew being involved with another ongoing investigation. Regardless of how petty the crimes are."

"My gut tells me there's meat on this bone." Phil looked back toward the house. "I think we need to look into Mike Todd. Is he creating a mystery around the lot in hopes of getting them to sell it to him?"

"Why would he kill Drew if that was the case? Sounds like Drew was helping him."

"We don't know *who* Drew was making the offer for."

"You've got a point there."

"I'm going back to Mike. The skullduggery around the lot is my case anyway," Phil said.

"Are you going to ask him if Drew was working for

him?"

"Not yet. I'll give him the chance to bring it up first."

"I agree. I'll go back through Drew's emails and texts, see if there's any hint of him working a deal. I'll also talk to his son. Maybe he mentioned it to him."

"Good idea. You want to head over and walk through that lot and see if we see anything of interest?"

"I can't imagine we will, but sure."

Twenty minutes later, we were both parked outside Samson Jordan's house. His wife came out, and we explained who we were and what we were doing there.

"I don't know how we're going to get all that paint off," she said, pointing at the cameras and the blue splashes of color on the red bricks.

"That's pretty high. I'd suggest you get a professional," Phil said, looking at the marks.

"You don't know my husband. He thinks he's a professional when it comes to anything around the house. I'm still mad at him for going out last night in the dark."

Phil and I told her we were just going to take a quick walk around the lot and would be out of her driveway in half an hour.

The lot comprised five acres of sparsely wooded land. There were several tall slash pines, three or four spreading live oaks and a few other oaks and sweetgums. The underbrush had recently been bushhogged, probably when the fence had been put up.

"This is just confirming my original impression. There's nothing here," I said.

"Not even any good places to hide," Phil agreed.

"I will say that the Mathesons are right. It is a great location for a house."

"Let's lock the gate and get back to real policework."

As soon as I got back to the office, I called Art King. He said his father had never mentioned any attempt to broker a deal for the Mathesons' lot.

"I actually just talked with the Mathesons," Art told me.

"We're trying to work it out so Dad's company can still build their home. But the way the HOA has it written up, Dad was specifically mentioned as one of the builders. Mike Todd said he didn't know if the board would approve the company without Dad as the owner and general contractor."

"How did Todd sound? Did he seem like he was trying to help or trying to stop the construction?" I asked.

"He seemed helpful, I guess. Even said he'd be willing to call a special meeting of the HOA to consider it. He did mention that there had been some sort of trouble around the lot."

"Did he?" I mused. "Thanks. Let me know when he contacts you again."

"He said he'd try and arrange a meeting of the board next week. I told the Mathesons."

I thanked him and hung up. Next, I pulled up the county property appraiser's site on my laptop to research the history of the lot. The Mathesons had bought it from the developer for a pricey ninety thousand dollars. The lot had been part of a bigger parcel of land bought by the developer five years ago. Since the developer had had the parcel map redrawn, I would have to go down to the property appraiser's office if I wanted to see who had owned the land before that. I put that on my to-do list, but not for today.

I headed for Lionel's office and found him in the middle of a complicated network upgrade that I couldn't begin to understand.

"I just want to get Drew King's texts and emails placed in a file where I can go over them again." Pete and I had already reviewed everything from the week before King's death, but it was possible that any communication about the Matheson lot could have occurred long before that.

"Can do. Let me finish with this update and I'll jump on it," Lionel said without taking his eyes off the monitors in front of him.

I thanked him and went down to records, where I picked up an inch-thick folder of Drew King's old reports.

Assuming that Pete had made it home from the hospital okay, my plan was to drop the reports off at his house after work.

An email from Major Parks was waiting for me when I got back to my office. Phil had told him he could meet this afternoon and Parks wanted to know if that also worked for me. Reluctantly, I typed "yes" and found myself committed to a meeting in less than thirty minutes. As tired as I was, I wasn't looking forward to a long meeting about responsibilities and duties.

However, the meeting wasn't as painful as I was afraid it would be. Parks, ever efficient, had prepared some handouts that reminded us of when we needed to accomplish certain tasks, like personnel reviews and budget requests. He also went over the procedures for disciplinary action if it became necessary to reprimand someone under our supervision.

I texted Pete as soon as we were done.

Exhausted but glad to be home, he responded.

When I got to his house, Pete looked as tired as I felt. Still dressed in a hospital gown, he was sitting in his favorite easy chair.

"I can't get real clothes on over these casts," he grumbled.

"It took three people to get him into his chair," Sarah said, looking thrilled to have him home.

"Two to hold me up and one to keep my gown closed so I didn't moon everyone." Pete grinned.

"I brought King's old reports." I held up the folder.

"Good. I'm so tired of TV and social media, I would have paid you to bring me real work." He held out his hand.

"That can still be arranged," I joked and pulled the reports back. He glared at me and I relented, handing him the folder.

"There's been an interesting development in the case," I said, and went on to describe what Phil and I had found out from talking to the Mathesons.

"Is there a tie-in to the Banks murder?" was Pete's first

question.

I stared at him. *Why wasn't that my first question?* I thought.

"I… don't know."

"You look like someone hit you on the head with a baseball bat," Pete said.

"I just remembered something that Andy Martel said at the station this morning. He lived in that area when he was a kid and remembered Banks living there too." I was kicking myself for just now remembering the conversation. I took out my phone. I didn't have Andy's number, so I called dispatch.

"Can you meet me at the property appraiser's office tomorrow morning?" I asked Andy, after I'd explained what I needed.

"Sure. I'm working night shift again. I'll just hang around and we can go over there when they open," he said. "Thinking about those days sure is bringing up some memories."

"Those memories are what I need," I said and thanked him.

Pete had started looking through the reports as I talked to Andy.

"I need my laptop." Pete pointed to the small table a couple of feet from his chair, looking frustrated that he couldn't get up and get it himself.

"What are you looking up?" I asked, moving the table within his reach.

"I need a map of the area. I want to cross-reference the addresses in these reports and flag any that are close to that lot."

"I'm glad your brain didn't get scrambled."

"Yeah, well, I never knew how much I liked to be able to walk and use my left arm," he muttered as he poked at the laptop keys with his right hand.

"Let me know what you find," I said and left him working away contentedly.

"I know he's tired. Still, I'm grateful to you for bringing

him some work. He's been worrying so much about his leg," Sarah said in a soft voice as she walked me to the door.

"I can hear you!" Pete yelled

"You have very selective hearing," she called back good-naturedly. When she turned back to me, she mouthed: *Thank you.*

As soon as I walked in the door at home, I got hit with the tired stick. Cara wasn't home yet, so I fed Ghost and Ivy, then laid down on the couch. Next thing I knew, Cara was asking me if I was all right.

"Just catching up on my sleep," I mumbled and stretched.

After dinner and a little adult entertainment, I went to bed with high hopes of a good night's sleep. Instead, I found myself wide awake at five in the morning, wondering if we would ever solve these murders.

I was at the property appraiser's office by eight the next morning. Andy was waiting for me in the parking lot and smiled when he saw me.

"I'm looking forward to seeing the plot maps for the old neighborhood," he said as we entered the building. We bypassed the counter and went back to find Cheryl Herrera, the property appraiser. She stood up when she saw us.

"Larry, what can we do for you? None of my employees are in trouble, are they?" Cheryl and Dad had become good friends as their terms of office were in sync, and they often shared the campaign trail.

"Nothing like that. We need to see some old plot maps." I went on to explain the time frame and area we were interested in.

"I'll turn you over to Carlos. He's a bit… gruff, but no one knows the books the way he does." We followed her over to a desk in a small backroom where metal racks held hundreds of books filled with plot maps.

"I got a dozen slips from surveyors," Carlos groused

when Cheryl told him what we needed. Middle-aged, with a furrowed brow and a perpetual frown, he looked at us the way I looked at cockroaches.

"You're lucky I know these stacks like the back of my hand," he said, holding up his hand to show us. If it had been anyone else, I would have thought he was making a joke, but I didn't detect the slightest hint of humor in this man.

"I'll leave you all in his competent hands," Cheryl said and left.

"Competent, my ass. She knows the rest of these idiots would take a year to find anything around here." He huffed and turned without another word to us. Five minutes later, he came back with two large books.

"I brought two 'cause there was a change made in one of the properties around the time you're talking about."

He opened the first book and, after a little back and forth, showed us a map that covered what was now the Pineland Trace subdivision.

Andy shifted the book around and took a minute to get oriented.

"There's our house." He pointed to a five-acre tract. "I think that one was Banks's house." He pointed to a lot two down from the one his parents had owned.

"I need to see where the current lot we're dealing with is located," I said.

"We don't do overlays." Carlos frowned. "I'll get the coordinates for the current lot."

Carlos walked out, leaving Andy and me looking over plot maps.

"Who else can you remember living nearby?" I asked.

"There were a couple of girls that lived in this house," Andy said, pointing out another lot. "Their daddy still farmed some of the area behind the house. I guess it would be these fifty acres. Their names were Dotty and... I don't remember the other. That's their surname, Burgess."

"I guess this is Robin's house." I indicated a one-acre

plot at the bend of the two-lane road. The name on the plot was Hennessy.

"That house is still there, just across from the entrance to the subdivision," Andy said.

I saw another name on a five-acre lot next door to Robin's house.

"What about this one, Wells? Do you remember anything about them?" I asked.

"No, not really," Andy said. "Though I remember the house, 'cause whoever lived there had a cool Mustang convertible."

The door opened and Carlos came back with a piece of paper in his hand.

"Here is the lot you're concerned with." He pointed to an area that was about three hundred feet inside of a hundred-acre tract.

"Is this a road?" I pointed to a dashed line that led from the main road to the spot he'd pointed out on the map.

"That's a dirt track. Most likely a hunting road."

"Can I get a copy of this map with the names of the owners on it?"

"Ha!" Carlos said. "You can get a copy of the plot map for twenty dollars." His tone didn't allow for any bargaining room. I hoped I'd never have to interrogate Carlos.

"We'll take two copies."

"You can pick them up this afternoon. Nobody is going to say moss grows under my feet," Carlos said grumpily.

"Can you remember anything about that spot of land from when you were a kid?" I asked Andy as we walked to our cars.

"No. I mostly stuck to the main road. There was a creek behind the girls' house and we'd go over there sometime."

"Do you remember Robin Hennessy?"

"Sort of. He was a couple of years older than me, so he wasn't interested in hanging out with me."

"Let me know if you remember anything odd or strange that happened back then."

I'd reached my car when I turned and called back to him.

"Did you or your parents know Drew King back in those days?"

"No. My parents had just moved to Florida and didn't know anybody," Andy said with a shrug.

Back at the office, I ran into Phil and gave him an update.

"I'm seeing a few avenues of investigation," I told him. "One is the Mike Todd angle. Is all of the high strangeness around that lot just some odd game that he and his neighbors are playing? Or is it connected to the murders? Second, is this all about something that happened years ago? It seems a strange coincidence that several of the players in the murders were living close to each other twenty years ago. Finally, maybe it's just what it seemed like from the beginning. Crazy people whose minds were addled by drugs and alcohol went on a killing spree."

"All we can do is pursue all leads until one of them illuminates the truth."

"That's good. Was that a quote of the day in the police gazette?" I joked.

"It's pure Eccles gold, my friend," he said smugly.

"I'm going to visit the worksite again. I'll show Drew's foreman all the pictures we've got of the people involved and see if he picks out any of them as having visited Drew at the worksite."

"Makes sense. I agree with the logic that if the murder was premeditated, then the killer must have known he'd find a suitable blunt object in the office."

After a little time in my office answering emails and following up on voicemails, I headed to the construction site. The crew had much of the foundation dug and were starting to sink rebar in preparation for pouring concrete. I found Dan Gunter working on a backhoe that had broken down.

"I'm lucky that I have some mechanical skills, 'cause these machines like to break down at the worst times. Have you got any leads in Drew's case?" He wiped his hands with a towel that looked like it would leave more grease than it would remove.

"We're looking at a couple of things. That's why I'm here. I want to show you some pictures, so you can tell me if you've seen any of these folks around here."

"Anything to help." He nodded.

He led me into the office, and I pulled up a virtual lineup on my laptop. It included photos of the Mathesons, Mike Todd, Robin, Malik, Samson Jordan, Natalie, Banks and half a dozen random pictures from our database. Dan picked out the Mathesons and Mike Todd, but that was it.

"I recognize those two from when you showed me their pictures before." He pointed to Robin and Natalie. "But I've never seen them here, except for that morning when I found him in the trailer." He pointed again to Robin.

"When did you see this guy?" I showed him the picture of Mike Todd again.

"A couple of times. I guess the last time was a few days before Drew was killed. They seemed friendly. I think we built his house."

That would explain how they knew each other. I needed to have another talk with Mike Todd.

Back at my office, I called Pete and filled him in on what we knew.

"Does your dad know you're keeping me in the loop?" he asked.

"Don't contact anyone and we'll be good."

"So that's a no."

"You're just a resource, like Eddie or Mr. Griffin."

"Great! You're comparing me to your crossdresser confidential informant and a history nut. I can't decide if I'm in good company or not."

"You're in the company you're in. Would you prefer that I come get those reports?"

"Uncle! I promise I'll quit looking a gift horse in the mouth. Now, about these reports. I've made a few notes. I focused on the reports centered around your victims and suspects. Reading between the lines of Drew's reports that include Douglas Banks as a witness, victim or perp, I'd say that Drew liked Banks and tried to help him. As a witness, he had some respect for what Banks had to say. There are none of the comments you'd expect from a deputy if he wanted to minimize Banks's side of a story."

Everyone who writes about their interactions with other people is able to find ways to let the reader know how they really feel. Deputies are no different. Most of the time you aren't just putting down the facts; you're also letting the reader know how you feel about the participants. This bias can be helpful or not, but as an investigator I preferred it when the writer let me know how he felt, for two reasons. One: the facts were only half of any story. Two: I liked to know the bias of the writer so I could take that into account when I was investigating a case.

"Banks was just an alcoholic who preferred living on the street," I said. "There's a difference between him and some of the predators that live among the homeless. Was there ever any mention of Banks being scared of anyone? Was he acting paranoid?"

"He'd be the only homeless person who wasn't. But specifically, no. There are several reports when he was heavily intoxicated where he tried to report his wife as missing. Some of those weren't Drew's reports. I pulled those up from more recent encounters."

"Did you find the original report he made about his wife?"

"Yes. She left him for another man, according to several of the neighbors. At least, she'd been stepping out on him. One deputy suggested that *Banks* might have killed her and the other man."

"Anything come of that?"

"It shut Banks up for a while. The deputy couldn't get much traction on that angle as the neighbors couldn't confirm any fights or arguments between Banks and his wife, and he seemed genuinely upset that she'd left him."

"Anybody check to see if she ever showed back up?" I asked.

"She didn't have any family, so there wasn't much follow-up."

"Maybe the wife has returned." I made spooky sounds.

"Don't underestimate a woman scorned."

"Though it sounds like Banks was the one who was scorned. What else have you got?"

"There were a mix of reports that referenced Robin, Natalie and Malik. Nothing that you wouldn't expect from those three. Malik only has a couple. One that led to a misdemeanor possession charge. Natalie had an assault charge that Drew was a witness to. She spat on and tried to bite Hondo before she managed to get her claws, literally, into another EMT that day. In the end, the charges were reduced to a second-degree felony. I'd have to pull the court records to see how it all played out. I know from her record that she was convicted, but none of the details of how they got there."

"What about all those older reports?"

"Just the Banks stuff. Our gruesome threesome doesn't show up before ten years ago. At least, they aren't in any of Drew's old reports."

"Go back far enough and they'd be juveniles. We'd need a court order to break the seal on those."

"I'll continue to dig."

"Thanks, big guy."

"You know what really sucks? I'm trying to stay on my diet with a leg and an arm in a cast. I should be slurping down milkshakes or something."

"Stay strong," I encouraged him.

I hung up and looked at the time, then remembered it was Friday and I needed to collect Mauser on my way home. Plus, I also needed to swing by and pick up the plot map from Carlos.

I forced myself to work the rest of the afternoon on my open cases, as well as to start a calendar for keeping track of my new responsibilities. I'd been reminded of the need for this after Major Parks sent over the personnel files of all the investigators under my supervision. Finally, I called it a day and headed back to the property appraiser's office.

Carlos had the plot map rolled up and waiting for me. I didn't take the time to look at it before heading over to Dad's, where Mauser came bounding over from the barn to greet me. I waved to Dad and Genie as I fended off the enthusiastic beast.

"Okay, that's enough," I told him after the third time he rammed into my hip. He turned and looked at me like I didn't understand fun. "I don't enjoy being beat up, buddy."

"He loves you like a brother." Dad had his arm around Genie, who gave me her usual make-you-feel-at-home smile.

"Thank you for watching Mauser tonight," she said.

"Tell Jimmy I'm proud of him, and that Cara and I are sorry we can't be there to celebrate with him."

"We'll have to have a big get-together for Easter," Genie promised.

"He's yours tonight. I babysat him last time," I told Cara once I'd brought the beast home and he was playing with Alvin.

"Liar. Last time you subcontracted the babysitting to Eddie."

"You got me. I guess we can share the chore."

As if he'd heard me, Mauser came over and leaned against us, tongue hanging out.

"There's an expert in living in the moment." Cara ruffled his ears.

"He just wants some of that pizza I can smell," I said, looking forward to the dinner that Cara had brought home.

After the pizza and clean up, I looked outside at the mellow evening sunlight.

"The sun isn't down yet. You want to take Mauser and Alvin out for a walk through the woods?" I asked.

"I'll get Alvin's leash." Cara had been more protective of Alvin since we'd started hearing a pack of coyotes in the woods. There had even been a recent spate of pets brought into the clinic that had been attacked by some form of canine. Dr. Barnhill couldn't say for sure whether it was a dog, fox or coyote.

"We'll put them both on leash and take turns with Mauser." Since Jamie had been working with him, Mauser was much better than he used to be. Still, it could be like having a bull on the end of a rope if he got the scent of something irresistible.

"Just switch arms so you don't end up with one longer than the other," Cara joked as she snapped the leash on Alvin. I managed to harness the rhino and out we went.

The weather was cool and breezy. Over the trees toward the west, the setting sun was turning the sky pink, orange and purple as we walked the trails through our woods. Mauser and Alvin spent the first leg of the walk with their noses down. Both would sniff and whip their heads from side to side, smelling all the animals that had recently crossed the path.

We'd reached the eastern corner of our property and were about to turn back when Mauser's head shot up, and it was all I could do to keep from going down on my knees as he surged forward.

"What's he going after?" Cara asked as she and Alvin watched Mauser half drag me through the palmettos.

Ten yards in, I smelled it.

"Something dead, very dead." I cringed and dug my heals in, only to be pulled up and almost over. Without a choice, I let him drag me another five yards to the rotting corpse of a deer. Shouting, I tried to keep him out of it. No luck. He dropped down and rubbed his shoulder and muzzle into the disgusting remains.

"Deer," I told Cara as I tugged and cursed at Mauser. Eventually he'd had enough, and I managed to get him away and back to the trail. "Great, now we have to give him a bath," I complained.

"Oh yes, you do!" Cara blanched at the awful stench coming from the big lummox, who was all smiles and lolling tongue.

It was well and truly dark by the time I got done hosing, soaping and scrubbing a resistant Mauser. He was quite upset that I was taking away all of his wonderful new smell.

"So much for a nice evening walk," I said when I finally brought him inside. "I need to put my clothes in the washer and take a shower."

"You do stink a little." Cara wrinkled up her nose in a way I found quite endearing.

"You could come help me scrub up," I said suggestively.

"Get the smell of death and wet dog off you and we'll talk." She smiled

CHAPTER TWENTY-ONE

Saturday morning didn't so much dawn as it drizzled. Spring in North Florida is even more schizophrenic than the other seasons. It can be cold, rainy, hot, sunny, threatening tornadoes or absolutely beautiful, all in the same day. Today, however, my weather app was predicting it would be dreary and wet until evening.

"Lovely day," Cara said, looking at the rain running down the windows.

"A good day to curl up and do nothing." I joined her at the window. "Who's going to break it to them that they have to go outside in the rain to do their business?" I looked over at the dogs, who were splayed out on the floor.

After breakfast, we settled into a relaxing morning of little more than reading and internet surfing, though I did manage to spend an hour looking over some information on my new responsibilities that Major Parks had sent me.

Cara made chili and the rich, meaty aroma filled the air by dinner time. The weather app was right on the money; a sliver of blue sky appeared just after five and, while the air wasn't dry, at least it wasn't actively dripping.

"A walk before dinner?" I wanted to stretch my legs and Mauser was getting restless. Alvin, on the other hand, looked perfectly content to stay curled up on his oversize pillow.

"Let's avoid the dead deer." Cara punched me in the shoulder.

"I'm not the one who has to go running off into the woods to find dead things." I looked hard at Mauser, who gave me his standard goofy grin.

I'd always marveled at how the human mind could mix and match words, sights, sounds, experiences and emotions to come up with new ideas or, on occasion, long-sought answers. I experienced this as we walked. Woods, dead things, Mauser's determination, the constant drumbeat of questions in my head about the murders, the similarity between our woods and the Mathesons' wooded lot… All of it swirled in my brain until an answer floated to the surface like one of those Magic 8 Balls. And once I had the answer, it seemed so obvious that it didn't occur to me that I could be wrong. Still, I wanted to turn it this way and that before I talked about it.

"A penny for your thoughts," Cara eventually said, bumping into me playfully.

"I know why someone wants to get onto that lot," I told her.

"Really?"

"There's a dead body buried there."

"What?"

"Probably the body of Douglas Banks's wife." I squinted my eyes and tried to decide if I was taking this flash of intuition too far.

"From the little bit you've told me, that seems like a stretch."

"Maybe. But think about it. Drew was about to start in on the foundation work on that lot. His being killed has delayed it. I think someone has been trying to get onto the lot at night with the intention of digging up what's left of the body."

"What about Banks?"

"Banks might have been killed to delay the identification

of the body if it was found."

"That makes a strange kind of sense," Cara admitted. "Do you know who this person is?"

"There's the rub. No. But this theory eliminates Robin, Natalie, Malik and anyone younger than about thirty-five," I mused. "I need to go over all the evidence again."

"Are you going to tell Pete and Phil?"

"When I've had a chance to think it through." I looked at Mauser. "I guess I owe you one, big guy," I told him.

"Inspiration can come from the strangest sources. That's actually one of my dad's favorite things to say."

We enjoyed our chili dinner, then Cara helped me load Mauser into his van for the trip back to Dad's place. Jimmy was there when we arrived, which gave me a chance to congratulate him on being named employee-of-the-month.

"And you're a sergeant now!" he told me with wide, happy eyes.

"Yep."

"Congratulations to you. Are you going out to dinner to celebrate?" Jimmy asked with just a hint that he was angling for an invite.

"I haven't had a chance to think about it."

"There are some great restaurants in Tallahassee." He then proceeded to give me a rundown of his favorites.

"If I do go out to celebrate, you'll have to come along and pick the place because you're clearly an expert," I said, and we exchanged high fives.

Back at the house, the first thing I did was unroll the plot map that I'd gotten from Carlos at the property appraiser's office.

I scanned the names again. Most murders are committed by someone close to the victim, both physically as well as emotionally. There were a number of familiar names on the map near the lot. Robin and his mom had lived only a few homes away, as had Andy and his family. There was also Alan Wells. I remembered he'd said he'd known Robin when they'd been neighbors. There were also half a dozen other names that I was going to have to chase down and cross-reference with our files.

Next, I pulled out the original report that Banks had made about his missing wife. Georgia Banks had been thirty-one at the time she'd disappeared in August of 1998. Drew wasn't the primary on the report, but he did help canvas the neighbors and wrote a report where he laid out a case for two scenarios.

In the first scenario, he'd suggested that she ran off with a guy. Backing this up were the neighbors' statements that she was unhappy with Banks and spent a suspicious amount of time away from the house. One neighbor, Tami Rice, had said she would knock on the door and, even though Georgia's car had been in the driveway, she wouldn't answer. Rice thought she was in the house, possibly with a lover. There were more innuendos from other friends and neighbors.

The second possibility that Drew had suggested was that Georgia had been murdered by Douglas Banks. He cited these same rumors as a motive.

It was seven o'clock when I decided to call Phil and Pete. With a little assist from Cara, I managed to make a conference call on my phone.

"Larry, you're killing me. It's Saturday night. Audrey and I could have plans."

"Do you?"

"Audrey does. She's gone out with her old college sorority sisters who are visiting Tallahassee. My plans involved watching some crazy, stupid sports event on TV while downing pork rinds and draft beer from my wet bar."

"Wow! Didn't mean to upset your exciting evening."

"I was going to spend the evening trying to scratch under my casts while not eating pork rinds and drinking beer," Pete said.

"Sorry if I have to break up the fun." I went on to tell them the theory I was patching together. When I was done, there was contemplative silence from both of them.

"It solves some problems and creates others," Phil said, breaking the silence.

"Finding the body of Georgia Banks would answer part of the mystery. It would give you a motive for the murders, but not who the murderer is," Pete said. "You've taken two murders and made them three."

"I thought about that, and we've been here before. If the three murders—"

"Assuming there *are* three murders," Phil interjected.

"Right. Assuming there are three murders and that they are connected, then it narrows the suspect pool down to people who are at least thirty-eight years old."

"And our best suspects are all younger than that," Pete said.

"Connected doesn't mean they were all committed by the same person," Phil said. "It might not be likely, but it's possible that someone might kill to protect another person. Just as an example, Robin kills to protect his mother."

"You mean if his mother had killed Mrs. Banks?" I asked.

"I know that's not at all likely, but the example holds."

"No, you're right," I agreed. "We need to look at everything."

We talked for another half hour, mulling over ideas.

"What did they think?" Cara asked when I got off the phone.

"They warmed to it." I was still lost in thought. Something was nagging at me.

"Still thinking about it?" She came over and started rubbing my shoulders.

"Can't let it go," I said, frowning.

"Go look over all your notes again. You know you want to."

"But I should be spending my free Saturday night with you," I said guiltily.

"Go."

"Thanks." I went back to the kitchen table and spread out all the reports and the plot map. Ghost decided to help, so I spent half my time picking him up and setting him back on the floor.

Alan Wells's name kept popping up.

I pulled up the video footage of his car dropping Robin off in front of the Supersave. The camera wasn't very good and had been aimed to pick up most of the large lot. Wells had pulled up near the entrance to the store, putting his car almost directly beneath the camera. Still, it was possible to make out Robin's head and shoulders as he got out of the car and walked away.

I watched the ten-second video a dozen times, trying to convince myself I was seeing what I thought I was seeing. Next, I looked at the doorbell cam footage of Robin walking away from his mother's house. Back and forth I went. The images were apples and oranges as far as the color and image quality.

"Can you come look at this?" I asked Cara.

I opened two windows and put the images side by side. "Watch."

I ran the videos a couple of times.

"What am I looking for?" she asked.

"What's he wearing in each video?"

"In the one where he's walking down the road, I can see loose-fitting brown pants, shoes and a tan jacket and sunglasses. In the other one, I can't see much." She leaned in and squinted at the image.

"Is he wearing the jacket in the second video?"

Cara frowned and looked again. "Can you clear it up any?"

"I can't. Lionel might be able to. I really don't think he's got the jacket on in the second video," I said, not knowing if I was trying to convince her or myself. "I think Robin left his jacket in Wells's car."

I checked the time and decided it wasn't too late to call Drew's foreman.

"I've got a couple more pictures for you to look at," I told him after apologizing for disturbing him on Saturday night.

"Truth is, it makes me feel good knowing that you're working around the clock to find who killed Drew," Dan Gunter said.

I texted him five photos. One was of Alan Wells and the others were random people. Gunter recognized Wells immediately and the hackles on the back of my neck stood up.

"I saw him at the construction site a few times. The last time, I noticed Drew was less friendly than the other times."

"How unfriendly?"

"Drew acted the way he did with time wasters, or people trying to sell him stuff he didn't want."

"How did Wells act?"

"Very friendly. I figured he was a salesman."

When I hung up, I knew I needed to talk to Alan Wells. I hit Phil's number on my phone. As I laid out my ideas, I could tell that Phil was intrigued.

"I want to talk to him. The sooner, the better," I said.

"There are pros and cons to going over to his place on a Saturday night," Phil said. "A con is that he could be irritated at the intrusion. A pro is that we'll take him by surprise, which might cause him to get tripped up."

"I know this is a bit of a fishing expedition."

"I don't see what harm it will do. If he's our guy, then he already has his back up. If not and he gets mad, so be it."

"I'll meet you at your house. It's on my way to the lake."

"I'll leave a note for Audrey."

The wind had picked up as I stepped out of the car at Phil's house. He lived in an older neighborhood on the south side of town. His brick ranch was framed by fifty-foot pine trees that swayed rhythmically in the light of the full moon.

"What's the plan of attack?" Phil asked as he climbed into my car.

"I just want to throw some questions at him and watch

his reaction."

"You can't always tell a killer by the way they act," Phil reminded me.

"But sometimes you can. In this case, I think the trick is going to be to pretend like we know a lot more than we do."

"That's how I always operate." Phil chuckled.

"It's colder than I was expecting," I said when we got out of the car at Alan Wells's house.

"The joke will be on us if he's out on a hot date tonight," Phil said as we walked up to the door.

"The lights are on," I pointed out. I wanted to get this out of my system, one way or the other. My gut was telling me that Wells had a part in the murders, while my brain was telling me to slow down. I listened to my gut.

When we got to the door, Phil and I looked at each other, then he let me ring the doorbell. We could hear the chime echoing through the house.

"He could be down at his dock." The words were just out of Phil's mouth when we heard footsteps crossing a wooden floor. Light came through the windows on either side of the door as someone flicked on a hall light.

"Who is it?" Wells asked in a tone that was neither accusatory nor hesitant.

"It's me, Mr. Wells. Sergeant Macklin. We met the other day."

The lock clicked and the door opened.

"And this is Lieutenant Eccles," I said with an apologetic smile. "We're sorry to disturb you, but we have a few questions we want to ask you."

Wells pursed his lips for a minute before stepping back from the door.

"I have some company," he said, "but come in." He was wearing sweatpants and a T-shirt, making me wonder who his company was. "We can sit in here." He pointed us to the kitchen, which had large windows overlooking the lake. Wells gestured for us to sit at the table.

"Can I get you some coffee or tea?"

"No, thank you." Phil took a seat at the antique oak table.

"You lived near Robin Hennessy when he was younger, is that right?" I wanted to make it seem as though our focus was still on Robin before we started to zero in on Wells.

"That's right."

"Do you remember anyone else who lived in the area?"

"A few of them, maybe."

"Could you give us any names that you remember?"

Wells smiled, then stood up and retrieved a pen and notepad from the kitchen counter.

"My memory is only so good."

"Just write down anyone that you can think of. We're trying to talk to everyone who has information about Robin's past."

When he heard that, he appeared to relax.

"I guess you need to work up a full profile of any suspects. I know I'm just a friend of the family, but I don't think he could commit a murder."

Wells wrote down names as we talked. With six names on the pad, he tore off the top sheet and handed it to us. "There's a few for you. I don't know how many of them are still around. Some might even be dead. It's been over twenty years."

I glanced at the list and saw the glaring omission. Douglas Banks's name hadn't been included. Was it possible that he just didn't remember? Phil and I exchanged looks. Neither of us believed that. The community was small, and Banks and his wife had represented some substantial drama at the time.

"How much longer do you think this will take?" Wells asked with a smile.

"Maybe thirty minutes or so. We want to go over a few points with you, since you've known Robin for a long time, and you gave him a ride the night that Douglas Banks was killed." Phil paused to give Wells time to react.

Wells just smiled. "I see. Then let me go tell my friend that we'll be awhile." He gave us a subtle wink and stood up.

"Of course," I said.

We watched him walk back through the house and down a hallway until he was out of sight.

"When do you want to ask him about visiting Drew at the construction site?" Phil asked.

"First, we'll remind him about Banks living in his old neighborhood. See if he'll even admit to knowing Banks."

After five minutes had passed, Phil and I exchanged looks.

"I didn't see any other car out front," I said.

"And I haven't heard the sound of anyone else in the house," Phil said, already moving down the hall. "We're idiots."

We came to a closed door and I knocked hard. There was no answer.

"Mr. Wells, we're concerned about your wellbeing," Phil lied. He tried the door, but it was locked. "We're coming in."

Phil put his shoulder to the door, but it didn't give. He stepped back and kicked it near the lock. There was a crack, and the door gave way a couple of inches. Phil gave it a gentle push and it opened into the master bedroom.

A quick look around told us that Wells had probably gone out the sliding glass door that opened onto a patio overlooking the lake. We ran out the door and stopped.

"Did he go around the house to grab his car, or down to the water?" Phil asked, looking right and left.

"He went thata way," came a voice from next door. I looked over and saw Tyler Diaz sitting on her back porch with a glass in her hand. She raised the glass in a salute and pointed down the hill toward Wells's dock.

We took off running. Sure enough, we saw him drop into a kayak and start paddling quickly away from the dock. The full moon illuminated the scene before us.

"Damn it!" Phil said as we came to a stop on the end of the dock. "Come back here!" he shouted uselessly, only to get a finger in the air from Wells.

I got on the radio and called for backup, directing them

to meet us on the other side of the lake from Wells's house.

"We can go around and meet them," I started, then saw the fiberglass canoe tied up beside the dock. "Come on."

Phil saw where I was looking. "I'm with you. Find some paddles." He started to untie the canoe.

"Got them." I'd found a couple of paddles on a hook beside the boathouse. "Do you know anything about canoes?"

"How hard can it be?"

"Take the front. I took canoeing in college."

"Are you serious?" Phil said as we clambered into the canoe.

"A PE elective is a PE elective." I pushed off the dock with the paddle. "Now dig in. He's got a big head-start. Don't worry about which side you paddle on; I can compensate."

CHAPTER TWENTY-TWO

We both paddled for all we were worth. Knowing that our backup would be on the other side, our goal was to stay as close to Wells as possible and not lose sight of him. The lake was over half a mile wide at this point. A cool light breeze ruffled the surface of the lake, causing it to glimmer in the moonlight.

"We're right behind you!" Phil yelled. It was a slight exaggeration. We were more like fifty yards behind. Our efforts had us gaining very slowly.

I saw Wells's face when he glanced over his shoulder. There was a fierce determination that made me think he wasn't going to just throw up his paddle and call it quits. Then I saw his kayak swing around and I thought I was wrong.

Phil and I were so committed to our paddling that it didn't register with us at first that the contest had changed from a game of chase to a joust. Wells brought his kayak to a standstill, then pulled out a rifle.

"Gun!" Phil shouted and ducked down so quickly that the canoe rocked violently, and I felt sure we were going to end up in the lake. After the first crack of the rifle shot, I wasn't sure if going into the water wouldn't be the best option. The bullet tore into the side of the canoe, leaving a hole that was just above the waterline.

We both pulled our guns when we heard Wells work the bolt on his hunting rifle. Phil fired a round that missed, as Wells began to rock his kayak to make himself a more challenging target. His next shot ricocheted off the aluminum ridge that ran along the top edge of our canoe.

With Phil in the front, it was difficult for me to get a clear shot at Wells. Off in the distance I could hear sirens, but I didn't know what good they were going to do us out in the middle of the lake.

Phil fired a couple more rounds, but Wells was rocking back and forth erratically.

"Bastard," Phil mumbled, trying to get a clear sight picture.

Wells's next round tore through the side of the canoe right below the waterline and exited through the other side, just missing me as it left a jagged hole in the fiberglass. Phil let out a startled cry, making me think he'd been hit.

"Are you okay?" I asked as he let out a string of curse words.

"Something hit my face and I dropped my gun over the side," he hissed through clenched teeth.

Water from the second hole was streaming into the canoe. It was only a matter of time before the canoe would be waterlogged enough that the first hole would start adding even more water.

"I'm done with this!" Phil kicked off his shoes and unbuckled his pants.

"What are you doing?"

"Give me some covering fire," he said.

"What?"

"Start shooting! If you hit the son of a bitch, all the better."

I did what he asked. I got up on my knees, exposing myself as I fired off half a dozen shots that landed close enough to make Wells duck down. As soon as Wells crouched to avoid my fusillade, Phil slipped over the edge of the canoe.

I saw Wells react as Phil entered the water, but he couldn't turn the kayak around without presenting his back to me. Instead, he pointed the rifle and fired another round into the canoe, which took another hit close to the waterline. Soon the canoe was half swamped with water.

I ignored the water and tried to take advantage of Wells having to work the bolt on his rifle to take another shot. When he saw me raise my gun, he rolled the kayak and two of my rounds sailed over the spot where he'd been. I did a tactical reload and got ready for him to reappear.

When Wells rolled back up, he didn't have the rifle anymore. Instead, he had pulled a pistol and fired two rounds at me. The waterlogged canoe was becoming a less stable platform to return fire, but I managed to get off two more shots, one of which nicked Wells's side. He cursed and brought his gun up in a fury.

As I pulled the trigger on another round, Wells rolled again. This time he didn't come up so quickly. The kayak was rocking back and forth violently, and I knew that Phil was there.

I needed to get to the kayak, but the canoe was nothing but a sinking liability at this point. My radio had fallen to the bottom of the canoe and was now underwater and useless. My phone was in my pocket and would be equally worthless. I pulled off my shoes, shirt and pants and jumped into the water.

It took me a couple of minutes to reach the kayak. When I got there, the kayak was still bottom up and Phil was holding onto it, breathing heavily.

"He's probably dead. If we could do CPR, maybe." Phil looked around. "But that's not going to happen."

"We need to get out of this water." The temperature of the lake was in the low sixties after a colder than usual North Florida winter. I could already feel myself becoming numb to the cold.

"Yeah, the sirens are over there, but that's a lot closer." Phil pointed to the nearest shoreline, where there were half a dozen McMansions on two- or three-acre lots.

"We need to roll the kayak over," I said.

"Guess it wouldn't look good with us using the kayak as a flotation device with him hanging underneath it."

We struggled to get it upright without Wells's body slipping out.

"I'm freezing," Phil said.

"You're crazy is what you are," I told him as we kicked our feet, pushing the kayak toward the nearest shore. "What you did was insane."

"Our position was becoming untenable."

"That sounds like something out of a report."

"It's going to *be* in my report. I didn't try and kill him, but the old guy was tough as nails. He was holding me under the water as much as I was holding him. I managed to headbutt his chest, which caused him to inhale water." As Phil talked, I could hear his teeth chattering from the cold.

I was feeling sluggish and fuzzy-headed as hypothermia crept up on me.

"Someone is going to have to salvage that canoe for the investigation," I pointed out.

When we reached shallow water, I tried to stand, but my legs were rubbery and numb and wouldn't obey my commands. Phil and I steadied each other and pushed the kayak onto the beach.

Once we were sure that the kayak was secure, we stumbled our way up the bank to where a house stood. There were two-thousand-square-feet of redwood decking along the back of the home.

Stiffly, we climbed the stairs and went to the double French doors and knocked. Neither one of us considered what someone would think seeing two men at their back door, dripping wet in their underwear. I'd lost my badge, phone and radio… everything except my gun, which I had tucked in the back of my underwear.

Lights came on above the deck and a boy of about fourteen pulled aside the curtains and looked out at us. His mouth mimed: *WTF*.

"Who are you?" he asked through the door, half laughing at us.

"We're deputies with the sheriff's office," I managed to say through chattering teeth. "We need to dry off and use your phone."

As soon as I said the word phone, his hand whipped one out of his back pocket. Instead of opening the door and handing it to me, he pointed it at us and started filming.

"I'm weak! If you are cops, this is going to be dank!"

"Open the door," Phil said in the most authoritarian voice he could muster under the circumstances.

"You got, like, ID?" He continued to film us.

"We got a dead body down by the lake," I told him. My sense of humor was fading quickly.

"Zing! This slaps!"

At that point, the unprofessional part of my brain reminded me that I had a gun in the small of my back. With effort, I forced myself to leave it there.

"Please," I said through clenched teeth.

He looked at us over the top of the camera like we were spoiling his vibe.

"Okay, boomer, I got you." He reached out and unlocked the door while continuing to film us.

"Boomer, my ass," I heard Phil mutter under his breath.

I pulled the door open and felt the heated air of the house envelop me. I swung the door wide so Phil and I could enter together.

"Please turn off the camera and get us some towels," I requested as politely as I could.

"Camera stays on, dude. But yeah, Mom will have a fit if she sees all that water on her floors."

He walked backward, laughing gleefully as he filmed us standing there in our underwear, blue and shivering.

"If it's the last thing I do, I'm going to find an

opportunity to charge that little cretin with a crime at some point in his life," Phil muttered.

"Don't say anything you'll regret with that phone filming you," I warned him.

"Even frozen, I'm not stupid." His face pulled back into a mockery of a smile. "See, I'm all smiles."

"What's your name?" I asked the kid when he came back with two of the largest towels I'd ever seen.

"Can you ask that?" he said as if we were busting him for drugs.

"I'm just being polite," I said, toweling off and feeling warmer by the moment.

"Is there really a dead body down on the beach?"

"Yes. Now what's your name… please."

"Jax."

"Last name?" Phil asked.

"Thorne."

"We need to call our friends," I said, reaching out for the phone.

"If I hand you my phone, does that, like, give you permission to look through my texts and pics?"

"No." I had my hand out, still ignoring the little voice in my headed reminding me that I had my gun.

Suddenly, we heard classical music chiming loudly.

"That's the front door," Jax told us without making a move to go find out who it was.

"Answer it," Phil said, obviously thinking the same thing I was. It was probably our backup at the door.

Jax frowned. "What's it worth to you? Do you want the phone or for me to answer the door? The phone is going to cost you more than me answering the door." He gave us a cherub-like expression that made me want to strangle him.

"Jax, ol' buddy. I don't think your father is going too take too kindly to your attitude," I said.

"My father's a lawyer and hates cops," he said flatly. "He's going to find this video hilarious."

A hundred different threats came to my mind, but I

wisely bit them all back.

"Recording someone in Florida without their permission is against the law."

"You're in our home and I haven't been doing it secretly. If you don't like it, you can leave." I thought he was going to say more, but instead he yelled, "Shit!" His eyes were glued to the French doors behind us.

I turned and saw, to my great relief, Julio Ortiz, Matti Sanderson and a highway patrolman. They were all smiles.

I turned back to Jax, who had finally lowered the phone.

"Thanks for your hospitality," I said, only slightly menacing. "I'll catch you later."

"Tell your dad 'hi' for us," Phil added. "Oh, and there's going to be a swarm of law enforcement officers in your backyard for a while processing the dead body. We'll make sure they all know how kind you were to us in our hour of need."

Outside, we suffered the obvious jokes and backslaps with good humor. As more deputies and the crime-scene van descended on the lake, we were given clothes, coffee and a ride back to the office to be thoroughly debriefed by Dad.

"We're going to have to call in help to recover all the items you decided to drop in the lake," Dad said when he saw us.

He interviewed us both separately, but it didn't take very long. We both stuck strictly to the facts of what had happened that night. We had always been instructed not to provide too many details about an action until after the adrenaline had worn off. Memories of a traumatic event were usually better recalled after a couple of days than immediately after the event.

After the interviews, Dad drove us both home. Sitting in the backseat of Dad's SUV with Phil, it felt like we were a couple of kids being driven home after getting into trouble.

Audrey was waiting in the driveway when we pulled up to Phil's house. She hugged him before playfully punching him in the chest.

"I had to cut my girls' night short because of your antics," she said with a mock frown.

"I owe you," he said and put his arm around her.

"Goodnight, boys," Audrey said over her shoulder as they walked up toward the house.

"Neither of us intended on going skinny dipping," I told Dad as we got back into his SUV.

"So…"

"You want what I suspect or what I can prove right now?"

"Tell me what you think happened."

"Can we invite someone else in on this conversation?"

"Who?" Dad asked with a skeptical look on his face.

I took his phone off the dash and dialed Pete's number.

After I put it on speaker and we all exchanged pleasantries, which included Pete calling me an idiot, I shared my theory with them.

"What I think happened is that Alan Wells and Georgia Banks had an affair and something went wrong. Maybe she got pregnant, or maybe he did something that she was going to report to the police. We may never know *why* he killed her," I explained. "But I think Wells *did* kill her and buried her at the end of a farm road, thinking that the property would always be wooded hunting land. Meanwhile, Douglas Banks went a little crazy since no one took him seriously when he reported his wife missing. Hell, it was worse when someone *did* take him seriously, because then Banks himself became the prime suspect."

"Where was Wells all this time?" Dad asked.

"He moved to Tennessee for fifteen years. By the time he moved back here, the land had been sold to a developer. Why he didn't go and dig her up right away before they started building, who knows? But he got lucky and the land she was buried on wasn't sold right away."

"We don't know if her body is there," Dad pointed out.

"I've got ten bucks that says it's there."

"No bet," he allowed.

"When Wells learned that the lot was going to be built on and that the construction company was owned by Drew King, a man who would know whose body they found, he first tried to buy the lot. When that didn't work, he decided to kill King and implicate a young man he knew was so addled by alcohol and drugs that he wouldn't be able to defend himself from a murder charge."

"Robin could easily be drugged and manipulated," Pete added.

"Right. I suspect that Wells gave Robin something to make him pliable enough that it was easy to convince him to go to Drew's office. When Drew let Robin in, he would have known him and, seeing what condition he was in, wouldn't have wanted him walking around the construction site, so he probably put him to bed on the couch. At some point, Wells showed up, probably explaining that he was a friend of Robin's mother and would take charge of him. Then when Drew let him in, Wells picked up the bat and killed him with Robin lying on the couch."

"What about Natalie?" Pete asked.

"I don't think Wells knew anything about Natalie. Maybe that she existed. Robin might have talked about her. But I don't think she figured into his plans. Wells just wanted Robin to play the part of a patsy."

"Can you prove that?" Dad asked.

"We know that it was Wells who drove Robin from his mother's house to town on the night that Banks was killed. Now that we know what vehicle we're looking for, I'm hoping we can find Wells's car on security cameras from the night that Drew was killed. Hopefully Lionel will be able to enhance the Supersave footage enough that we can prove that the coat found at the Banks murder scene was left in Wells's car. I think he talked Robin into taking the coat off with the intention of leaving it with the body. Of course, we're still waiting for Robin's blood analysis from both the night Drew was killed and the night that Banks was murdered. I'll talk to Dr. Darzi about exactly which drugs we should request the labs to test for. We're looking for something that is both a sedative and one that can cause lapses in memory. Date-rape drugs like Rohypnol and GHB are the most common, but there are others and Wells might have chosen one that would be less likely to be tested for.

"He's nodding," I said so Pete would know that Dad was on board so far.

Dad rolled his eyes. "With the suspect tucked into the cooler at the morgue, I need to be confident that we have the murderer. We won't be having a trial where we can lay out all the evidence for the media and public to see."

"Finding the body of Mrs. Banks will go a long way toward confirming our suspicions," I said.

"Even if Wells buried the body, he might have been wrong about exactly where he buried her," Pete said. "Maybe she's not on the Mathesons' lot."

"I've already talked to them and they're willing to let us to do a thorough search."

"Did they have any stipulations?" Dad asked.

"Not after I made a few *Poltergeist* references. When I hung up with them, they were positive that they didn't want to build their house on or near the body of a murdered woman." I smiled.

"That's low." Dad chuckled as he turned onto the road to my house.

"All's fair in love, war and law enforcement," I said.

"Hey, we're saving them from having blood running down their walls and flies swarming in the bathroom," Pete said and hung up.

It was my turn to ask Dad a few questions. "Have you heard if they found any physical evidence at Wells's house?"

"Shantel recovered a hoodie which is similar to the one worn by the person who was captured on the video before the fence was cut," Dad said. I'd suggested they look for that. "They also took all the gloves they could find."

"With luck, the fibers that Dr. Darzi got from the murder weapons will match a pair of his gloves."

Dad pulled through the gate and up the driveway to my house, where a light was shining on the small porch.

"Remember that both you and Phil are temporarily on leave with pay, but don't get used to it. We're going to get through the investigation as quickly as possible so you can get back to work," Dad told me.

"No dog-sitting duties this time?" I asked, not being able to resist a little smart-assery.

"You're always going to be Mauser's reserve babysitter." He patted me on the back as he pushed me out of the SUV.

I crawled into work the next day to some clapping, jokes and headshaking. Though Phil and I were off duty until the internal affairs investigation cleared us in the death of Alan Wells, I came in to make sure Julio, Lionel, Shantel and Marcus were all on the same page with what needed to be done to wrap up the investigation.

When Major Parks reminded me that I really shouldn't be hanging around the office while under investigation, I walked across the street to the jail to fill Robin in on everything that had happened.

He was glad to see that his tunnel had a light at the end of it, but he couldn't understand why Natalie wouldn't be set free any time soon.

"She almost killed people," I explained.

"Almost," he whined.

"Little people. And she's going to be charged with *almost* killing people, not *actually* killing people, thanks to Sergeant Henley. But no matter how you slice it, she's not getting out for years."

Robin looked like a kid who'd dropped his ice cream cone.

I tried to convince him to use this time as a new beginning. I don't think he even heard me talking. I called his mother on my way home and told her that her son wouldn't be facing any serious charges. I could almost see her rubbing the cross that she wore around her neck as she fretted about his future.

Over the next week, the recovery of the rifle and the canoe were strong evidence that Wells had posed a danger to us and others, so Phil and I were both cleared by IA.

We collected more surveillance footage from Pineland Trace at the time of both the fence-cutting and the paintball incident so we could look for Wells's car. At his house, we retrieved a paintball gun from underneath the boat dock. We were able to thank the observant retired police officer for that one. She'd witnessed him on several occasions putting something up under the deck.

Ground-penetrating radar picked up an anomaly on the Matheson lot a hundred feet from Mike Todd's house. The next day, an archaeological forensic team put together by the Florida Department of Law Enforcement unearthed the remains of the long-dead Georgia Banks. After a few conversations, Dad agreed to host a fundraising effort to bury the Bankses in side-by-side graves in Rose Hill Cemetery.

We also had the dive team from the Leon County Sherriff's Office do a second search of the lake in the hopes of recovering more of the stuff that Phil and I had lost.

"Did they find your phone?" Cara asked me that night when she came home.

"No. They did recover my star and ID. Phil's is still missing, though he was happy to get his gun back. The radios and Phil's phone were wasted. The Glock was fine."

"I still can't believe that he jumped in and drowned Wells!"

"I can't decide whether he's crazy or one of the bravest people I've ever met. Of course, I have to include Pete 'I'll-smash-into-another-car-at-ninety-miles-per-hour' Henley into that mix. Which brings up something I wanted to talk to you about. You remember when you were worried about marrying a deputy because of the *not coming home alive* part?"

Cara pulled me close. "I still worry. But, yeah, Sarah

made me feel better about the risks."

"You might have to return the favor. Pete says she's gotten spooked by the crash."

"That's understandable."

"It is. Still…"

"Is he going to be able to go back on active duty?"

"That depends on how well his leg heals. I know it's going to crush him if he can't. It's not helping his attitude to have her… It's probably not fair to say that she's *wishing* he doesn't fully recover, but she keeps talking about all the other things he could do and it's taking its toll."

"What about Jenny and Kim?" Cara asked.

"Kim is fully on Team Pete. She still wants to be in law enforcement herself. But Jenny is on her mother's side."

"I can find an excuse to go see them."

I leaned over and kissed her. She returned the kiss, then gave me a stern look.

"It would help if y'all would stop putting yourselves in harm's way."

"I promise to try harder," I said, holding her tight.

Larry Macklin returns in:

Memorial Day's Escape
A Larry Macklin Mystery—Book 19

ACKNOWLEDGMENTS

As always, thanks to my wife, Melanie, for her editing skills and support; to H. Y. Hanna for her inspiration, assistance and encouragement; and to all the fans of the series. Larry never would have come this far without all of you!

In addition, I owe a special thanks to the designers and staff of My Irish Jeweler for permission to use the image on the cover of this book. The pendant is from my wife's own personal collection and is one of many pieces we have purchased from this jeweler over the past several years. If you have a love of the Emerald Isle, or just appreciate lovely, well-crafted jewelry and great customer service, check out their website at myirishjeweler.com.

Original Cover Concept by H. Y. Hanna
Cover Design by Florida Girl Design, Inc.
www.gobookcoverdesign.com

ABOUT THE AUTHOR

A. E. Howe lives and writes on a farm in the wilds of North Florida with his wife, horses and more cats than he can count. He received a degree in English Education from the University of Georgia and is a produced screenwriter and playwright. His first published book was *Broken State*. The Larry Macklin Mysteries is his first series and he released the Baron Blasko Mysteries in summer 2018. His most recent series, the Mortician Murder Mysteries, was launched in 2022.

The first book in the Macklin series, *November's Past*, was awarded two silver medals in the 2017 President's Book Awards, presented by the Florida Authors & Publishers Association; the ninth book, *July's Trials*, was awarded two silver medals in 2018. Howe is a member of the Mystery Writers of America, and was co-host of the "Guns of Hollywood" podcast for four years on the Firearms Radio Network. When not writing, Howe enjoys riding, competitive shooting and working on the farm.

www.ingramcontent.com/pod-product-compliance
Lightning Source LLC
Chambersburg PA
CBHW061543210726
48287CB00006B/2063